SPEAK
THE DEAD

GRANT McKENZIE

SPEAK THE DEAD

Copyright © 2015 by Grant McKenzie
Cover, jacket and interior design by Damonza

ISBN 978-1-940610-54-2
eISBN 978-1-940610-62-7

Library of Congress Control Number: 2015939841

First hardcover publication: September 2015
1201 Hudson Street
Hoboken, NJ 07030
www.PolisBooks.com

POLIS BOOKS

OTHER BOOKS BY GRANT MCKENZIE

Writing as Grant McKenzie

No Cry For Help
Port of Sorrow
K.A.R.M.A. (Polis Books)
The Fear In Her Eyes (Polis Books)
Speak The Dead (Polis Books)

Writing as M.C. Grant

Angel With A Bullet
Devil With A Gun
Beauty With A Bomb

For
Karen and Kailey
who I love
even more
than wine gums

"Oh wow, oh wow, oh wow."

— Apple founder Steve Jobs' final words
on his deathbed

TWENTY-FIVE YEARS AGO

The blast shattered the night's silence, ripping the six-year-old girl from restful slumber into blind, terrified panic. Sally bolted upright, her heart hammering so fast that it pained her ribs.

She strained to listen… heavy footsteps in the hall shuffling along the floor as though fighting gravity. Something hard and meaty slammed into her bedroom door, cracking the wood and rattling the flimsy brass handle. She covered her mouth and froze in place, but whoever was outside didn't seem intent on entering.

A mumbled curse escaped unpliant lips before the unknown intruder shoved away from the door and shambled on.

In its wake, Sally grimaced at the uncomfortable wet warmth that seeped around her, soaking through her cotton nightdress and pooling on the protective rubber sheet her mother had fitted over her mattress. This time it wasn't one of her night terrors, however. This was really happening.

Sally climbed out of bed, both embarrassed and afraid.

Before looking for a new nightdress, she crept to the door and carefully turned the knob. The handle wasn't locked—it didn't have the capability—and it opened both silently and easily. Whoever had fallen against it could have entered her room with no effort at all.

Despite her growing fear, Sally peeked into the hallway and gasped—a bloody handprint oozed down the shiny white surface of her painted door. Its finger trail elongated as the handprint slid, becoming something other than human.

Sally fought her panic as she glanced up and down the dark hallway. The washroom light was on, and she could hear the sound of heavy grunting, like an animal.

She didn't want to see what was making the noise.

Instead, Sally darted in the opposite direction and pushed open the door to her parents' bedroom at the rear of the house. The room was in darkness except for a shaded bedside lamp, and what it illuminated filled Sally with overwhelming despair. Her eyes filled with tears as she rushed forward to climb on the four-poster bed beside her mother.

With her ravaged nightdress drenched in blood from a double-barreled wound that had ripped open her chest with unimaginable, close-range fury, Sally's mother was no longer contained within her shattered, fleshy shell.

Sally wept as she cradled her mother's limp head against her tiny chest, mindless of the blood and the cloying stench of death. She closed her own eyes, wanting it to be nothing more than a nightmare, a horrible dream that she could wake from and everything would be okay again—when her mother's trapped voice finally released in a pent-up groan: "Run, Sally! Run!"

Her skin prickling with painful, electrified goose bumps, Sally stared open-mouthed into her mother's lifeless green eyes. Another face seemed to stir underneath the dead flesh, and without moving a muscle it repeated the warning.

Sally released her mother's head back onto its pillow and scrambled off the bed. At the bedroom door, she turned around again, unsure. Her mother hadn't moved. The other face was no longer visible, but its urgent warning still echoed inside her head.

"Be brave," she told herself. "You're a big girl now. Do as your mother tells you."

Sally opened the door and started down the hallway toward the stairs. When she neared the washroom, she slowed, fear making every footfall sound like the clatter of a dropped soup pot as her bare feet struck the floor.

"Just run," she told herself. "Don't look inside."

Sally glanced inside and saw her father standing in the bathtub. He was wearing drawstring pajama bottoms, but no shirt. His bare torso was covered in blood, and the twin barrels of a well-oiled shotgun were jammed in his mouth. The glistening oil mixed with dribbling blood to turn his saliva into a frothing purple beard.

Her father's eyes were rolled back in his head, the orbs white and stormy. A dark shadow filled the room and the incessant chanting of a repetitive voice echoed from every direction.

Sally hesitated, wanting to stop and help, to wake her father from this seizure, to save one of her parents—but the urgency of her dead mother's warning propelled her onward. As Sally bolted down the stairs, racing toward the front door, a final bone-jarring *BOOM* erupted behind her.

With tears streaming down her face, Sally did the only thing she could.

She kept running.

SIX MONTHS AGO

The woman ran until her lungs threatened to burst. She had lost both her shoes in the undergrowth when she diverted off the footpath, and now the soles of her feet were cut, bruised, and bleeding with every step.

Leaping over a mossy log, her feet sank ankle-deep into marshy soil—and stuck.

She screamed as her right foot twisted and the sickening *snap-crunch* of cartilage ripping from bone fired a white-hot jolt of pain directly into her brain.

The woman collapsed face first in the dirt, unable to breathe, the crippling hurt blurring her sight, her reason, and her will to survive.

Dammit! Dammit! Dammit!

The river was close. She could hear it. She scrunched up her face and gritted her teeth.

An escape. People. There were often fishermen wading in the shallows in their ridiculous rubber pants. She had made fun of them so often, but now—

Come on! Get up! You're tougher than this!

Whimpering, she ran her hands down her leg to gently pull her injured foot from the soft ground. She did the same with her other foot and then rolled over onto her back. She wanted to lie in the cold mud forever, allow the pain to subside and her breath to catch, but she couldn't. With a prayer on her lips and her face awash in cold sweat, she found the strength to sit up and cradle her twisted ankle in her hands.

The pain, the dirt, the cold, the fear… it was too much.

And why?

Walking home from work, she took the same path through the woods that she traveled every day, her ever-present iPod drowning out the birdsong and the labored gurgling of the Spokane River.

She didn't hear the stranger approach.

Suddenly, a gloved hand wrapped around her mouth and the terrifying lick of cold steel pressed against her throat.

She froze, her mind unable to fathom what was happening. And then the stranger spoke: "If you run, I'll slit your fucking throat."

It was the kind of warning that screams: *You're dead.*

The woman drove her elbow hard into the stranger's gut and took off down the path at full speed. The knife had slid across her skin and blood had flowed, but she felt the wound wasn't deep, no worse than her legs had suffered when she first learned to shave.

If she had been wearing runners, the stranger wouldn't have stood a chance, but the damn heels she wore to the office to make her butt look pert beneath her tight skirt were useless.

She lost the shoes when she diverted off the path and into the thick, bug-infested foliage. The stranger's panting breath was so close behind her that she hadn't dared turn around.

She had simply run.

Pushing up from the dirt, the woman attempted to stand. She placed most of her weight on her left foot, but the moment she tried to balance herself with her right, pain brought her back to her knees with an agonized squeal.

The crunch of breaking branches nearby made her swallow the pain and crawl toward the river. If she couldn't make the water, maybe she could at least find a large bush or a fallen tree to crawl under. Hide until the stranger gave up.

She pulled herself along the ground, nails digging into the soft earth, fingers clawing for purchase. Desperate.

The river was close. The noise of it. The smell of it. The cool—

A heavy weight landed on her back, hard knees on either side of her spine, the surprise load crushing her chest into the dirt, snapping ribs.

She opened her mouth to scream, but a second weight pushed down on her skull, forcing her face deep into the moist earth. Dirt and worms and dead leaves flowed into her mouth and up her nose.

She couldn't breathe.

She couldn't ask why.

The stranger yanked her head out of the dirt before she lost consciousness. The woman spat and struggled, but her efforts were so pitiful that she felt ashamed.

"I told you not to run."

The woman's eyes went wide as the knife stabbed deep into her neck and was pulled hard across her throat.

When released, her head flopped onto the ground, her breathing strangled, her blood pouring out to stain the earth. She wanted to speak, but her mouth, her body, no longer worked. Only her brain was alive, and that wouldn't be for long.

She was flipped over onto her back.

"You're not her are you?" asked the stranger, disappointed.

The tip of the knife flicked toward her eyes.

With her larynx severed, the woman couldn't scream.

ONE WEEK AGO

Sister Fleur wept tears of blood.

The monster stood above her, his breathing labored, his face spattered in sweat and gore.

Beside her, Sister Emily had stopped moving, her throat grotesquely swollen and her battered face locked in agony rather than the serenity she deserved.

Mercifully, she was beyond pain now.

Sister Fleur stared up at a visage ripped from nightmare and prayed for him to stop. His fists were a storm of agony, each blow measured to inflict maximum humiliation and pain.

The left side of her attacker's face was smooth and handsome, but the right side sunk fear into her heart. Twisted and torn, folds of rubbery, dead-belly skin drooped over a lifeless eye and sunken cheek. Muscle and fat had been eaten away as if by rats, and his ear was nothing more than a ragged hole.

It was the face of evil or hell or the devil himself.

"Where's Salvation?" the deformed man screeched.

It was a question he had asked a dozen times, and with every shake of her head he had landed another blow. Sister Emily had endured the worst, but Sister Fleur couldn't make herself answer.

Gasping for breath, the man grabbed Sister Emily's leg and dragged her close. Her unseeing eyes stared at Sister Fleur as the man's large hands tore at her clothing. Hot spittle flew from malformed lips.

"I'll rape her corpse while you watch," he threatened. "And that is not yet the worst I can do."

Sister Fleur shook her head in panic. No more, please Lord, no more.

"Where's Salvation?"

And, God forgive her, she told him.

1

Talking to the dead isn't as creepy as people might imagine.

Sally knew most people liked to think of the dead as empty vessels; the corpse nothing but leftover meat, fat, and juices that the soul leaves behind like unwanted baggage after it has moved on to bigger and better things. She just happened to disagree.

The dead had feelings. They responded to music and speech and the touch of the living. She didn't know what it was, leftover energy maybe? But when she talked to the dead, they responded in subtle ways. The gray flesh became more pliant, the air around them grew less frigid, and this allowed the makeup—foundation, rouge, eyeliner, lipstick—to go on smoother and emit a more natural glow.

Sally often got the feeling that the time she spent with a guest was the first he or she had been touched by a gentle hand in a long, long time.

"Isn't that right, Mrs. Shoumatoff?" Sally said as she rinsed shampoo from the dead woman's brittle hair.

Mrs. Shoumatoff was having her funeral that afternoon, but the director had confided in Sally that he didn't know if anyone was going to attend. No one had responded to the notice he wrote and placed in the local newspaper, and so he was planning to contact the local Mourners Club to see if it could send some members to fill a few seats.

Mr. William Payne, senior director of Paynes' Funeral Home, disliked an empty funeral. But with the promise of pots of coffee and Earl Grey tea, china cups, and his wife's delicious home baking, he could usually guarantee at least a half-dozen, white-haired or blue-rinsed mourners on short notice.

Using the parlor's much advertised and very popular installment package, Mrs. Shoumatoff had paid for her funeral in advance. She had requested an open coffin ("If possible," she wrote in the contract). Her handwriting was elegant and spoke of a formal European education, but under occupation she had written: *cleaning lady, retired.*

Her husband hadn't known about the funeral arrangements. It was the county coroner's assistant who found the contract for Paynes' Funeral Home inside Mrs. Shoumatoff's apron pocket. She had been wearing the apron when she died and, according to her husband, was rarely seen without it.

In the death certificate that accompanied Mrs. Shoumatoff from the morgue the coroner had ruled the death as accidental. Mrs. Shoumatoff had tripped on the living room carpet and struck her head on the corner of a brick fireplace. Death was not instantaneous but neither was it lingering. The only puzzle was why, especially for a retired cleaning lady, was she rushing through the living room with her apron and hands covered in white flour.

When the husband was told of the funeral arrangements, he asked if he could go with a cheaper option instead, and have the difference refunded to him in cash. Mr. Payne politely informed him that was not an option.

Mr. Shoumatoff had not taken the news well, and when Mr. Payne asked if he would like to provide one of his wife's favorite dresses for the funeral, he had cursed the Payne family lineage and stormed out.

Mr. Payne did not believe he would return. Not even for the funeral.

This was not an entirely new situation. Sometimes it was grief, other times it was anger or denial or bitterness. Sally had even known jealousy to play a part. Whatever the reason, Sally never allowed her guests to look anything but their best.

To that end, she had established a wonderful rapport with the ladies at the Salvation Army thrift store, conveniently located less than half a block from the funeral home. This afternoon, Mrs. Shoumatoff would be wearing a lovely green dress with subtle gold accents. The lace embroidery on collar and hem—which the Sally Ann ladies had mended perfectly—had a definite European flavor, and Sally believed Mrs. Shoumatoff would approve.

Her one dilemma was the apron. It had become so much a part of the woman's identity, but Sally didn't know if that was of her own choosing. She could tell from the scars on the woman's body as she cleaned and dressed her that life had been a hardship, but Sally didn't know if the apron brought her comfort or was yet another form of domestic bondage.

"What do you say, Mrs. Shoumatoff?" Sally asked as she combed the corpse's damp hair.

As was to be expected, Mrs. Shoumatoff didn't answer.

Sally rubbed in another dab of conditioner and combed out the last stubborn flakes of dried blood. It had taken a thin layer of molding wax and a few extra dabs of foundation to fill the dent from her fall. The flesh had split down to the bone, but it was nothing that couldn't be fixed, especially in the talented hands of the parlor's lead mortician, Jesús Moroles.

"I think we'll leave the apron off," Sally said.

She touched Mrs. Shoumatoff's cheek. The flesh was stiff and cold.

"But I'll put it in the casket beside you, how's that?"

Sally touched the woman's cheek again. A barely perceptible warmth had softened and relaxed the skin. Sally beamed.

After gently blow-drying the woman's hair and adding a few soft curls with an iron, Sally moved on to makeup.

As Sally explained to Mrs. Shoumatoff, makeup for the dead is not the same as for the living. The skin—which is just another organ, albeit with a surface area of around two square meters—no longer breathes; it is kept chilled and the natural dehydration that begins at death destroys elasticity.

To preserve the body, as decomposition happened faster than most people thought, a surgical tube was inserted into the carotid artery, giving direct access to the heart. Approximately two to three gallons of formaldehyde-based embalming fluid was then pumped into the arterial system. This procedure flooded the capillaries and forced all the blood in the body out of a second tube in the jugular vein. At Paynes, the embalmer added a special pink dye to the fluid as a way to counteract death's dull pallor. The pungent fluid looked rather like Pepto Bismol.

After embalming, Sally's secret to reviving natural beauty was done in four stages. The first was a hydrating layer of cold cream. The second was a flesh-colored layer of oil-based foundation, applied carefully to hands and face in short, quick strokes.

Once the base was dry, the third stage was a translucent water-based cosmetic that allowed for a variation in tone to show through. This was the layer that returned life to the bloodless skin.

The fourth stage was what separated the cosmetician from the artist.

In the living, the first things Sally tended to notice were the eyes. Being a window on the soul, a sparkle in the eye expressed so much. But with the dead, the eyes are closed, and necessarily so. Shortly after death, the eyes, which are mostly water, begin to collapse. To preserve the illusion of peaceful slumber, special gel-coated discs were inserted under the eyelids before they were sealed with a needle-thin line of glue.

With the eyes closed, it was the mouth that became the most crucial area.

Sally had learned the reason the dead tend to look sad was because the round muscle of the mouth relaxed at death, causing the corners to droop. To correct this, Sally used more of her special adhesive to hold the lips together and then applied a colorless wax to shape and soften the line. At Madame Tussauds' famous wax museums, the artists made the stars' smiles fill a room, but at Paynes' Funeral Home, Sally's job was to simply make the dead look at peace.

A grinning corpse could give mourners nightmares.

The finishing touch was a dab of oyster-shell gel that Sally created herself to bring warmth and shine to the lips.

Once the mouth was complete, Sally lightly brushed a subtle coral blue onto the natural hotspots—jaw, cheeks, and eyelids—to add shadow and depth.

"Nearly done, Mrs. Shoumatoff," Sally said cheerfully. "Thank you for being so patient."

Being careful not to overdo it, Sally lifted a ball pump and antique glass decanter from her cosmetics bag and sprayed a mist of fine powder across the surface of the dead woman's skin. The powder was used to seal the cosmetics and flatten out any distracting shine.

Satisfied with her work, Sally smiled down at her guest. Mrs. Shoumatoff looked ready for a night of cheek-to-cheek dancing and one last stolen kiss.

With a contented sigh, Sally glanced up at the clock on the wall. Three a.m. It seemed later, somehow.

After returning Mrs. Shoumatoff to cold storage, Sally decided to brew a fresh pot of coffee before wheeling out her next guest, Mr. Lombardo.

The men never took as long as the women.

In death as in life, she supposed.

2

With a wide grin splitting his face, Jersey Castle soaked in the raucous applause and ear piercing whistles from the amped-up audience as he brought his drum solo to its head-banging crescendo. Sweat flew in all directions as, with a final crash of the cymbals, he tossed a pair of hickory drumsticks into the air.

At the front of the stage, dressed in head-to-toe black leather, chromed spikes, and face piercings, John "Johnny" Simpkins, lead singer of *The Rotten Johnnys*, was snarling at the crowd, the index and middle fingers of both hands raised and parted in rude defiance.

"What ya cheering for, ya wankers?" Johnny yelled in his horribly fake British accent. "We were crap!"

The crowd roared its approval.

Still grinning like a fool, Jersey slid out from behind his drum kit and exited the stage. In his form-fitting, black leather pants, ripped T-shirt, and bandoleer of rusted chain, he was perspiring like a junkie in the holding tank and badly needed re-hydrating.

"Great set, Skunk," said Malcolm "The Mouse" Malkovich, the Rottens' publicist and manager. He handed Jersey a large bottle of water. "I thought you were going to burst those skins."

Jersey gulped the water greedily, not caring as the cold liquid dribbled out of his mouth and onto his sweat-drenched chest.

"I'm getting too old for this," he said.

Pouring water into his palm, Jersey splashed it across his close-cropped black hair. His stage name, Skunk, came from a natural streak of premature white that began just below the peak of his hairline before zigzagging off in a lightning bolt pattern to a spot above his right ear. It made him look like the love child of Frankenstein's Bride and Pepé Le Pew.

He nodded in the direction of the audience. "Most of them look underage."

Malkovich shouted to be heard over the crowd as Johnny continued to abuse his fans. "That's what keeps you young. If you were playing to a load of seniors, I'd tell you to hang it up, but punk is big with the kids again. Five years ago, a tubby bastard like you wouldn't be allowed near a stage, never mind drumming in a sold-out gig."

"Tubby?" Jersey protested.

"Hey!" Malkovich held up his hands, allowing his fake diamond rings to catch the light. "Just a figure of speech."

"You do remember I'm licensed to carry a gun, right?"

"Come on, lighten up, you know I love you, man."

Jersey looked Malkovich up and down, taking in the vintage 1970s crocodile-print suit, purple silk shirt opened to just above the navel, and a half-dozen assorted gold chains tangled in a nest of graying chest hair.

"That's what I'm afraid of."

Johnny and the rest of the band—Fudge on bass, Tick on guitar—joined them in the wings.

"You two fighting again?" Johnny swept his drenched hair out of his eyes, rivers of sweat running black from the excess dye he used to keep a firm rein on his receding youth. Comically, the gold chain that ran from a piercing on his lip to another on his left nostril had snapped in half and dangled from his nose.

"He implied I was fat," said Jersey.

"You threaten to shoot him?" asked Johnny.

"I did."

Johnny turned to Malkovich. "He'll do it, you know? He may be a chubby bastard, but he's a damn good shot. Even has a medal for it."

Jersey tried to make his grin look fierce. "You should remember that, too, Johnny, instead of prancing around like a Bond villain."

"A Bond villain?"

Jersey grinned wider. "Yeah, *Gold Booger*." He touched the side of his nose. "Look in the mirror."

Johnny reached up and discovered the broken chain.

"Ah shit, when did that happen? I must have looked a right idiot."

"You?" Jersey's tongue burrowed into his cheek. "I can't imagine."

"Ha, Ha." Johnny stormed off to the green room at the rear of the club.

As the crowd took the hint that there would be no second encore, the house DJ flooded the bar with mellower go-home music. Relaxing, the four men followed Johnny's lead. Inside a storage closet that had been converted to seat six with folding chairs, a large mirror, and a small bar fridge, the Rottens cracked open a chilled six-pack of Heineken.

Jersey took a long pull of Dutch lager. "You know what I was thinking?"

"How good my ass still looks in these pants?" quipped Johnny.

"Besides that."

Johnny unclipped the chains from his piercings and dropped them into a purple velvet drawstring bag that had once contained a bottle of Crown Royal Canadian whisky. "Tell me?"

"The crowd really got into *God Save the Queen* on the encore, so what if we tried a Rotten version of *Star Spangled Banner*?"

Johnny shrugged. "The Pistols never did it, but I guess if the

New York Philharmonic can play it in North Korea… I don't see why not."

"We could throw in some light and sound effects," Tick jumped in excitedly. "You know for *rockets' red glare* and *bombs bursting in air*."

Johnny started to laugh. "And maybe a few 'Fuck Yous' after the line, '*where is that band who so vauntingly swore*'."

"Yeah, that's the spirit," Jersey agreed. "With the right inflection we could make it an anti-war anthem."

Malkovich turned pale. "Err, guys, that could get us in trouble."

"We're a punk band, Mouse," said Jersey. "Trouble is our business."

"No," argued Malkovich. "Getting people to pay to watch you old farts relive some other band's glory days is our business."

Johnny laughed harder. "Get us some more beers, Mouse. The boys did Rotten proud tonight."

3

Sally fastened a plastic diaper around Mr. Lombardo's hips and began to whip up a small bowl of shaving cream.

When she was satisfied with the consistency, she brushed the thick cream on his stubbled cheeks and chin with an old-fashioned shaving brush made from genuine badger bristles. She had found the brush along with a matching mother-of-pearl straight razor in an antique shop, and couldn't resist the impulse to buy. It had taken her a while to first sharpen and then master the proper technique of the straight razor, but felt that her guests deserved the best for their final shave.

Besides, even if she wasn't perfect, the odd nick here and there didn't really matter. Her guests didn't bleed.

Once Mr. Lombardo was stubble free, Sally produced a thick sponge and a bottle of liquid detergent to clean any leftover medical residue from his body and legs.

Earlier, his widow had delivered a favorite gray herringbone suit along with a beautiful new silk tie in light turquoise that, in life, would have complemented his eyes. The suit had been dry-cleaned and pressed at Mr. Lombardo's own shop, a downtown fixture since the early Fifties. It almost seemed a pity that Sally would have to slice the suit open in the back before the fitting, but it just never laid properly otherwise.

Sally had just begun dabbing the sponge across Mr. Lombardo's bird-like chest when a loud, piercing scream shattered her serenity. She spun to the small basement windows high on the rear wall that, if they had been clear rather than painted black and barred in iron, looked out on the alley behind the funeral home.

Another high-pitched scream punctured the silence, but this time it was accompanied by the roar of a powerful engine and the ominous squeal of tires.

Instinctively, Sally dropped her sponge, snapped up her straight razor, and ran up the concrete stairs to unlock the rear fire exit.

A third scream was cut short by the sickening slap and crunch of metal upon flesh.

Sally yanked open the heavy door and vanished outside.

ON THE ABANDONED stainless steel table in the mortuary basement, detergent leaked from Sally's sponge in tiny rivulets of phosphorescent green.

The liquid flowed through the coarse, dry hair of Mr. Lombardo's inert chest and spread across his sunken bleached-white stomach.

As the lemon-scented chemical soaked into dead flesh and flowed around old surgery scars, several shimmering words became visible on the corpse's stomach.

The detergent didn't reveal every letter, but anyone with a passing interest in word puzzles would have been able to decipher the two simple words scrawled in a childish hand: *He knows!*

4

Jersey was already rushing toward the heavy fire doors at the rear of the club when the woman's third scream was cut short.

A fresh rush of adrenaline instantly made his pulse race faster. When he burst through the exit, he was clutching a Glock 26 semi-automatic handgun. Even in uncomfortable leather pants, Jersey never left home without his sub-compact 9mm snugged in an ankle holster.

A flare of brake lights at the end of the alley was accompanied by the ear-piercing squeal of burning rubber as a large four-door, American-made sedan took the corner at a high rate of speed and vanished from view.

Jersey briefly considered chasing after the vehicle when a door directly across from him burst open and a petite woman in a blue lab coat rushed out.

Her exit triggered a pair of bright security lights above the door, and in their dazzling radiance Jersey was taken aback by short, spiky hair the color of fresh snow, a button nose, and perfect Cupid's bow lips. Most startling of all, however, were her eyes. Large with fright, they were the most vivid shade of green he had ever seen.

Although distracted by her understated beauty, Jersey wasn't blinded enough not to notice she was clutching an old-fashioned straight razor in an aggressive don't-fuck-with-me grip. And lying on the ground between them was the broken, unmoving body of a well-dressed woman in a black trench coat.

"Stay back," Jersey shouted. His gun felt unexpectedly heavy in his hand as he aimed it mid-mass on the attractive arrival.

The white-haired woman stared at him through those enormous eyes, her feet frozen in place, her face pale with fear.

Jersey suddenly remembered what he looked like.

"It's okay," he said quickly. "I know I don't look it right now, but I'm a cop. Do you work in that building?"

The woman nodded.

"You heard the scream?" Jersey asked.

The woman nodded again.

"Can you put the blade away?"

The woman looked down at the razor clutched in her hand, and her face flushed with embarrassment. She quickly snapped the razor into its handle and dropped it into a pocket of her lab coat.

Satisfied that she wasn't a threat, Jersey lowered his gun and moved to the crumpled form lying on the gravel road. He pressed his fingers to the victim's neck, although the angle of her head and a spreading pool of blood suggested there was little point.

As he expected, there was no pulse.

When Jersey looked up, he found the attractive woman kneeling close beside him, staring in fascinated wonder at the recently deceased.

"Her neck's broken," said Jersey. "Nothing we can do."

The woman wiped a stray tear from her eye and Jersey felt an instant, irrational attraction. He was used to the public recoiling in horror, screaming hysterically, or even vomiting at the sight of death, but this tiny stranger displayed none of that. And for someone who dealt with violent death on a daily basis, her reaction was a powerful, if not totally appropriate, aphrodisiac.

Jersey tried to clear his mind, to focus on the dead rather than the living. It didn't work. While the woman's gaze was riveted on the victim, Jersey's was focused on her. This lovely stranger was a good eight inches shorter than his own six-foot-two-inch frame, but there was a palpable heat in her fragile beauty that made his breath catch in his throat. He instantly wished they were meeting in a different place at a different time when he didn't look like such a clown and there wasn't a dead woman on the ground between them.

He foolishly tried to inhale the scent of her, but all he could smell was blood, excrement, and death. Jersey forced himself to break away.

"I'm going to call it in," he said. "Don't touch anything."

The woman offered a gentle smile and simple nod that made Jersey feel light on his feet and eight-feet tall.

Jersey rolled up his pant leg to expose an ankle wallet containing a cellphone, his detective's shield, a credit card, and a couple of neatly folded twenties. He removed the cellphone, stood up, and made the call.

INSTEAD OF RETREATING, Sally inched closer to the dead woman for a better look.

She was in her early sixties with professionally colored and styled auburn hair. Her moderately expensive periwinkle pantsuit, flowing black raincoat, and simple but elegant jewelry reflected a comfortable stage of life. Her eyes were open and clear, but her face reflected the pain she had experienced at death with lips curled in an agonized grimace.

It was a frightening way to leave the world and not a visage, Sally believed, she would want to leave her children.

The dead didn't frighten her, but Sally was never around them this close to the moment of death. She wondered if she could alter the muscles before they became locked in place by rigor mortis.

Sally reached out to touch the woman's lips, undisturbed by

the blood that pooled in her mouth and overflowed at the corners. But the instant her fingers connected with the woman's mouth, a flash of impossibly bright light exploded in her brain.

Sally tried to scream, but she was no longer in control of her own body. In fact, she didn't believe she was still *in* her own body. She lifted a hand and squinted against the glaring light. Shadows appeared around the edges and a shape began to form.

The sight made her gasp.

A large car was hurtling toward her, the chrome grill of its radiator like the teeth of a hungry shark. There were two people in the front seat, but before she could make out their faces, the car struck her legs and sent her flying over the hood.

The pain in her shattered limbs was blinding, but before it could fully register, her head hit the windshield with a sickening crunch. Sally's neck twisted beyond the breaking point and then her body went limp as it skidded lifelessly over the roof and crumpled to the ground behind the vanishing car.

And then, she was somewhere else.

The light faded and Sally found herself alive and kneeling safely beside the dead woman. The oddly dressed detective was crouched beside her, his strong hands gripping her shoulders to hold her steady. He had removed her hands from the woman's mouth and wiped the blood from her fingers with his ridiculous T-shirt.

Sally shivered from a cold sweat, her teeth near chattering as though she had been doused in ice water.

"ARE YOU OKAY?" the detective asked. "You went awful pale."

Sally nodded numbly, her vocal chords refusing to work.

"I asked you not to touch anything," he said, but his concerned tone betrayed no anger. He sighed. "Do you need a bottle of water or something?"

Sally swallowed. "Sure." Her voice was much softer than she planned.

The detective turned toward the club just as another leather-clad punk rocker opened the door and stuck his head out, curious.

"Get me some water, will you, Johnny?" the detective called.

"What's going on?"

"Hit and run. Get me water."

"Okay, sure thing."

Johnny disappeared inside the club.

"Come on." The detective lifted Sally to her feet. "There're a couple crates we can sit on while we wait for the lights and sirens brigade."

Sally allowed herself to be escorted across the alley to a pile of wooden beer crates stacked outside the nightclub.

She hugged herself as she sat on an overturned crate, while the detective made himself comfortable on another. He tilted his chin to indicate the building across the alley.

"That's a funeral home, right?" he asked.

"Yes."

"You always work so late?"

Sally shrugged. "I get the guests ready for the day's services. I like to work when it's quiet."

"Guests?"

"The dead."

"Oh."

Sally lifted her gaze and took in the husky man with the unusual streak of white in his hair. His villainous wardrobe and smeared ebony eyeliner didn't suit him at all. The corners of her mouth lifted in a smile.

"You don't look like a cop."

The detective grinned back.

"I moonlight in a band. We were playing tonight." He indicated the fire door behind him. "In there."

"What are you called?"

"The Rotten Johnnys."

Sally laughed. "Are you that bad?"

"Yeah." The detective grinned wider. "Actually, we try not to be. We took our name from the Sex Pistols as we do a lot of covers of their stuff. But we also throw in some other cool bands: a little Clash, if we're feeling ambitious; dash of The Monks; Electric Chairs; Dead Kennedys; Ramones; Boomtown Rats; Joe Jackson… whatever gets people boppin'. We're also trying out some angry Celtic stuff that I really enjoy: Flogging Molly, The Pogues, that kinda thing."

The fire door opened and Johnny appeared with two bottles of water. When he handed them over, his eyes went wide as he caught sight of the broken and bloodied woman lying alone in the middle of the alley.

"Jesus Christ, Skunk! Is she dead?"

"Hit and run. I told you."

"You didn't say she was fucking dead. Why aren't you doing anything?"

"I called it in. There's a unit on the way."

Johnny sputtered. "B-b-but she's dead and you're chatting up a groupie like there's nothing—"

The detective jumped to his feet and shoved Johnny against the metal door. "She's not a groupie. She works across the alley in the funeral home. She's a witness."

"Okay, okay, take it easy, shit." Johnny scrunched up his face as if he was about to be sick. "I'm going back inside."

Johnny slammed the door behind him, and the detective returned to his crate.

"Sorry about that, Miss, err…"

"Wilson," said Sally. "Sally Wilson."

The detective offered his hand. "Jersey Castle."

Sally took his hand in hers and gave it a gentle squeeze. His grip was firm and dry without being so loose as to be insulting or too strong to be intimidating. In fact, Sally thought, it was just right.

5

Two patrol cars, an ambulance and a fire truck arrived simultaneously, followed within minutes by an ugly brown Ford with twin dented front fenders and a long, paint-blistering scratch running horizontally across the driver's side.

Jersey cringed when he saw the Ford and absently began tucking his ripped T-shirt into his leather pants. The rapid movement made the chain bandoleer that crossed his chest jangle noisily. He quickly pulled it over his head and tossed it out of sight behind one of the wooden crates.

When Lieutenant Noel Morrell stepped out of the Ford and stopped to stroke his impressive ginger moustache, everybody stopped breathing. Despite the lateness of the hour, the lanky lieutenant looked as though he had stepped fresh out of the Hugo Boss catalogue—all sharp lines and aggressive stance. With shined shoes and pleated slacks, Morrell took a few moments to process the scene before striding forward at a brisk and measured pace.

The other officers on the scene didn't start breathing again until after he strode past. When he stopped in front of Jersey, the detective reluctantly lowered his eyes in supplication.

"What in tarnation are you wearing, Detective Castle?"

"I'm off-duty, sir."

"Is that what I asked?"

"No, sir."

"So answer the damn question."

"It's my stage costume."

"Costume?"

Jersey shrugged.

"Are you a closet fairy, Detective Castle? Do you enjoy being chained and whipped by degenerates?"

"I play drums in a punk band, sir, but I don't believe you're allowed to question my sexuality, whatever it may be."

"Is that right?"

"Yes, sir. I recall the memo."

"Quite." Clearing his throat as though to dislodge something distasteful, Lieutenant Morrell turned his attention to the dead woman's mangled body in the middle of the alley. He wrinkled his nose. "So what do we have here?"

"Hit and run."

"You saw the vehicle?"

Jersey squirmed. "Just the tail end as it turned the corner. Four door, American made. Possibly a Dodge."

"Registration?"

Jersey glanced at the club's rear entrance, searching for the tell-tale sign of a close-circuit security camera. Something he should have paying attention to instead of… becoming distracted.

"Not yet," he said. "I—"

Sally stepped between the two men and handed Jersey a piece of crumpled paper.

"This might be the license plate you're looking for," she said.

"You saw it?" Jersey asked.

Sally nodded, her eyes looking away.

"But you came out after—"

"Well," Morrell snapped. "Is this the registration or not?"

"I believe it is," said Sally cautiously. "It took me a moment to remember. Detective Castle was very patient."

Morrell snorted. "Hmmm, well, good." He turned to the closest uniformed officer. "Get a BOLO alert out to all patrols on this number immediately."

Morrell turned to Jersey and stroked his moustache again. "Good work, detective. Just don't let this punk business interfere with your caseload."

"No, sir."

"I'll be watching."

Morrell spun on his heels with such precision he could put a Marine Corp drill sergeant to shame, and marched back to his car. As he started the engine to back out of the alley the other officers held their breath again.

A sudden squeal of brake and crunch of metal made everyone cringe as a large trashcan was sent flying off to one side. Morrell reacted by stepping harder on the gas and quickly backing the rest of the way out of the alley.

"Amazing," said one of the uniformed officers after Morrell's car had vanished from sight. "He only hit one can."

The other officers laughed, including Jersey.

Sally looked at him quizzically.

"He's the worst driver you've ever seen," Jersey explained. "No peripheral awareness. His car has been under the hammer more times than I've been out of tune. When he's driving, fire hydrants get so scared, they leak."

Sally's eyes sparkled in amusement. "He's keeping strange hours for a senior officer."

"His daughter is about to give birth and has moved back home," explained Jersey. "He's feeling useless there, so he's driving everyone crazy out here instead. The other night he decided to inspect a stakeout that Vice was running and nearly blew the whole operation."

Jersey turned as he caught sight of the Emergency Medical

Technicians moving toward the body with a stretcher. He rushed forward and held up his hands.

"We're treating this as a potential homicide," Jersey said. "We need photos and a full work-up before transport. Sorry, guys."

The EMTs looked disappointed as they retreated to their ambulance and sat on the rear bumper to wait for the coroner and a forensics crew to arrive.

Jersey turned back around to ask Sally how she had managed to see the car's plate number, but she was gone.

6

Closing the fire exit behind her, Sally fastened all three dead-bolts and sank to the floor. Cold radiated from the shallow concrete landing as she wrapped her arms around herself and squeezed.

What the hell was she thinking? How could that possibly be the correct license plate? The cops would be furious at her for wasting their time, but it had seemed so real...

All she had done was touch the woman, and she had... what? Relived the last thing the woman experienced before she died.

That didn't make any sense. Sally had been working with the dead for years and apart from... Sally hesitated, remembering. When she had touched her dead mother all those years ago, she had still been warm, her life just ended. But Sally hadn't left her own body and witnessed her mother's death. Instead, her mother delivered a warning. She told Sally to run.

And I've been running ever since.

Maybe she'd inhaled too many fumes, Sally thought as she glanced across the room at the ancient exhaust fan sputtering in the far corner. *That could explain everything.*

Feeling better with that explanation, Sally rose to her feet, shook off the chill, and returned to Mr. Lombardo. The poor man had been left alone with nothing but a plastic diaper to protect his dignity.

The detergent from the sponge had evaporated, leaving odd-looking green chicken scratch on his stomach. Sally rinsed the sponge in warm water and gave the body a quick wipe to remove the marks.

After drying him, Sally peeled away the thin plastic dry-cleaner wrap from around the fresh suit his widow had delivered and began the process of dressing him. As she feared, she had to slice the suit jacket down the back and stitch it together with safety pins to get just the right fit. But once she was done, Mr. Lombardo looked like a successful businessman who had fallen asleep on a stainless steel tray.

The only exception, as is the case she found with most men, was his hands. Those could have belonged to a potato farmer.

Sally stretched a kink out of her neck and glanced at the clock before picking up nail clippers and an emery board to make Mr. Lombardo's hands match the rest of the presentation.

She was just adding a final touch of metal polish to his gold wedding band—something his widow insisted be buried with him—when there was a firm knock on the rear door and a man's voice called out her name.

7

Detective Jersey Castle stood in the alley and knocked on the door once more.

"Yes?"

Sally's voice: firm yet tentative; soft but not defensive. *A voice,* Jersey thought, *one could fall asleep to and still be thrilled to hear upon awakening. Seriously?* he chided himself, *you just met the girl. Snap out of it, man.*

"It's Jersey." He made his voice firm and deep. Strong. Not soppy at all. "The Medical Examiner has removed the body, and I just have a few final questions."

"Hold on."

When he heard the locks being turned, Jersey felt a joyfulness stir in his soul that he hadn't experienced in far too long. Never married nor engaged, Jersey had contentedly lived his life, never contemplating loneliness until this exact moment as he waited in anticipation of the green-eyed woman behind the locked metal door.

When the door swung open, Jersey wiped the excited grin off his face and replaced it with a serious, and what he hoped was a manly, for handsome was probably a stretch, expression.

Sally held the door and looked up at him. She appeared worried.

"It's okay," Jersey blurted in an attempt to put her at ease. "It's just routine."

"Do you want to come in?" Sally asked.

"Sure, that would be great."

Jersey winced at his own enthusiasm as he stepped through the door and followed her down concrete steps to the chilled basement below.

At the bottom of the stairs, Jersey took in his surroundings: plain off-white walls, unimaginative linoleum floor in a speckled black-and-white gravel pattern, gleaming stainless steel fixtures, two large walk-in refrigerators at the far end, and an elderly corpse in a smart-fitting herringbone suit.

"Nice place," he said.

Sally burst out laughing and it was so infectious Jersey couldn't help but join in.

"Sorry," Jersey said as the laughter died down. "I guess that was lame."

"Not to worry." Sally walked over and lightly touched his arm. "For an inner-city mortuary, it does have its charms."

Sally moved past him and grabbed the occupied gurney.

"Can you get the door?" she asked. "The cooler on the right."

Jersey crossed to the giant refrigerator and pulled open the heavy steel door, which allowed Sally to wheel the gurney inside. Once the body was parked, Sally covered its head and upper body in a light cheesecloth veil to protect against dust or other contaminants wrecking her work. When she was done, she closed the door.

"So," Sally moved to pack up her supplies, turning her back to him, "what questions did you have?"

Jersey cleared his throat and fumbled open a small fake-leather notebook.

"Just the one really," he said. "How did you see the vehicle's plate?"

SALLY DIDN'T KNOW how to answer.

The truth seemed ridiculous: she had noticed the car's registration while watching the hit and run through the victim's own eyes.

It was the one part of her experience that really bothered her. All the rest, the woman's legs being broken, her neck hitting the windshield… it didn't take a detective to piece together what must have happened. The state of her body told that story. It would have ignited anyone's imagination.

But how did she explain the license plate and the two faces she glimpsed through the windshield?

"Ms. Wilson?" Jersey's face radiated concern.

"Sorry." Sally smiled. "I drifted off for a second."

"You look worried. Are you feeling okay?"

"Yes, I'm fine. Just… tired."

"It can be a shock," said Jersey, "seeing a thing like that. It hits me, too, sometimes. I'll be working a case, wading through bodies, thinking I'm invulnerable to it all, and then, *wham*, I need to sleep for about twenty hours just to get things back in perspective."

"My guests are easier," Sally said. "More at peace than yours."

Jersey grinned. "I've never thought of my cases as having guests, but maybe I should start." His eyes reflected a gentle warmth and Sally felt something inside her stir. "Then maybe their faces wouldn't stay with me so long."

Sally reached out and stroked his arm again, her fingers becoming hooked in a rip in the sleeve of his ratty T-shirt.

"How did you get that hair?" Sally asked. "The white streak."

Jersey blushed. "Natural curse, I guess. My grandfather had it, which never endeared me to my father as he hated the son of a bitch."

Sally laughed, but quickly covered her mouth. "Sorry."

"No, don't be," said Jersey. "I can be a son of a bitch, too, if the mood strikes."

"I find that hard to believe."

Jersey smiled wider. "You might be surprised."

"I think I'd like that," said Sally.

"Like what?"

Sally grinned playfully. "To be surprised."

Jersey blushed again.

"Why Ms. Wilson," he said in a weak attempt to sound like Rhett Butler, "are you hitting on me?"

Sally feigned indifference. "Would you like me to?"

"With all my heart."

Jersey's sincerity was so unexpectedly earnest, Sally felt her own cheeks grow warm.

The awkward silence that followed was broken when Jersey's cellphone burred.

"Sorry." He answered the phone. When he hung up, he said, "They've found the vehicle and need me on scene."

"Good news?"

Jersey shrugged. "Didn't sound like it."

"Pity," said Sally. "Your work day is just beginning, while mine, thankfully, is at an end."

"Don't rub it in."

Sally laughed and punched his arm. "I wasn't."

Jersey crossed to the steps leading up to the rear door.

"Lock up behind me, will ya? It's a crazy world out there."

"Don't I know it."

Sally followed him to the door.

Jersey stepped into the alley, but before taking off he did something completely out of character—he turned and kissed Sally on the lips.

Sally was startled, but secretly pleased.

"Just in case." Jersey headed down the alley and disappeared from view.

BACK IN THE mortuary, Sally bustled to pack up the rest of her supplies and finish cleaning the equipment and tables.

It had been too long since she had found a man who wasn't either completely freaked out about her occupation or had a morbidly disturbing fascination with it. Jersey hadn't seemed to give it much thought either way. He had been more interested in her than with what she did to pay the bills.

The discovery of the hit-and-run vehicle was also good news. If they had found the car maybe Jersey wouldn't realize that she never told him how she saw the vehicle's plate.

8

When Jersey arrived at the scene of the suspect vehicle, discovered in an alley less than eight blocks from the nightclub, he covered his ripped T-shirt with a navy blue windbreaker that he kept stashed in his trunk.

The word POLICE emblazoned on the back of the nylon jacket in large, glowing white letters reflected any available light. The jackets were great for rainy night traffic stops but, as Jersey liked to joke, not recommended for undercover work.

There was nothing he could do about the leather pants and tattered biker boots, but at least the windbreaker made him look slightly less like an overweight thug with a leather fetish.

"Nice pants," said the uniformed officer manning the barricade at the mouth of the alley. "Vice got you cruising gay clubs?"

"Just your wife's bingo hall," Jersey fired back.

The officer laughed. "In those pants, she'd eat you alive and spit out the zipper."

"Sounds like domestic bliss."

The officer sighed. "If only."

Jersey went around the temporary plastic barricade and continued down the alley to a small crowd of uniforms mulling around a large, four-door Dodge sedan.

"We know who owns it?" Jersey called out to the crowd as he reached the rear of the vehicle.

"We think it's this guy's." The answering voice carried the smoky undertones of a seductive Portuguese lilt, but it took a practiced ear to truly enjoy it.

Jersey turned to see his partner, Detective Amarela Valente, as she popped her head out of the open front passenger door on the opposite side of the car. She was dressed head to toe in black—form-fitting slacks, tapered blouse, sensible shoes, and a shiny bomber-style leather jacket. Unlike him, however, she pulled it off with aplomb. It also didn't hurt that she was athletically slim and possessed a perfect heart-shaped rear that could make a Spanish bullfighter cry—and probably had.

This morning she had twisted her sable black hair into a serious ponytail and was wearing disarming cat's-eye glasses. She was also nodding impatiently in the direction of the car's interior.

Jersey shouldered past two uniformed officers who were so distracted by every movement Amarela made that, despite his considerable size, they hadn't registered his arrival. Jersey figured they were probably hoping she would offer to spank them after class.

"Forget it, boys," Jersey muttered. "She doesn't know you're alive."

The two officers flashed him sour looks as Jersey bent down to peer through the driver's window. The seat was occupied although it was difficult to make out the driver's face due to the amount of blood that splattered the glass.

"We got a gun?" Jersey asked.

"Still in his hand," said Amarela.

"Angle of entry?"

"Stand up and see for yourself."

Jersey straightened and noticed the bullet's exit puncturing the car roof less than an inch above the top of the window.

Instinctively, he tried to follow the bullet's trajectory, but the alley hadn't yet been graced by the morning's slowly rising sun.

"We'll need that bullet," he said to no one in particular.

The sour-faced officers ignored him.

Jersey walked around the car's enormous front hood, careful to avoid several muddy puddles slicked with oil, their depth and contents unknown. He leaned over Amarela's shoulder to look inside.

The dead man's gun was a snub-nosed .38 revolver with blued metal finish and handsomely polished walnut grips.

"Not a bad choice for suicide," said Jersey. "It sucks for just about anything else."

"Don't diss the snub .38, Jers," warned Amarela. "Some of us are too embarrassed to carry Baby Glocks." She made the word "baby" sound, well, babyish.

Jersey grinned. "It's all about being comfortable with your own sexuality, partner. Some of us don't need to compensate."

"You *have* sexuality?"

"Oh, don't be modest, girlfriend. I saw you checking out my butt in these pants."

Amarela snorted. "I was just trying to figure how tight you had to tie the girdle."

"Ouch."

Jersey snapped on a pair of blue latex gloves and leaned further into the car, putting his weight on his knuckles so he didn't fall face first into the corpse's lap. When Amarela wriggled in beside him, the situation became cozy, except for the bloody dead man in the seat beside them. Amarela smelled of Dove soap and peppermint shampoo; the dead man didn't.

"So what brings you out so early?" Jersey asked in a low voice to avoid being overheard by the bored uniformed onlookers.

Amarela shrugged. "Couldn't sleep. Went for a drive and heard your name over the radio. I was heading to the hit-and-run when the report came in on this."

Jersey studied his partner. "You feeling okay?"

"I'm fine. Just couldn't sleep. No biggie."

"Okay," he said softly. "If you say so."

"I do. Besides, why are you so damn chipper? You've obviously come straight from the club. The gig go well?"

Jersey nodded. "Real well. Crowd loved us. Only three fights, and the mosh pit was writhing."

"And?"

"And what?"

"And what else? Usually before a gig, you get all stoked and happy, but you crash right after, like a kid coming off a sugar rush, and turn into Mr. Grumpy Pants for at least twenty-four hours."

"I do not," Jersey protested.

"Do, too. It's like male PMS. So fess up."

Jersey sighed. "I met a girl."

"At the gig?"

"No. After. In the alley."

"A hooker?"

"No! A witness. She works in the funeral home across the alley from the club. She's the one who saw the car's plate."

Amarela grinned wide, showing a full set of nearly perfect white teeth. Rebelling against its sisters, the perfection of the smile was marred by a single eyetooth that stuck out at a slight angle. Amarela's choice not to get it fixed had been one of the first things that endeared her to Jersey when they were partnered together five years earlier.

Amarela said, "You met a mortician in an alley over the body of a dead woman and now you're all gaa-gaa?"

"I'm not gaa-gaa!" Jersey spoke too loudly and several of the officers outside leaned down to look in the windows at them.

Jersey gritted his teeth to avoid blushing and glanced over at the dead man. "We can talk about this later."

Amarela shrugged. "Suit yourself, but we *will* talk."

THE DRIVER WAS in his mid to late sixties with a good head of silver hair. He appeared reasonably fit in a soft but still slim way, and wore a tailored, designer-label suit. The shirt and tie, however, looked slightly off as though he had been in a hurry to get dressed.

"How come he looks rumpled?" Jersey asked.

Amarela snorted. "He just blew his brains out and you expect him to tuck in his shirt?"

Jersey rubbed the side of his nose with a latex finger. "You wear a three-thousand-dollar suit, you want to look your best. You tuck in your shirt, you straighten your tie, you make sure the Windsor knot is just right…" He let the thought trail off.

"He just drove over someone," said Amarela. "That can make a guy twitchy. He starts to sweat, he loosens his tie, starts grabbing at his shirt, the man's a nervous wreck."

"Hmmm," said Jersey. "Then what?"

Amarela shrugged. "Then the remorse kicks in, so he pulls into an empty alley, digs out his gun and buys a one-way ticket to the hereafter."

Jersey leaned closer to the victim and sniffed.

"I don't smell booze," he said. "Why run if you're sober? The alley outside the club was dark. It could have been an accident."

Amarela didn't answer, so Jersey hunched lower to get a better view of the entrance wound in the side of the dead man's temple.

"Get forensics to check the angle, just to make sure it was self-inflicted."

"Why?" asked Amarela. "You thinking car-jacking gone wrong? Those assholes don't tend to leave guns behind. Guns cost money and jackers are scavengers."

Jersey locked eyes with his partner and kept a serious face. "It's only a crappy .38."

Before Amarela could protest, Jersey backed out of the car and stretched his back. "We got an I.D.?"

Amarela exited the car and stood beside him. The top of her head was not quite level with his shoulders.

"The car is registered to a Nicholas Higgins. Whether or not that's Mr. Higgins hogging the driver's seat will have to wait until we get him out of there. I didn't see a wallet."

"He wouldn't want to ruin the line of his suit," said Jersey. "You check the glove box?"

Amarela sighed. "I *was* just about to do that before you strolled up like a Billy Idol wannabe and wanted the back story."

Jersey stepped back and held up his hands. "I wasn't criticizing. And just so you know, Billy's *White Wedding* is still a huge hit with the fans."

Amarela popped open the glove box and carefully removed a thin, calfskin wallet. She kept her eyes averted from Jersey's smug grin as she flipped it open and removed an Oregon driver's license. She compared the photo I.D. to the dead driver.

"Looks like Mr. Higgins won't need to renew," she said. "The license was set to expire at the end of next month on his... " she did a quick mental calculation, "sixty-fifth birthday."

"About the same age as the woman he ran over." Jersey moved to the rear window and pressed his face close to the glass. A dark object wedged behind the passenger seat caught his eye.

"There's something behind your seat," Jersey said. "Can you unlock this door?"

Amarela leaned over and flipped the lock. Jersey opened the door and pulled out the object. It was a woman's leather clutch purse.

"You want the honors?" he asked.

"Embarrassed by what you might find?"

Jersey rolled his eyes, opened the purse and plucked out a wallet. When he opened it, he found another Oregon driver's license. This time the I.D. matched the woman lying dead behind the club.

"It seems," said Jersey as he showed the I.D. to his partner, "that Mr. Higgins drove over his own wife."

"That could definitely make you suicidal," said Amarela.

"True," agreed Jersey. "But if you loved your wife so much that you couldn't live without her, why would you leave her for dead in the first place?"

9

A shriek of hastily applied brakes made everyone turn to see a dented brown Ford slide into the barricade and narrowly miss the scrambling officer on guard duty.

Lieutenant Morrell climbed out of the Ford to survey the damage caused by hitting the barrier. He turned an evil eye on the pale-faced officer who had just narrowly missed becoming a hood ornament.

"You! Tell the garage I want them to do another check on this beast as soon as I return to the station."

The officer remained tongue-tied, but managed to nod.

"And," Morrell continued, "straighten this damn barricade."

The lieutenant flicked a finger across his moustache to flatten any stray hairs and marched down the alley to the crime scene.

The crowd of officers parted like the Red Sea and some of them suddenly discovered they were no longer needed on the scene. They departed as inconspicuously as possible.

Morrell stopped at the car and bent to peer through the driver's window.

"Damn mess," he said. "We have a weapon?"

"In his hand," said Jersey.

Morrell straightened up and glared across the roof at the detective.

"Still in costume, I see, Detective Castle."

"Yes, sir," said Jersey.

"And what is your sidekick dressed as? Zorro."

Amarela opened her mouth to protest, but Jersey grabbed her arm and squeezed.

"We were just wrapping up here," said Jersey. "It appears that Mr. Higgins, he's the gentleman with the ventilated skull, was married to the woman he drove over in the alley."

"Hmmm, interesting," said Morrell in a tone that suggested he wasn't interested at all. He bent down to peer through the window again. "Is that leather interior?"

"Corinthian," said Jersey with a straight face.

"Blood makes a real mess of leather."

"It does," Jersey agreed.

Morrell straightened and finger-brushed his moustache.

"Forensics on its way?" he asked.

"Yes, sir."

"We'll need the bullet."

Jersey nodded.

"Good, good, fast work, detective. Keep me informed."

Morrell turned on his heel and marched back to his car.

Once he was out of earshot, Amarela snarled, "Zorro?"

Jersey grinned. "I would have put you in the Catwoman camp, myself. You know, sleek, sexy—"

"Dangerous," snapped Amarela.

"Definitely," said Jersey, his grin widening.

There was another crunch of metal and plastic from the mouth of the alley as Morrell's car jerked forward into the resurrected barricade before quickly switching into reverse and backing away. The officer on guard duty flashed Jersey an exasperated look as he bent to fix the barricade once more.

All Jersey could do was shrug his shoulders in sympathy.

JERSEY AND AMARELA were walking to the barricade when Jersey came to a sudden stop and spun around.

"What?" Amarela asked.

"Can you read the plate?"

Amarela peered down the alley and shook her head. "There's something covering it."

Returning to the vehicle, Jersey lifted a ragged strip of waterproof black cloth that half covered the license plate.

"This is from the victim's coat," he said. "It must've snagged when she came sliding off the back."

"So?"

"So how could anyone have seen the plate with this flapping in the way?"

Amarela rolled her eyes and turned back toward the barricade. "There's another plate on the front, Doofus. Did your witness say which one she saw?"

"No, but…" Jersey allowed his words to drift, but he was troubled.

The only way for Sally to have seen the front license plate would be if she were standing in the alley *before* the victim was struck. *But how was that possible?* He had seen her enter the alley at virtually the same time he did.

With a heavy sigh, Jersey snapped open his cellphone and dialed the club. After six rings an answering machine picked up with a rather punk "leave a message or fuck off" greeting.

"Hey, Les, Jersey here. I need to know if you guys have CCTV on the door facing the alley. If so, I need to see it, so don't erase this morning's footage. Call me back as soon as you get this."

Jersey left his cell number and hung up.

Amarela flashed him a sideways glance.

"I know, I know," Jersey said defensively. "I should have secured the tape when I was at the scene. But I was…" He hesitated.

"Distracted," Amarela finished for him.

10

Sally opened her apartment door to the pitter-patter of tiny feet. A longhaired Calico, its fur a chaotic blend of orange, black, and white, instantly wrapped itself around her ankles and began to purr.

Locking the door behind her, Sally dropped her coat and a small leather travel pouch on the floor and bent to pick up the cat. The purring grew louder as the cat climbed onto her shoulder to begin nuzzling her cheek and bumping the side of her head with its own.

Sally laughed delightedly.

"You want breakfast, Jiggy?"

Jiggy—short for jigsaw, as in puzzle; not the Will Smith *"Getting' Jiggy wit It"* song—licked her cheek. The cat's tongue was so rough it could have removed five layers of makeup in one swipe if Sally ever bothered to wear any.

Sally prepared a bowl of food for the cat: a generous dollop of disgustingly pungent soft food surrounded by crunchy, tuna flavored morsels of hard.

With the cat occupied, Sally started a warm bath, changed into a fuzzy white robe and slippers, and poured herself a glass of red Chilean wine. The wine was as rich in color and full of body as fresh blood, but with a lighter, fruitier, and more palatable flavor.

Sally took two long swallows of wine before turning her attention to the fridge. The glass shelves were mostly bare, but a plastic container of leftover Pad Thai from the local Noodle Box looked appetizing. She gave it a sniff to make sure it was still edible before zapping it in the microwave.

After another large swallow of wine, Sally topped up her glass and carried it to the bath along with her lukewarm container of Thai noodles in spicy peanut sauce.

When the tub was nearly full, Sally added a splash of foaming bath salts. She let the water run for an extra minute before switching off the taps and stepping in.

The water soothed her muscles, the wine soothed her mind, and the exotic food made her feel wonderfully decadent. Sally closed her eyes, the rim of the glass resting upon her lower lip, the rich bouquet smelling of volcanic soil, exotic fruit, and a hint of dark chocolate.

Her thoughts drifted lazily until, behind her eyelids, her pupils widened in alarm as the car's ferocious grill was suddenly bearing down on her again.

No, not on *her*, she told herself to ease a rising panic, the dead woman in the periwinkle pantsuit and black raincoat.

Sally forced herself to stay calm, knowing the vehicle couldn't hurt her. This was the past, not the present.

She glanced at the license plate and then looked into and through the windshield.

Two faces. Both men.

The driver, an older gentleman with silver hair, looked terrified, his eyes wide and filled with tears. The passenger, face in profile, nose like a shark fin and skin a sickly white, was talking incessantly at the driver. His thin lips were flapping with such force that foam and spittle bubbled at the corners. There was also something wrong with his eye... like it was sliding down his cheek.

She didn't recognize either man.

The car rushed forward and she braced herself for impact—

Something warm splashed her cheek…

Sally's eyes snapped open. Jiggy was dipping her paw into the bath water and shaking it before licking and repeating.

"Thanks," Sally said with a relieved sigh. She lifted her free hand out of the tub to stroke the cat under its chin. "Once is enough to be hit by a car, even in a dream."

The cat purred and flicked its paw again, sending water spraying.

A LITTLE DRUNK from the wine and exhausted by her night, Sally stumbled from the bathroom with her eyes half-closed and crawled into bed. The embrace of a goose down comforter wrapped around her like a lover, while the warmth brought blissful weight to her eyelids. Not one to be left out, Jiggy kneaded the blanket at her human's feet before curling up behind her knees and joining her in sleep.

AS THE STEAM in the bathroom began to dissipate, three finger-painted words appeared on the bathroom mirror above the sink.

The message read: *Run, Sally! Run!*

11

Jersey made a quick stop at his condo on the northern edge of Old Town to drop off his car and grab a change of clothes.

Buying the condo was one of the smartest moves Jersey had made. Old Town had been in the early stages of transformation from forgotten to trendy when he raised enough for a down payment and locked himself into a long-term commitment he never thought he'd have the nerve for.

Located a short walk from popular Waterfront Park and nestled in an inner-city neighborhood that boasted some of the best restaurants Portland had to offer, Jersey's condo was now worth close to double what he paid for it. If he had actually known what he was doing, rather than being blessed by dumb luck, he could be the new poster boy for police smarts.

With hair still dripping from a quick shower, Jersey dashed out the front door and climbed into the passenger seat of Amarela's unmarked, department-issue, four-door cruiser parked illegally at the yellow curb.

Dressed in clean blue jeans, white sneakers, plain black T-shirt, and a midnight-blue blazer, Jersey looked like a huskier version of Billy Joel from his *Glass Houses* tour. Unlike the piano man, however, Jersey wore the jacket to cover a regulation Glock 17 automatic attached to his belt in a flat combat holster specially designed for concealed carry. The jacket also helped move eyes away from the unwelcome bulge of his belly.

Jersey liked to think of the Glock 17 as his deterrent gun since it had the size and heft to make the smarter criminals think twice. They didn't always have that reaction to his backup piece, the so-called Baby Glock, even though it was just as deadly. Perception can be everything.

Jersey finger-combed his wet hair. "Thanks for the pit stop. I feel human again."

"No problem." Amarela put the car in gear. "Dressed like you were, I would've had to make you ride in the back."

"Now that's cold, I know what kind of people ride back there." Jersey paused for effect. "Mostly your exes, right?"

Amarela's right hand was a blur as she released it from its two o'clock position on the steering wheel and punched Jersey hard on the upper arm. Her knuckles were like tiny pickaxes.

Jersey winced as his muscle spasmed from the attack, but he covered it with a laugh.

"Why so sensitive?" he asked. "You and Clarissa break up again?"

"Don't talk to me about Clarissa." Amarela repositioned her hands in the ten o'clock and two o'clock positions. "That bitch is out of my life for good."

"Isn't that what you said last month before you took her back?"

"That was different."

"How?"

Amarela pouted. "It just was."

Jersey saw he was treading in dangerous water and decided to back down.

"This why you couldn't sleep?" he asked in a gentler tone.

Amarela shrugged.

"After work," Jersey continued, "we'll go to my place, order pizza, open a bottle of Scotch, and trash talk the fairer sex until you turn straight."

Amarela laughed. "It'll take more than a bottle."

"I'll open a cask," said Jersey.

Amarela released one hand from the steering wheel and held it palm up to her partner. Jersey slapped it in a high five.

"SO TELL ME about this girl you met." Amarela steered out of the busy downtown core, heading for the crowded interstate. "She gorgeous?"

Jersey grinned. "More exotic, actually, with spiky blonde hair that I swear is as white as my kitchen cabinets, and she has the most amazing green eyes."

"Ooh, la, la. She sounds out of your league, partner."

Jersey shrugged. "Probably is, but…"

"But?" Amarela prodded.

"But there was something… a connection. It was weird, but we met over a dead body, and it just seemed right. She wasn't freaked out by it, you know?"

"Because she works with dead people in the funeral home?"

"Yeah," Jersey agreed. "I guess that's it."

"So your 'special connection' is being cool around corpses?"

Jersey scowled. "It's more than that. She… I…"

"Spit it out."

"I kissed her," said Jersey. "It was a crazy impulse and a shock to both us." He winced. "I just hope I haven't scared her away."

"Well, well, aren't you the romantic? A first kiss over the body of a warm corpse, how can this be anything but destiny?"

Jersey slumped in his seat. "I'm not talking to you if you're going to mock."

"Okay, I'm sorry. I'm happy for you. Really. What's the point in looking good in leather pants if you're not getting laid?"

Turning his head away, Jersey gazed out the window. "That's your apology?"

"Come on, Jers," she coaxed, stifling a laugh. "I'm sorry. What can I do to prove it?"

Jersey shrugged.

"Breakfast," she said. "I'll go through the drive-in and get you one of those greasy egg pancake things you like."

"With a hashbrown and large coffee?"

"Yes!"

Jersey turned forward again. "That's a start."

THE LATE MR. and Mrs. Higgins owned a modest four-bedroom, two-story home in the tiny city of Maywood Park perched high on the east bank above Interstate 205.

Surrounded on all sides by the sprawling city of Portland, Maywood Park was a unique, all-residential community that boasted a population of fewer than eight hundred, yet was still tenacious enough to fight several attempts over the years to be annexed by its expansive neighbor.

With only three hundred homes spread across a total area of 0.17 square miles, it didn't take Jersey and Amarela long to arrive at the Higgins' residence. Amarela parked in the empty driveway of a double-car garage, the ubiquitous basketball hoop in the peak looking lonely and disused.

"You bring keys?" Jersey swallowed his last sip of coffee and dropped the empty container into the dashboard cup holder—one of only two in the whole vehicle. Felons were not invited to enjoy backseat beverages during transport.

Amarela lifted a clutch of keys from her pocket and made them jangle. "I left the ignition key in the car and took the rest."

Jersey looked up at the gleaming, power-washed vinyl siding and sighed. "Let's go see what suburban bliss was trying to hide."

The home's open front porch was wide enough to accommodate

a couple of slope-backed Adirondack chairs and a round table perfectly sized for a pitcher of lemonade, a plate of tuna-fish sandwiches, and a bowl of potato chips on lazy Sunday afternoons.

Amarela tried the keys in the front lock, while Jersey surveyed the quiet street lined with mature trees and mowed lawns.

The neighborhood wasn't cookie-cutter fresh like the latest subdivisions that continued to spring up around Portland's borders. In fact, some of the homes were in sore need of TLC, but the mature shrubs, wide roads, and solid concrete sidewalks gave it a bygone character that Jersey found appealing.

It was the kind of place where kids could still play street hockey without worrying about being run over by short-tempered drunks or drag-racing punks. Then again, judging by the age of the curious faces that peered out at him from behind twitching polyester curtains, Jersey didn't know if there were any actual kids left in Maywood Park.

"Got it." Amarela pushed open the front door. "Don't see an alarm system, so we're good to go."

Jersey turned to follow his partner inside the house. "The neighbors are nosey. We may get company from the county sheriff's office. This is their jurisdiction."

"Oh, goody," said Amarela with a lascivious smirk. "I love me a girl in uniform."

"Oddly enough," said Jersey. "So do I."

Amarela rolled her eyes. "I'll take upstairs."

Jersey proceeded through an open archway on his right that led into the living room. Even though Mr. and Mrs. Higgins hadn't been expecting unannounced company in the form of two homicide detectives, the place looked perfectly and unexcitingly normal.

The square room was carpeted in a stain-resistant shade of milk-coffee Berber with matching three-person couch and two reading chairs. The furniture was aimed at a wood-burning fireplace with a dark-stained oak mantle, but the twin chairs could also catch good reading light from a large bay window dressed in elegant, though out-of-date, floral curtains. There was no television.

Instead of the high-definition delights of real fake housewives, fly-by-night psychologists and naked, bug-eating survivalists, the Higgins' main form of entertainment was found through a second archway at the rear of the room. Where a formal dining room had once been set to accommodate a large family, the solid oak table and eight matching chairs had been sent packing to the garage and replaced by wall-to-wall IKEA bookshelves.

Each shelf was loaded with an eclectic assortment of non-fiction tombs, most of which focused either on obscure Biblical studies or historic sea voyages to the Arctic Circle. Jersey wondered why there didn't appear to be a definite His and Hers division in the reading material, but decided there was a possibility they actually shared the same interests.

There was also no obvious sign of discord in either room. No broken furniture, smashed plates, blood spatter, or torn-up credit card receipts for binge shopping or lunches with mistresses. Whatever had led Mr. Higgins to drive over his wife, it hadn't started here.

Jersey returned to the living room to study family photos spread out along the fireplace mantle. The photos told him the Higgins took great pride in their two grown children, one of each gender, both university graduates. The daughter's photos were all semi-professional, individual portraits with flattering light and air-brushed skin, while the son preferred random snapshots showing a split-level family with a beautiful wife, teenage daughter, and a baby boy.

The baby looked like his grandfather—especially around the eyes—except for a darker olive complexion and sharp Persian nose descended from his mother. The teen didn't resemble either side of the family as a single extra chromosome had given her a flat face, slanted eyes, and small ears that bespoke the telltale characteristics of Down Syndrome.

The smiling teen appeared in a majority of the other photos, and it was clear to see the love her grandparents lavished on her.

It's hard to imagine doting grandparents turning their hand to murder and/or suicide but, as Jersey well knew, it happened.

Jersey moved into the kitchen that, like the living room and library, was clean and normal and boring. There wasn't even a dirty cereal bowl in the sink to get somebody's morning off to a bad start.

The house's main phone rested in a wooden hutch beside double-paned glass patio doors that led to a beautifully landscaped, and surprisingly secluded, backyard. Jersey crossed to the phone and picked up a leather address book. He flipped it open to 'H' and saw the names of the Higgins' children. The son lived in Portland, but the daughter had moved to New York.

Jersey wrote their phone numbers and addresses into his notebook as Amarela descended the stairs.

"Anything?" he asked.

"Nada. Clean, tidy, nothing out of place. They shared the same bed, so they must've got along. You?"

"Same." He held up the notebook. " I got the NOKs, at least."

Amarela scrunched her nose. Nobody liked to inform Next Of Kin that a loved one was gone.

"So what you thinking here?" she asked.

Jersey shrugged. "Based on what we've seen, I'd write it up as domestic murder-suicide." He paused. "Except for location, timing, and choice of weapon."

Amarela nodded. "Why get dressed up and go out on the town in the middle of the night to a secluded, yet still public, spot when you could kill your wife in the privacy of your own home?"

"And why use a car if you own a gun?" Jersey added. "The

hit-and-run angle only makes sense if you wanted it to look like an accident."

"And you would only do that if you hoped to get away with it," Amarela interjected.

"And if you planned to get away with it," Jersey released a heavy sigh, "why kill yourself after?"

12

The man with the slippery eye and shark-fin nose broke the lock on the rear entrance to the punk club and made his way inside.

The club—so anti-trendy it was simply called The Club, although its signage boasted a wooden bat adorned with sharp iron spikes dripping with blood—was empty except for the lingering and pheromone-rich stench of booze, rage, sex, and sweat.

It was a stink only humans could exude.

Assured by the silence that he was alone, the man crept down a narrow hallway until stopped by his reflection shimmering in a large full-length mirror where the performers took a few final seconds to adjust themselves before taking the stage.

In front of the mirror, he removed a tiny squeeze bottle of artificial tears from his pocket.

His face drooped with the waxy pallor of a decorative candle placed too close to a neighboring flame. The left side was nearly flawless so long as he didn't try to smile or otherwise pull on the overly tight skin. His left eye was a glassy brown marble flecked with fiery orange, its dark iris so intense few people could stare directly at it without feeling a shiver run down their spines.

The right side didn't fare so well. Although his strong nose was unmarred, the area that ran from hairline to the far corner of his mouth was a rippled mass of sagging skin. His wrinkled forehead drooped over his right eye, which resembled a smoldering ember adrift on an infected red tide; his cheek had collapsed inwards, the plump muscle eaten away, leaving only a sunken hollow of corrugated flesh.

The right ear was missing its outer flesh and cartilage housing, leaving only a dark hole.

An eye patch would have gone a short way to making his façade less frightening, but the man knew his deformity made people so squeamish they could barely look at him. If a witness to his many crusades ever came forward, they would only be able to articulate one singular thing about him: *ugliness*. And as he had witnessed many times in this world, ugly was not a rare commodity.

The man squirted the saline solution into his dead eye and returned the bottle to his pocket before moving on.

Inside the manager's office, a quick survey revealed no videotape or digital recorder for the security cameras. Instead, a coiled mass of black USB cables snaked down from holes drilled in the ceiling and into an eight-port hub. The octopus hub, in turn, was plugged into the back of a squat mini-tower computer nestled under the desk.

The man hit the power switch on the PC and waited for it to boot. Within a few seconds, a monitor flickered to life and the Windows icon appeared. The man waited patiently while the computer ran its checks and balances. When the floating Windows icon finally disappeared, it was replaced by a flashing security sign. The sign asked for a finger to be placed on a print scanner. To one side of the keyboard, a flat plastic pad, no larger than a credit card, pulsed with a soft red glow.

The man would have smiled if his skin had allowed it.

Scrounging around the office, he picked up a roll of transparent tape and a pencil sharpener. With strong hands, he broke open the sharpener and dumped a thin layer of graphite dust onto the shiny curved surface of the computer mouse. The fine dust clung to the oily swirls and sworls left over from the owner's hand. He blew the excess away with a gentle puff from the side of his mouth.

The man tore off a tiny strip of tape, placed it over a clean, dark print of the mouse-clicking index finger and placed the tape on the scanner. He covered the tape and scanner bed with the back of a plain white business card to turn light escaping transparent into readable opaque.

After hitting the Enter button, the scanner read the lifted print without a single hiccup, and the computer's welcome screen appeared.

From there it was a simple job to locate the digitally encoded video files for the rear entrance camera and find the time-coded entry. A double-click opened the tiny movie while a tap on the spacebar made it fill the screen.

The man watched in passive silence as the large sedan mowed down the screaming woman. She had simply stood there, not believing her husband could possibly do what the man told him to. She hadn't known just how convincing the man could be.

After the car sped away, the man watched as Sally entered the alley from the mortuary. She had grown into a beautiful woman with the inherited shock white hair of her father and the mystical green eyes of her mother. The straight razor looked cumbersome and silly in her small, delicate hand, but the man was pleased that she possessed a fighting spirit.

When Sally crossed to the discarded woman, the man tensed and leaned forward to peer even deeper into the monitor. The scene was darker than he had hoped, the funeral home's security lights focused too narrowly to encompass all of the body, but there was enough ambient spillage to read the cosmetician's body language.

The man watched Sally reach out and touch the body.

Sally froze. Her body became as rigid as a statue, and the man wished he could see her eyes, but the camera's resolution was too low and the light too dim.

The moment finished too quickly as the heavyset leather-clad punk broke Sally's trance, but the man felt a stirring deep in his soul.

Had she seen?

She must have.

But could she understand what *she saw without the interpreter?*

He lifted his cellphone and dialed.

The phone was answered on the second ring.

"Yes?" An older man's voice. Alert and awake.

"I've found her."

"Are you sure this time, Aedan?"

"It's her," he said confidently. "It has to be."

The phone was covered and Aedan heard whispered voices conferring.

After a few moments, the older voice returned. "Bring her home. We'll be waiting."

13

Jersey's phone rang as he and Amarela wound their way out of the suburban maze of Maywood Park in an effort to avoid the traffic jam that made up the interstate.

The locals liked to blame the continual congestion on the Canadians as they flooded across the border into Washington and down through Oregon to California in a greedy blitz for bargains and sunshine. But from what Jersey could see, most of the license plates still boasted Pacific Northwest roots.

When Jersey answered the phone, a nasally voice—the kind that only comes from repeated blunt-force trauma—said, "Did you break into my club?"

"Now why would I do that, Les?"

"To get the CCTV footage. You called about it."

"If I was going to break into your club why would I call first?"

Les grunted. "Yeah, okay. Well someone did. The back door was kicked open and my computer don't work."

"The surveillance footage is on the computer?"

"Yeah, 'course, that's why I bought the damn thing. VCRs are for shit."

"I'll stop by and take a look. I know a thing or two about computers."

"Figured you would," Les said. "You got that geek vibe about you."

Jersey turned to Amarela. "Can you drop me off at the club and do the NOK without me?"

"Ah, shit, Jers," Amarela whined. "You know I hate that job. People get so damn emotional, and clingy and snotty… always with the snot, you notice that?"

Amarela actually had a good whine: all pouty lips and large eyes and the ever-present hint of sex if you did her bidding. Fortunately, it hadn't taken Jersey five years to become immune. The first two were tough though.

"And what?" Jersey argued. "I like it?"

"No, but people take it better from you. You've got that cuddliness about you."

"Cuddliness?"

"Yeah, you know? They see me, they think 'skinny bitch with a great ass has it all going on', but they see you and—"

"They think 'fat fool *with a decent ass* doesn't have a clue.'"

Amarela grinned. "No, I'm not saying… it's just people naturally trust you more."

"Cause I'm cuddly?"

"Because you *appear* cuddly. People don't want to cuddle me."

"No, they want to—"

"Don't!"

Jersey sneered without malice. "Suck it up and drop me at the club. I ain't nobody's teddy bear."

JERSEY PRESSED THE power button on the PC.

"I tried that," Les grumbled. "What, you think I'm a moron?"

Les had been owner/manager of The Club for the last five years and had led the format change from black leather biker bar to black leather punk club. The reason for the change was simple—he couldn't stand listening to Johnny Cash every night.

"Man was fucking depressing," he told Jersey one night between sets. "All religion and righteousness, but with a voice that chews out a little piece of your soul and spits it on the ground. That cover he did of *Hurt*? Jesus Christ, stick a gun in my mouth already."

To blend with his club's image, Les had buzzed his premature gray hair, leaving a two-inch-wide Mohawk that ran down the center of his head like an exploded zipper. He dyed it different colors to match the various holidays: green for St. Paddy's; orange for Halloween; red, white and blue for Fourth of July, and so on. Today, it was purple. Whether or not that was for the Queen's birthday, Jersey didn't want to know.

To further complement his anti-establishment punk credo, Les wore a tight pair of black jeans and a loose-fitting black T-shirt with the slogan *Punk Sucks* in a metallic shade of purple to match his hair. Les owned at least a hundred black T-shirts, all with different slogans that ended in either *Suck* or *Sucks*, like iPods Suck, Death Sucks, and Pandas Suck.

On his hands and knees under the desk, Jersey discovered the computer had come unplugged from the wall socket. Rolling his eyes, he plugged it in and hit the power switch again. Instead of the expected triumphant Windows launch tune, however, the computer beeped in protest and flashed a cryptic BIOS message on the screen.

"It can't find the hard drive," Jersey said. "You got a screwdriver?"

"Bit early for me."

"Not the drink. The tool."

"Okay, but you sure you know what you're doing?" Les started digging through drawers and cabinets.

"I've been building these things for years."

"Building them? What the fuck for?"

"For fun. It's a hobby. Challenges me, you know?"

"Well, that's stupid." Les pulled a fat red multi-purpose

screwdriver from a dusty drawer. "They come already built from the store."

"Yeah, I know." Jersey sighed. "But I like to customize them. You know, bump up the RAM, add a killer video card, slip in an over-clocked processor or water-cooling. Mod the case, some neon lighting…"

"Yeah, like I said, stupid."

Les handed Jersey the screwdriver. "You want that drink now?"

"It's ten in the morning, and I'm on duty."

"I'm just talking a screwdriver. Vitamin C is good for you."

"Make it virgin, and I'll take you up on it."

"Suit yerself."

When Les left the office, Jersey unscrewed the top of the screwdriver, found the right bit, and slipped it into the stem.

When Les returned with his orange juice, Jersey said, "I've found your problem."

Les looked down at his computer lying open on the floor, a tangled mess of electronics and multi-colored wires.

"What the fuck did you do?"

"I just opened the case," Jersey explained. "But I wasn't the first. Your hard drive is missing."

"Well it must be in there somewhere."

Jersey grinned. "No, it's not. Someone took it."

"Well, crap. All my records are on there. Payroll, work schedule, inventory, everything."

"You have a backup?"

"A what?"

"An external drive where you backup all your files."

"I don't know what you're talking about," said Les. "I had the computer. It does all that stuff."

"Not anymore," said Jersey. "Sorry."

"Well, fuck. I knew I should have stuck to using recipe cards.

You never see good ol' pen and paper giving you this much grief. Fucking technology, who needs it?"

Les took a long gulp of his orange juice, grimaced and handed it to Jersey.

"That's yours," he said. "Tastes horrible without the booze."

Jersey accepted the glass and took a tentative sip. Surprisingly, it tasted fresh squeezed.

"So can I still get the Internet?" Les asked.

"Without a hard drive, you can't do anything. Can you think of any reason why someone would want it?"

"Can't see it being any good to anyone but me."

"Did you watch the footage from the hit-and-run last night?"

"Didn't even think of it. The camera catches a good part of the alley, so it was probably on there. You think that's why I got broken into?"

Jersey shrugged. "We found the driver, but it couldn't have been him. He's dead."

"Maybe it was the Feds. I downloaded some movies the other week, just Asian porn, but still."

Jersey laughed. "I don't think the Feds are interested in your peccadilloes."

"What? No, it was nothing like that. Just some girl-on-girl stuff."

"Well the action's over until you get a new hard drive. I know a kid who'll sort you out. I'll ask him to call."

Jersey brushed the dirt off his knees, handed back the empty glass, and headed for the rear door.

"You'll need a new lock on here as well," he called over his shoulder. "This one's buggered."

Standing in the alley, looking across the potholed gravel at the dark windows of the mortuary, Jersey pulled out his phone and dialed dispatch.

When the call connected, he said, "Darlene? I need an address."

14

Sally awoke to a persistent rapping of knuckles on her front door.

She yawned and stretched before sliding out of bed and slipping into her bathrobe and slippers. Jiggy, having migrated from the foot of the bed to curl in a fluffy ball with her head on the spare pillow, opened one lazy eye, blinked, yawned, and went back to sleep.

"It's okay for some." Sally left the bedroom and shuffled to the front door.

JERSEY'S PHONG RANG as he waited outside Sally's door. When he answered, Amarela said, "We've got a problem."

"What?"

"The son went nuts when I broke the news. No tears, no quick stop on grief, just straight to pissed. What the fuck is that about? Both your parents are dead, and *I'm* the bad guy."

"We all react—"

"Save it," Amarela snapped. "He was a fucking asshole. I told you I hate doing this."

Jersey turned away from the apartment and headed down the stairs. Sally would have to wait.

"Okay, calm down," said Jersey. "He's pissed. That's not our problem."

"No? The lieutenant wants to see us."

"Why?"

"The asshole called the mayor, direct. Had the number on speed dial. Made me fucking stand there while he did it, too."

"And the mayor called Morrell?"

"Duh. My phone started ringing at the same time the fucking NOK is slamming the door in my face. I should have Tasered the prick."

"I'll grab a taxi and meet you at the station."

"Screw that, I'm not walking in there by myself. Where you at? I'll pick you up, and we'll go in together."

As he pushed open the lobby door of the low-rise apartment building, Jersey gave his partner the address of a nearby *Grind'm If You Got'm* coffee shop that made a synapses-firing Red Eye. His caffeine level was dropping uncomfortably low.

WHEN SALLY OPENED the door, there was nobody there.

With an irritated sigh, she relocked the deadbolt and padded across the room to the front window. She looked down and saw a husky figure walking away. The breadth of his shoulders and the fit of his jeans told her it was Jersey, the detective who had so unexpectedly kissed her on the back steps of the mortuary.

She still didn't know quite what to make of that but, despite the boldness of his actions, his lips had been soft and his eyes so very gentle. Hmm, maybe she did know after all; she liked it... liked him.

She wondered if he had stopped by to ask her out, but lost the courage at the last moment, or if the knock had been strictly work related. If it was business, why had he walked away? And, more importantly, if he hadn't walked away, what answers could she give him without sounding like a complete loon?

Sally snugged her dressing gown tighter at the collar and padded into the kitchen to brew a pot of coffee. She liked to start the day with a few strong cups while she watched *The View* to catch up on what had annoyed the ladies lately.

She actually had a recurring daydream where she was a guest on the show promoting a small book she had always contemplated writing entitled, *Beauty Tips for the Dead.* The only problem was that she couldn't imagine any living person—outside of the funeral businesses—wanting to buy it, and the dead didn't have active credit cards.

IN THE STAIRWELL outside the apartment, Aedan descended from the floor above where he had silently fled when the beefy cop arrived unexpectedly. Moving close, he pressed his left ear against Sally's door.

He could hear the television. Women arguing.

He inhaled the air, catching a lingering scent of shampoo and soap.

She was the one. She had to be.

15

With a caffeine buzz from his morning Red Eye—two shots of tar-like espresso topped up with fresh brewed dark roast coffee—Jersey felt bright eyed and hopeful. His partner, however, was floating a dark cloud on his parade as they rode the elevator to the thirteenth floor of the Portland Justice Center.

Located in the heart of downtown, the eighteen-story tower was home to not only the Portland Police Bureau, but also four courtrooms and the maximum-security Multnomah County Detention Center. For criminals, that meant the journey from being arrested to incarcerated was a short one.

"I hate getting called into the boss's office," Amarela muttered. "Makes me feel like a rookie again."

"Ah, the good old days," said Jersey.

"Speak for yourself. Lecherous old men always wanting me to go undercover as a hooker or porn star? It was like walking naked through a safari park."

Jersey smiled. "Somehow I don't see you as a victim."

"No, but I had to crush a lot of nutsacks to get that message across."

"Men are pigs," said Jersey.

Amarela burst into laughter. "Amen."

"Shouldn't that be A-wo-men?"

"Damn. When a woman gets elected Pope, she'll need to fix that."

When the elevator door opened, the partners marched out with sober faces and made their way through a maze of desks to the lieutenant's corner office.

LIEUTENANT NOEL MORRELL steepled his hands as the two detectives entered his office. He still looked as crisp and fresh as he had at four that morning.

"Ah, detectives Castle and Valente," he began. "Nice to see you finally got dressed, Detective Castle, although a dressier pair of pants, proper fitting shirt, and a decent pair of shoes wouldn't go amiss."

"Yes, sir," said Jersey with an unconscious flexing of mouth muscle that hinted at a smile. "But apart from that?"

"You also need a haircut."

"Yes, sir."

"You've been investigating this morning's hit-and-run?"

"We have."

"And your progress?"

"Well, as you know, I was first on the scene after the victim was struck and killed by her husband's car. Detective Valente was on the scene for the recovery of the vehicle and its driver. It appears at this time that the driver committed suicide after killing his wife. However—"

Lieutenant Morrell held up a hand.

"I want to stop you there," he said. "I have received an urgent request from the son that the bodies of his parents be immediately released to the funeral home. It seems his parents didn't believe in embalming and the family wants an open coffin, so they need to hold the service as quickly as possible." He flattened his hands on the desk. "The bottom line is this; do you have any evidence that this is anything other than a domestic murder-suicide?"

"Evidence? No," said Jersey, "but it feels wrong. The location, timing, and choice of weapon don't add up."

"I agree," said Amarela. "There's more to this than it appears."

"But you have no evidence to suggest third-party involvement?"

Jersey shook his head. "Not at this time, but—"

"I'm releasing the bodies to the funeral home," said Morrell. "The victims' son is a close friend of the mayor's son, and I can't see any benefit to getting into an argument over religious rights and freedoms without something solid to back it up."

"But," Jersey protested, "if you release the bodies now, there won't be time for an autopsy. At least let me request a drug screen."

"The decision is made, detective. That will be all."

Amarela grabbed Jersey's arm and pulled him toward the door. Before he exited, Jersey turned and asked, "What funeral home are the bodies being shipped to?"

Morrell glanced down at a sheet of paper on his desk. "Paynes Funeral Home. Both victims had those pre-paid plans you see advertised on TV. I've actually been thinking of getting one for Mrs. Morrell. Our anniversary is coming up and with the new baby…"

Morrell stopped. He was talking to himself.

16

In the chilled basement of Paynes Funeral Home, Sally removed the crisp sheet from the dead woman's face.

The basement felt different during the day—colder somehow. Despite the blacked out windows, Sally could sense movement all around her: creaks, scrapes, and sighs descending from the viewing parlor and sales office above; rumbles, horns, and grumbles colliding on the streets outside.

It was unsettling.

At night, her workshop was a calm oasis—just her and the guests.

But when Mr. Payne phoned with a special request, how could Sally refuse? In fact, she was delighted to help. The Payne family had always been so good to her.

Sally looked down at her guest again. Any sign of recognition that she expected to feel wasn't there. The woman was a stranger.

It disturbed her that she had watched this woman die and yet her face hadn't imprinted itself. Sally mostly remembered her clothes—the periwinkle pantsuit and black raincoat now blood-soaked and bundled in a clear plastic garbage bag under the gurney.

She also recalled in horrifying detail the shock and pain as the woman's neck twisted beyond the breaking point. But everything had been viewed directly through the woman's eyes rather than from a spectator's point of view. Sally had barely looked at her face, except when she touched her mouth. She remembered the mouth.

Jesús had done a wonderful job on her: smashed skull restored with wire mesh and liquid polymer; twisted neck straightened, the metal screws and plastic supports hidden from view so long as nobody rolled her over; flattened nose splintered back into shape; and her broken front teeth hidden behind a thin, opaque mouth guard.

Jesús told her he was trying to convince the Paynes to invest in a 3D printer that would allow him to reconstruct guests' faces from scanned photographs.

"Everyone could have open casket," he had enthused to her, "even burn victims or those ravaged by disease. Imagine? I could print ears, noses, even whole faces, and you could use your magic to make everything natural."

Although she didn't quite understand the technology behind three-dimensional printing, Sally had to agree, it was a brilliant idea.

Still, even without a special printer, Jesús's work was that of a master artist. Working underneath the flesh, he left her a clean canvas marred only by tiny stitches in her guest's cheek, forehead, and nose. Even the once-torn scalp was smooth with the skin stretched over the wire frame he'd built, and the stitches as close to the hairline as he could manage.

Sally would be able to cover the stitches with a smudge of wax before she applied the foundation, although she would need to take extra care with her airbrush to remove the harsh bruising around the eyes.

With trepidation, Sally reached out and touched the woman's smooth cheek. The explosion of light and the weightless feeling of leaving her body didn't come. There was no vision, nothing but the stiffness of cold flesh.

Sally sighed with relief. It had just been a fluke, she thought, a glitch, a weird supernatural blip on her otherwise very dull and normal life. The last thing she needed was to be having visions of her guests at their final moments. That was the sort of thing that used to get women burned at the stake.

Without embalming, Sally didn't waste any more time. After plugging her iPod into a portable speaker system and choosing a melodic playlist, she got to work cleaning the body with disinfectant soap, washing and styling the auburn hair and applying foundation. Once all Mrs. Higgins' flaws and stitches were covered, Sally moved on to her true passion of using makeup to achieve a natural look.

When Sally was done, Mrs. Alison Higgins looked serene. To preserve the image, Sally gently covered the woman's face and hands in a layer of fine cheesecloth. As the family hadn't yet delivered any fresh clothes, Sally draped the body in a sheet before wheeling it into the large meat locker on the left. That locker was kept at a colder temperature for the un-embalmed and extra care had to be taken to ensure the flesh didn't overly dehydrate.

As was her habit, Sally brewed a fresh pot of coffee before wheeling out her next guest, Mr. Higgins.

Again, she thought as she sipped her coffee, Jesús had done a wonderful job. Gunshot wounds always brought their own challenges. The small entry wound was usually not a big deal as a simple wax plug and makeup could do wonders, but the large exit wound often posed difficulties depending on its location and the caliber of bullet.

Mr. Higgins was lucky in that the bullet was a small, soft-nosed .38 and it had exited the side of his head above the left ear. This allowed most of the damage to be covered by packing the skull with pressed cotton, stitching the folds of torn scalp back together and adding just a small graft of color-matched wig. The bullet, or more likely a fragment of shattered bone, had nicked the left ear, slicing a healthy chunk from its tip. Jesús had fashioned a replacement out of wax, but it was Sally's job to make the pale addition match the skin tone of the real ear.

Sally stripped the sheet off Mr. Higgins and dressed him in a plastic diaper before filling a small metal basin with warm water and disinfectant soap. She was just about to wash him when there was a loud knock at the rear door.

Sally glanced at the clock. Time had escaped her. It was already after six.

Curious, Sally rested her bowl on the counter, put her iPod on pause, and climbed the concrete steps to the door.

"Who is it?" she called.

"It's Jersey, Sally. Can I come in?"

Sally unlocked the three deadbolts and opened the door.

Jersey stood in the alley, the collar of his jacket turned up against a cold drizzle, his mouth set in a firm line.

Sally smiled and beckoned him inside.

"I'm afraid it's not much warmer in here," she said.

"That's okay," said Jersey. "I dressed in layers."

As she relocked the deadbolts, Sally felt a coldness emanating from the detective that had nothing to do with the weather. She wondered if he was regretting their stolen kiss.

Jersey walked down the stairs and stopped in front of the body of Mr. Higgins.

"You fixed the wound already," he said, clearly annoyed. "Can't even tell there was a gaping big hole in his skull."

"That's Jesús's work," Sally explained with pride. "He's very skilled. He has an art exhibit opening next week at a small gallery. Sculpture. Metal and clay, I believe." She hesitated for just a fraction of a second, but then the words gushed out. "We could go together if you like? I'd love to see what he creates outside of body parts."

Jersey turned to stare into Sally's viridescent eyes, but instead of sharing her excitement, his face was as rigid as kiln-fired clay.

"How did you see the license plate?"

Sally took a step back, unsettled by his tone.

"I thought the investigation was closed," she said. "When your station released the bodies—"

"*I* still want to know."

"So it's personal?"

"I don't like loose ends. Do you have something to hide?"

Sally crossed to the body of Mr. Higgins and picked up her metal bowl of soapy water.

"I'm not hiding anything," she said coldly.

"But you're not telling me everything."

Sally dipped a sponge into the warm water and washed the corpse's chest.

"It's not what you think," she said.

"And what do I think?"

"That there's something, I dunno, sinister going on."

"Is there?" Jersey asked. "It seems an odd coincidence that a woman is murdered outside this funeral home and then the very next day she's brought here for burial."

Sally shrugged. "She bought one of our pre-paid packages, or her husband did. For both of them. They're quite popular."

Jersey sighed and allowed his face to soften slightly.

"Sally, I want to be honest here. I like you, and I would like to see more of you, but I really need to know what you're hiding."

Sally's voice became very quiet as she absently dabbed her sponge across Mr. Higgins' stomach. "You'll think I'm weird."

Jersey's façade crumbled. "How much weirder can it get? Every time we meet there's a dead body between us."

The birth of a fresh smile froze in place as glowing green words suddenly appeared on Mr. Higgins' flesh.

Written in a childish scrawl, the message read: *He's here. Run!*

17

Sally gasped at the sight of the words.

"Did you write that?" she blurted.

"No! How could I?"

"It must be a horrible joke," she said. "Somebody at the police morgue, maybe?"

"Not likely, they're a serious bunch. Does it mean anything to you?"

"You're the only one here. Do I need to run?"

"No." Jersey pulled out his phone and snapped a photo of the words even as they began to fade. "I know you weren't involved, Sally, but I just can't figure how you saw the car's plate."

"It was a guess."

"A guess?" Jersey was incredulous.

"Well, okay, not a guess exactly. But I didn't really *really* see it. Not in the way you mean at least."

Jersey sighed. "Just spit it out. Please?"

"Okay, but don't—" Sally took a deep breath, swallowing the unspoken words. Either Jersey would believe her or he wouldn't. "When I touched her... Mrs. Higgins... in the alley, I just wanted to fix her mouth. It was all... all misaligned, but I had, I don't know what you'd call it... a vision."

"A vision?"

"Yes!" Sally snapped, but then blushed, flustered. "I saw the accident through *her* eyes. I saw the car, the license plate, the two men in the front seat, and then I was hit, or rather *she* was hit by the car, and I felt her neck break and then I was back in my own body and looking out my own eyes." Sally sucked in another deep breath. "I know it sounds crazy, and that's why I didn't want to tell you."

Sally closed her eyes and waited. She could hear Jersey breathing. It was steady and deep and the only sound in the room.

"Maybe there's another explanation," he said after a moment. "Maybe you saw more than you thought, but in the panic of the situation, a woman dying in front of you, it became muddled... mixed up."

Sally opened her eyes and fastened onto Jersey's face.

"It's happened before," she said. "It was a long time ago. I was only a child, but..." She paused, struggling, and then shook her head. There were tears in her eyes. "Maybe you're right," she added, finding Jersey's explanation easier to accept. "Maybe I was confused."

Jersey took a step closer, and Sally thought he was going to reach out and hold her, but he stopped before crossing into her personal space. His eyes narrowed, crinkles deepening like fault lines across a bleak desert.

"Even if you were confused," he began, "you gave us the correct registration. And now you're saying there were *two* men in the front seat?"

Sally glanced down at the body on the gurney. "Mr. Higgins was driving. He looked so sad. But there was another man beside him, talking to him, urging him on."

"Did you see what this other man looked like?" Jersey asked.

"A nightmare," she said. "An ugly, ugly nightmare."

18

Jersey jotted down Sally's description of the second man. The unusual scarring on his face would make him easy to identify if he had ever been entered into the system. Sally's explanation of how she had seen him, however, was troubling. The district attorney would never give him an arrest warrant based on a vision.

That was a bridge, he decided, he'd cross at a later time. For now, the most troubling aspect of the crime was the writing on the body.

Most of it had already faded back into the flesh, and he didn't have any authority to stop Sally from completing her work. He called the lieutenant's personal cell, but it went straight to voice mail.

Sally agreed to a compromise. She would wash the rest of the body and apply makeup, but would also protect the area with the writing.

After pouring them both a coffee, Sally indicated Jersey could sit on a metal stool off to one side while she returned to work. In her element, Sally moved with the fluid grace of a dancer, and she smiled a lot as though sharing funny stories with her dead.

Jersey found her manner endearing. She was flightier and far less serious than the women he was usually attracted to, although the whole vision thing was disturbing. And, yet, there was a calm radiance about her that made him feel strangely at ease. It was as if when he was in her presence, even if her focus wasn't trained on him, he never experienced doubt about what an important part he played in her world. Her smile was a lure, but the hook was how she made him feel, and Jersey liked that feeling.

The detective took a long sip of coffee, not entirely positive he wanted to voice aloud the troubling thoughts pinging in his brain. In the end, however, he couldn't imagine a better sounding board.

"When I first came across our corpse here," Jersey began, "I mentioned to my partner that he appeared unusually rumpled, like he had been in a rush to get dressed."

Sally lifted her gaze. "So you're thinking that maybe Mr. Higgins wrote this message on his skin before he killed himself?"

"That would be one explanation."

"And another?"

"That the second man you saw wrote the words after he killed him."

Sally's eyes grew large. "Why?"

"Who knows? Playing games, maybe."

Sally's eyes narrowed. "But if it was murder—"

"Double murder, actually," said Jersey. "Your description of the scene inside the car makes it sound like Mr. Higgins didn't necessarily want to drive over his wife, that this second man was making him, or at least encouraging him. Then, with the wife out of the way, the second man kills the driver."

"But why would someone do that?" Sally asked.

Jersey sighed. "That's the million-dollar question."

"Could it be an insurance scam?" Sally ran a tiny comb through Mr. Higgins' thick eyebrows. "If the wife is insured for a large amount of money and the husband is bored of her, he could have hired someone to kill her."

Jersey grinned. "Now you're thinking like a detective. The killer decides he needs some assurance that Higgins won't go to the cops after his wife is dead, so he makes the husband do the deed."

"And then," Sally continues, "the killer double-crosses the husband, but…" Sally wrinkled her nose.

"But?" Jersey encouraged.

"It still doesn't explain why he'd write a note on the body. It reads like a warning, but a warning for who? The only people who would be likely see it are—"

"The coroner and you," Jersey finished. "Any psycho ex-boyfriends I need to know about?"

Sally blushed slightly. "None that I left alive."

"Good to know." Jersey laughed. "Besides if the note was meant for you, then the killer would need to know the bodies would be transported here."

"The pre-paid plans," Sally blurted. "Everything is kept on the computer in Mr. Payne's office."

Jersey was impressed, but he could also tell that her imagination was beginning to frighten her. "The message wasn't meant for you, Sally," he said with confidence. "Where's the payoff?"

Sally sighed and the tension eased from her shoulders. "I prefer my job," she said. "My guests come to me when their story is complete, but yours have had the final pages torn out."

SALLY FINISHED WITH Mr. Higgins and wheeled him into the large cold room.

"That's me for the night," she announced.

"Thank God," said Jersey. "I was getting tired of looking at wrinkled old flesh."

"I hope you're talking about Mr. Higgins!"

Jersey grinned. "So you feel like going for a drink?"

Sally gasped in mock surprise. "Why, detective, are you asking me on a date?"

"If you'll have me."

Sally beamed. "I know this great little bakery that pulls its first batch of muffins from the ovens around now."

Jersey's stomach gave an audible grumble, which made Sally laugh.

"I'll take that as a yes."

19

Aedan watched from his vehicle as Sally and the detective left the funeral home. They were walking close together, huddled against a chill rain.

Aedan's breath fogged the window. He didn't like this detective's interest in Sally. The Higgins case was closed. Murder-suicide, end of. Domestic bliss turned homicidal. Happens every day. He couldn't have made it any cleaner. Sally shouldn't even have been a blip on the man's radar after she gave her witness statement.

Could she have told him her secret? The possibility needed to be considered, but could she even comprehend the ramifications of it? Without the interpreter…

No, Aedan thought, this detective was after something else.

Something he could never have.

Salvation.

20

Sally entered her apartment feeling tired and awake in equal measure.

Jiggy ran to meet her at the door with a mixed greeting of purring happiness and pitying mewl.

Sally kicked off her shoes and hung her coat in the closet. "You hungry, baby? I have muffins."

Sally held up a bag of oatmeal-rhubarb-chocolate-chip muffins, smiling to herself over how Jersey had insisted on buying a dozen fresh from the oven.

The warm chocolate had made a mess of their hands and mouths as they ate. And, if Sally was being honest, added a sweet, electric jolt to the delicious attraction she felt sparking between them. They had walked and talked for hours with no clear destination in mind. But eventually, with her feet aching, Jersey had dropped her in front of her apartment with a lingering, tender kiss and a promise of...

Jiggy looked at the bag of muffins with what appeared to be feline disdain, which made Sally laugh. She knew the cat preferred sour-cream doughnuts.

"Okay, okay," she relented. "Your usual, milady. Table with a view."

Sally mixed a batch of crunchy and soft cat food in a bowl and placed it upon Jiggy's favorite spot, the kitchen windowsill where she also kept a potted catnip plant.

With the cat content, Sally entered the bathroom and turned on the taps. As the bathtub filled, she headed to her bedroom, stripped off her clothes, and wrapped herself in a white terrycloth robe. With a yawn, she strolled to the kitchen, poured the last of the Chilean wine into a glass, and returned to the bath.

Sipping her wine as the tub continued to fill, Sally studied her reflection in the mirror above the sink. Was she too skinny, she wondered, untying her robe and letting it drop to the floor around her feet. She cupped one of her breasts in her free hand. Were her breasts too small? And what about her hair? It had always been this horrible, ancient white. Did its lack of pigment make her look older than her years? Did it make her less appealing than the blondes or the brunettes or, especially, the redheads? She had always wanted to be a redhead, but her hair never held dye for more than a day.

As she contemplated her appearance, the bathroom filled with steam and the mirror began to change from clear to opaque. It was as if she was becoming invisible.

Sally took another sip of wine and turned toward the tub when something out the corner of her eye made her stop.

She turned back to the mirror and gasped.

A message was scrawled on its surface in the same awkward hand as on the body of Mr. Higgins.

This message read: *Do you remember?*

21

Jersey was parking in the underground garage of his condo building when his cellphone rang. Hoping it might be Sally calling to say she already missed him, he answered without looking at the display.

"What the hell do you think you're doing, detective?" blasted the voice of his boss, Lieutenant Morrell.

"Err, I—"

"I just received a phone call directly from the mayor. His son's friend has accused you of interfering with the recently departed Mr. Higgins."

"Interfering? What the heck does that mean?"

"You were at the funeral home?" Morrell barked.

"Yes, but—"

"I warned you to back off? Didn't I say the case was closed? So what in darnation were you—"

"There's writing on the body," Jersey interrupted.

"Writing?"

"A message on the victim's stomach. It was in some kind of invisible ink that became visible when—"

Morrell cut him off with a growl deep in his throat. "What did the message say?"

"*He's here. Run!*"

"Who's here? What does that mean?"

"I don't know, but when I re-interviewed the witness—"

"The one who gave us the license plate?"

"Yes."

"And she works at the funeral home?"

"Yes."

"The same funeral home where the bodies are being prepared for burial?"

Jersey sighed and worked his jaw to stop from clenching. "When I re-interviewed her, she remembered seeing two people in the car when it ran over our first victim."

"A third party?"

"Yes."

"And you believe this message was what? Some kind of threat?" Morrell asked.

"Possibly," said Jersey cautiously. "But I admit it's a strange way to go about it."

"Strange indeed." Morrell paused, and Jersey could imagine the clanking of gears over the airwaves. He wondered if the lieutenant's pajamas came with a designer tie and starched collar. When Morrell spoke again, his voice had softened. "How did you know this message was on the body?"

"I didn't," explained Jersey. "I stopped in to see the witness just to clear up a few things for my final report. She was preparing Higgins' body at the time and when she washed his stomach, the message appeared."

"Intriguing. I don't like it. We should have the lab take a closer look at this message."

"The funeral isn't scheduled until the afternoon. We can still get access to the bodies in the morning."

"Arrange for that. I'll handle the mayor."

"Yes, sir," Jersey said quickly before Morrell could change his mind. "But there's one other thing. The funeral home was closed when I got there, so I entered through the rear door. How did the son know I was anywhere near his father's body?"

"Good question," said Morrell. "Perhaps that's something you should ask him yourself."

22

Naked, Sally dashed into the kitchen to grab the wall phone. She had only punched in the first five numbers of Jersey's number when she felt a presence behind her.

Sally spun around to face a nightmare.

The man she had seen in her vision was standing in the doorway. He was holding her cat in his arms, stroking it with one hand while holding it tight by the scruff of the neck with the other. Jiggy was struggling, but the man's grip was too strong.

"You shouldn't leave the water running..." His voice was slightly slurred by the hindered movement of his disfigured mouth, "... the tub could overflow."

Sally had never felt so naked, so alone, or so vulnerable. She reflexively covered her breasts with one arm and twisted her hips to shield herself. In her free hand, she still gripped the phone. It was an old-fashioned Bakelite receiver and held some heft, but she doubted it would make much of a weapon.

"W-w-what do you want?" she stammered.

"There's no need to be afraid," said the man. "Hang up the phone, turn off the taps, and put on your robe. You've certainly grown into a very beautiful woman, cousin, but I'm sure you would feel more at ease with some clothing."

Sally glanced around the kitchen, her gaze flicking over

everything that could be used as a weapon: knives, pots, a spice jar of Cayenne pepper. The man was taller than her, likely stronger than her, although he might be surprised, moving dead bodies around the funeral parlor wasn't for the weak.

"I'm not here to hurt you," he said as though reading her thoughts. "But please don't do anything foolish."

Sally fastened her gaze on the man's face and steeled her voice. "Let my cat go, and I'll do what you ask."

The man bowed slightly and released Jiggy. The cat landed on its feet and immediately scampered under the protection of the television stand where she arched her back and hissed.

"A show of good faith," he said.

Sally let the phone fall from her grasp and bounce on the end of its tether as she headed into the bathroom to turn off the taps and pull on her robe. Alone in front of the mirror, she glanced down at her half-finished glass of wine. Another weapon? She could smash the glass; use it like a knife. Sally lifted the glass and took a long sip to calm her nerves.

When she returned to the living room with glass in hand, she felt more angry than afraid.

"Who are you, and what the hell do you want?" she asked.

23

Jersey rapped on the apartment door and waited. When it opened, a disheveled California blonde looked him up and down before yawning in his face. Once you got past the over-bleached hair, artificial tan, and too-white teeth, the blonde was mostly legs, and today they reached all the way up to a peekaboo hint of blue bikini panties before disappearing beneath a rumpled Wonder Woman T-shirt.

"Oh," said the blonde with clear disappointment. "It's you."

Jersey opened his mouth to offer a witty rejoinder, but the blonde had already turned her back to him. "Your teddy bear is here," she called out while walking away. "And he's staring at my ass."

"I'm not staring," Jersey blustered, the color rising on his cheeks. "And... teddy bear?"

The blonde stopped and glared over her shoulder. "What?" She jabbed her hands onto cocked and boney hips. "You prefer Fuck Buddy?"

"I'm not—"

"Ignore her." Amarela appeared in the doorway, hurriedly slipping her Smith & Wesson semi-auto into a belt holster. "She always wakes up bitchy."

Jersey frowned. "I thought you two—"

"Bye, Babes." Amarela cut him off mid-sentence as she gave the half-dressed blonde a quick kiss on the lips before shoving Jersey out the door and closing it behind them.

Before Jersey could protest, Amarela headed for the stairs. "You're early."

"And your roommate is—"

"She's not my roommate," Amarela cut him off again. "Why are you early?"

"We have an errand to run."

"Oh?"

"Remember the asshole you spoke to yesterday? Next of kin." Amarela nodded.

"He tried to drop me in it last night."

"How?"

"That," said Jersey, "is exactly the question I want an answer to."

THE SON OF the recently departed Nicholas and Alison Higgins lived in a two-story, off-white spackled house with a suspect moss-covered roof in a gentrification-coming-soon suburb in the city's diverse northeast quadrant.

Despite its outward appearance, the solid 1940s-era house had all the earmarks and potential of a smart fixer-upper rather than a woe-is-me hard luck story. The house itself sat on a large grassy lot directly across the road from the fenced ninth hole of the one hundred fifty acre Rose City public golf course.

Jersey rang the doorbell. It sounded like someone choking a crow.

"If he gets snippy again, can I shoot him?" asked Amarela dryly. Jersey's mouth twitched. "Sure."

Amarela studied the tired, working-class neighborhood as they waited. "You think his inheritance will come in handy? Mom and Dad had a nice big house, probably cash in the bank, maybe insurance. There's just him and the sister."

Jersey started to answer when the door was opened by a slim man in his mid-thirties with a groomed five-day stubble that made him look like a wannabe actor or gigolo. He completed the look with a monotone dark suit over a charcoal T-shirt and matching sneakers. When he saw Amarela, he released an audible sigh of irritation.

"Peter Higgins?" Jersey asked.

"Yeah, but I'm burying my parents today, so if you don't mind leaving me the—"

Jersey placed both hands on the man's chest and shoved him into the house. Peter back-pedaled, swinging his arms in an effort to maintain his balance. When he finally succeeded in staying upright, Jersey and Amarela were standing in the entrance hall with the front door closed behind them.

"What the hell do you—"

Jersey held up his hand to silence the protest. "Where do you get off assaulting an officer of the law?"

"Assault? I never—"

"Detective Valente. Did this man just swing his arms at me in a threatening manner?"

"Yes, Detective Castle, he did." Amarela's smile was thin and cruel. "Both physically *and* verbally."

"You won't get away with this," Peter protested. "I know—"

"You know too many people, Mr. Higgins," snapped Jersey. "But if collecting the insurance on your parents is important to you, then I'm only interested in one."

Peter licked his lips and glanced up the stairs behind him. Jersey wasn't sure if he was planning to make a run for it or just checking that his wife wasn't listening.

"Which one?" he asked.

"Who told you I was at the funeral home last night?"

Peter's shoulders relaxed. "So you were there. What did you do to my father's body?"

"I never touched him," said Jersey. "I was interviewing a witness, but how did you know I was there?"

Peter licked his lips again. "I received a phone call. He didn't leave a name."

Jersey reached up and pinched the flesh between his eyebrows. "An anonymous call? You expect me to buy that?"

"Yeah, it's the truth. There was no Caller ID either. I checked 'cause he sounded kinda creepy."

"In what way?"

Peter shrugged. "He made these slurping sounds, like he was speaking through a mouthful of spit."

"And what did he say?"

"Just that you were—"

"He mentioned me by name?"

"Yeah. Detective Castle."

"Go on."

"He said you were at the funeral home and you were doing stuff to the bodies."

"Doing stuff?" Jersey asked.

"Yeah, interfering he called it. Interfering with the bodies."

"So you called the mayor?"

"Well, I mean what would you do? Christ, those are my parents."

"Did he mention anything about a message?" Jersey asked.

"A message? No. What message?"

Jersey turned to his partner. "I'm done. You can shoot him now."

24

In the car, Amarela chuckled.

"The look on his face was priceless," she said. "I thought he was going to shit himself."

Jersey rubbed the knot between his eyes again. "He's probably already on the phone to the mayor's son, who'll tell the mayor, who'll tell the commander, who'll tell the lieutenant, who'll—"

"Take us off the case that he's already taken us off of?" Amarela asked.

Jersey grinned. "Something like that."

"So we should avoid going into the office, then?"

Jersey's grin grew wider.

AS THEY TRAVELED back across town, Amarela asked, "So what do you know about the insurance on his parents?"

"Nothing. It was a bluff. I took what you said about the money coming in handy and thought 'what the hell.' Even if he's completely innocent, his parents dying at a time when he needs the dough is bound to make anyone feel guilty."

"It made him a sweat a bit."

"I noticed that, too."

Jersey shared Sally's late-night theory about a killer being hired to murder the wife, but then double-crossing the husband.

"Nice theory, but instead of a double-cross, what if the killer was hired by the son instead?" said Amarela. "Both parents dead in an apparent murder-suicide, the kid inherits, and everyone gets paid."

Jersey squeezed the steering wheel. "And if you have the right contacts to skip the autopsy, the bodies are buried before anyone becomes suspicious."

"And no one *is* suspicious," began Amarela.

"Except us," finished Jersey.

Amarela stared out the window in silence for a few moments before adding in a quizzical tone, "And why are we suspicious again?"

Jersey laughed. "There's someone I want you to meet."

ON THE SECOND floor of the four-story building, Jersey knocked on Sally's apartment door.

When there was no answer, he pressed his ear to the wood. He could hear the low drone of a television inside.

He knocked again. Still no answer.

"She could've gone out shopping or something," said Amarela.

"She was tired," said Jersey. "She's only been home about two hours."

"Oh?" Amarela queried.

"We went for coffee and muffins. Nothing devious."

"Muffins? You *are* a teddy bear."

Jersey groaned. "Don't give me a hard time for being normal. What was up with *Dawn of the Dead* Barbie at your place? I thought you and Clarissa split."

"Short story," said Amarela. "I was horny."

Jersey blanched and knocked on the door again. This time he heard a cat's meow.

"I would say that's probable cause," said Amarela with a snicker. She reached out and turned the door handle. The handle was unlocked and the door swung open. She looked at Jersey, her expression serious. "That's not good."

Jersey's jaw clenched tight as he withdrew his weapon and followed Amarela into the apartment.

"Sally!" Jersey shouted. "Sally, you in here?"

A multi-colored cat hissed at Jersey before scampering under the television stand to hide behind a box of DVDs. Its ears were tucked low and its eyes were filled with distrust.

Amarela moved to the bathroom and nudged the door open with her foot.

"Tub's full of water, but no naked girl."

Jersey eased over to the bedroom door and turned the handle. He entered in a combat crouch, but apart from a pile of discarded clothes and a rumpled bed, the room was unoccupied.

"All clear," he called before making his way back to the main room.

"There's nobody here." Amarela joined her partner and nodded at a near empty glass of wine sitting on a coffee table. "Looks like she was planning a relaxing bath before bed, but either changed her mind or was interrupted."

"No sign of a struggle?" Jersey voiced aloud.

"Nothing. Maybe a boyfriend stopped by and made her a better offer."

Jersey's eyes narrowed.

"Hey," said Amarela, "I'm just saying. You've only known her one day. You don't know what she's into."

Jersey entered the kitchen and found the wall phone dangling by its cord. He lifted the receiver and hit redial to watch the last number called appear on the base's tiny digital screen. Only five of seven numbers appeared, but Jersey knew the number well—it was his own.

"Bag the wine glass," he called out, needing to displace his rising panic with action. "I want it tested for GHB or its ilk." GHB was an acronym for gamma-Hydroxybutyric acid, a colorless, odorless liquid known by many names on the street, such as Easy Lay or Grievous Bodily Harm, but was most commonly referred to as the date-rape drug.

Jersey cursed under his breath. Sally was missing, and he couldn't get over the feeling that it was all his fault.

25

A wakening in a dark, cramped and uncomfortable place, Sally's first thought was, *When did I fall sleep?* The last thing she recalled was the glass of wine and the odd thought that her consonants slurred before a heavy, incoherent weariness had suddenly fallen over her. After that, her memory was frighteningly blank.

Now her tongue was thick and wooly, her throat parched, and her ears stuffed with cotton. The aftereffects of a drug.

She cursed and blinked, making sure she was truly awake. The darkness remained undisturbed.

Stay calm, she told herself, but even her inner-voice was shaky. As panic made her breath quicken and her heart race, the terrifying image of being trapped inside a coffin filled her thoughts.

Sally bolted upright, her stomach muscles doing all the work, and smacked her head with a loud bone-on-metal clang. Sally cried out as something sharp bit into her scalp, and with a whimper, she collapsed flat on her back again. A warm wetness dripped from a painful gash in her skull.

Cursing again, Sally tried to move her arms and legs, but they were bound together at ankles and wrists. She moved her head to the right and saw only a deeper darkness, but when she moved it to the left there was a pinprick of dim red light. Raising her bound arms, she felt the lid. The hard metal was flocked in a thin layer of cloth, not that it had done her head any good.

Concentrate. Where am I?

Taking a deep breath, Sally tasted stale, sickly air. Beneath her, rhythmic waves radiated through tense muscles like a boat on a choppy lake. But the steady rumble and occasional jolt wasn't that of a boat.

She was in the trunk of a car, she reasoned, her head was throbbing, and she needed to pee. Badly.

Rolling onto her left side, Sally drew up her knees and kicked backwards with bound feet. Her feet hit the metal and plastic barrier between trunk and rear seat with a satisfying crack. She lashed out again and a second crack was followed by a loud snap.

Suddenly, the red light in her periphery flared brighter and she was thrown into the barrier with muscle-numbing force. As the car quickly came to a halt, the crunch of loose gravel replaced the steady thrum of tarmac.

Sally braced herself as a key entered the lock and the trunk lid lifted to reveal a dark silhouette against the backdrop of a beautiful sunny day. A thick cloud of dust floated behind the silhouette in a billowing cloak.

"You're awake," said the silhouette, his words moist and slurred. "Sorry for the cramped accommodation. I thought it best to let you sleep."

Sally blinked until her eyes adjusted and the nightmarish face of the man who had been in her apartment came into focus. She curled her lips, fighting against fear.

"You're bleeding," said the man, his voice concerned.

"I need to pee." Sally tried hard to sound defiant and strong— anything but terrified and weak.

"Of course."

The man reached in, grabbed her by the shoulders and pulled

her from the trunk. Sally was surprised at the strength of him, but relieved to be standing on her own two feet on solid ground.

The man bent to the nylon strap binding her ankles and cut it with a tiny stainless-steel knife that appeared in his hand as if by magic. When he stood back up, he nodded at a small hedgerow just a few steps from the road and handed her a small travel pack of paper tissue. She held her bound hands out to him, but he made no move to cut those bonds.

Lowering her hands, Sally glanced around at their location— an empty country road surrounded by endless fields of pasture. There was no other traffic and no signs of any people; she couldn't even see a farmhouse. She looked down at herself. *Not naked, at least.* The jeans and T-shirt she was wearing had come from a pile of clean laundry that she had been meaning to put away for the last two days. As such, the pockets wouldn't even contain a piece of lint never mind anything useful.

"How long have we been traveling?" she asked.

"A few hours. I have water and snacks in the car once you've done your business. I also have Band-Aids for—"

Turning her back, Sally closed her ears to the man's false concern, and trudged to the bushes.

He never took his eyes off her for a moment.

THERE WAS NOWHERE to run, Sally thought as she squatted behind the bushes. No homes with telephones, no farmers with guns, no lead-footed drivers with fast cars and a romantic notion to play Prince Charming.

She reached up to her torn scalp, feeling rivulets of blood beginning to congeal under her fingers.

What could she do with that? she wondered. *Leave traces on the bushes in case Jersey sent a bloodhound to track her down?*

The thought was ridiculous. Jersey wouldn't even know she was missing. No one would.

26

When Sally returned to the car, she was more composed, but thirstier than ever.

"Would you like to ride up front?" the man asked.

His voice sounded completely unthreatening, despite having drugged, kidnapped, and driven her to god knew where in the trunk of his goddamn car.

Sally stared into the man's one good eye. It was so dark, it was like staring into a black hole; and there was something else, too, she realized, something not quite human.

"Did you dress me?" she snipped.

The man nodded.

"You drug me, too?"

"I needed you to come with me."

"And you couldn't ask?"

"Would you have come?"

"Not without a good reason."

The man's mouth twitched, and a small pool of drool dribbled from the twisted lips. His dead eye looked incredibly sad.

He said, "I couldn't risk the detective coming back before I could explain."

"Did you hurt him?" Sally asked quickly.

"I made sure he was distracted. He's perfectly fine."

Sally sighed in relief. "I could use that water."

The man opened the car door and ushered her into the front passenger seat. The car was large, a late-model Cadillac with a roomy interior and plush electric seats.

"There's just one thing." The man leaned over as though to fasten her seatbelt, the unmarred side of his face passing so close she could have bit him.

The nylon strap around her wrists was severed, but before she could enjoy the freedom her left hand was slipped into a metal handcuff that had been chained to a bar under the seat. She opened her mouth to protest but was distracted when the man grabbed her right hand and fastened a handcuff around that wrist, too. The second handcuff was attached to a slightly longer chain, giving her right hand more movement.

"I apologize," said the man. "But I must take precautions." He handed her a bottle of water and twisted off the sealed top. "You'll be able to eat and drink, and this is more comfortable than the trunk. However, if you make me regret this upgrade, I won't hesitate to return you to the darkness."

Sally flared her nostrils, but bit back a stream of profanity. She didn't want to waste her energy on something that would so obviously fall on deaf ears. Instead, she tilted the bottle to her lips and began to drink. She couldn't remember the last time water had tasted so good.

THE MAN SETTLED into the driver's seat and started the engine.

With his profile exposed, Sally studied the full extent of his misshapen face. In her original vision of the man, when she had watched him manipulate Mr. Higgins into driving over his own wife, Sally thought his flesh was melted and burned from a close encounter with fire, but up close she could see that it was actually a rubbery curtain of excess skin. It was as though the skin had grown to cover a large subcutaneous growth or tumor. When the tumor was removed or shrunk, gravity had pulled down that side of his face like an empty pocket.

She wondered why anyone would allow such a disfigurement to go untreated in this day and age of discount plastic surgeons in every neighborhood mall ready to nip, tuck, suck, and staple while one's spouse shops for key chains and batteries at the Dollar Store next door.

Sally rattled her chains to remind herself that she was the prisoner in this car, not him. He wasn't one of her guests, and it wasn't her job to fix him.

"Where are you taking me?" Sally asked.

The man turned to her, his mouth twitching again. Sally wondered if that was his way of smiling. If so, it was both disgusting and disturbing.

"I'm taking you home," he said.

"Yeah, well, you missed a turn," Sally snapped. "I live in the city."

"I mean your real home," he said calmly. "Where you were born and where—"

"I don't remember that place," Sally snapped again. "Couldn't even tell you its name. How do you know anything about it?"

"I know everything about you, including your real name. Sally Wilson is so plain for what you were raised to become."

Sally narrowed her eyes. "That is my real name."

The man shook his head. "That's the name you adopted. You must have been too traumatized to tell anyone your true name when they found you on the outskirts of Bismarck. The family didn't know how you made it there on foot. You had been missing for two weeks. By the time we finally tracked you down, you had been shipped out of state, and your records were sealed. We've been looking ever since. It has taken us twenty-five years and many false leads. Someone didn't want us to find you."

"Who is us?" Sally asked.

"Your family."

The image of her mother lying dead on the bed, and her father in the bathtub with a shotgun jammed in his mouth, flashed before her eyes.

"I don't have a family."

Reaching into a breast pocket, the man retrieved a small bottle of artificial tears. He squeezed several drops into his right eye. The excess liquid ran down his sagging cheek and dripped onto his shirt. He didn't seem to notice.

"That's not true. You have a large family. The Blues were—"

"The Blues?" Sally asked.

"Your family name. You were born Salvation Blue on the first of June, 1984. Your mother called you Sally for short, but your father preferred the full Christian name, Salvation."

"And you know this how?"

The man's mouth twitched again and a pool of spittle dribbled down his chin. He dabbed at it with a paper tissue from a travel pack he kept in one of the cup holders.

"The day you were born," said the man, "was also the day we were betrothed. I'm Aedan. Your husband."

IT TOOK SALLY a moment to adjust to the news.

"Husband?"

Aedan nodded. "That is why I never gave up looking for you. It was my duty."

Sally didn't want to believe what she was hearing. "This is fucked up. I've never seen you before today and... " she could hardly spit out the words, "marrying a baby is just sick."

"We wouldn't have lived together until you came of age," said Aedan, his tone sounding hurt. "But we were promised to each other. The ceremony was—"

"Ceremony?" Sally blurted.

"The wedding ceremony. I have photos that I can—"

"Let me out of here," Sally demanded, her teeth gnashing so tight her jaw threatened to snap.

"I can't do tha—"

"Let me out!"

Aedan's face turned a dark shade of gray as he turned and fixed her with his good eye. The black hole seemed to crackle with energy.

"Do I need to drug you again?" His tone still sounded calm despite the storm in his eye.

"Fuck!" Sally slammed her hand against the door panel and turned to stare out the side window. Although she fought back tears, her shoulders slumped in defeat.

"You'll understand better when we reach home."

Sally shook her head. "There's no way I'm ever going to understand this shit."

Aedan sighed. "You'll see."

27

"It's not good news," a forensics technician told Jersey and Amarela when they entered the cold basement of Paynes Funeral Home.

"Let me guess," said Amarela dryly. "The victim's dead?"

The technician, a skeletal man in his early fifties with a bad comb-over and a silver moustache so thin it could have been drawn with an eyebrow pencil, snorted loudly.

"The message?" Jersey asked impatiently.

"Nothing left but residue. It wasn't meant to be permanent and as soon as it got wet it began to break down."

Jersey sighed heavily. "Any idea what it was made from?"

"I can run a few tests back at the lab, but my guess is a simple vegetable dye designed to react to water. The breakdown process would make it glow for just a few minutes. Nothing complicated. A kid could make it."

Lieutenant Morrell entered the steel and porcelain room from a second set of stairs that led down from the lobby of the funeral home. "So there is no way to prove the message was directed at your witness, Detective Castle."

"It was meant for whoever washed the body," said Jersey.

"Which could have been your witness or the coroner or even a family member," said Morrell. "I was just talking to the funeral director upstairs and he tells me that it's not unusual for family members to request that they wash the body before burial as part of the grieving ritual."

"Did either of the Higgins children make such a request?" Jersey asked.

"No."

"So it's still suspicious, then?" said Amarela.

"It's unusual," agreed the lieutenant. "But not enough to delay the funeral."

Amarela leaned close to Jersey. She whispered, "The mayor must have stood his ground."

The lieutenant's eyes narrowed. "It was Mr. Higgins' lawyer, actually, Detective Valente. And he offered me his full cooperation if we had a good enough reason to delay the burial. But we don't."

"Sally's missing," blurted Jersey.

The lieutenant arched his eyebrows. "Your witness?"

"We just came from her apartment, and she's gone."

"Were there signs of struggle?"

"Nothing definite, but—"

"Let me get this clear, detective," said Morrell firmly. "You have no evidence of foul play except some woman told you she *might* have seen another man in the speeding car when Mr. Higgins drove over his wife. To further cement her story, a mysterious message appears on a body that she's handling in a mortuary by herself. And now when half my forensics team is scrambling around a cold basement and finding nothing, she disappears?"

Jersey cringed. "Well it sounds bad when—"

"It sounds very bad!" Morrell scolded. "This case is closed. Leave this family to bury its dead, and get back to work before I forget why I employ you." He glared at Amarela. "Both of you."

AMARELA WAITED UNTIL the lieutenant had stomped back upstairs.

"That was uncalled for," she said.

Jersey nodded. "He practically accused Sally of—"

"No," Amarela interrupted, "I meant the boss lumping me in with you. You're the senior detective. If you go off on some wild goose chase it doesn't mean I should share the blame."

Jersey's mouth twitched as he bent down close to his partner's ear.

"I need you to do me a favor," he whispered.

"What, here? The stiffs making you—"

Jersey groaned. "Just convince the techie to take enough blood to run a tox screen, will you?"

"Why me?"

"Because, partner, you could talk a man into shaving his butt for you."

"Disgusting," she said, while crinkling her nose, "but true."

28

When the car left the secondary road and merged onto a fast-moving freeway, Sally finally had an idea of where she was. The first road sign they passed told her they were traveling on the I-90. It was followed by a large sign that proclaimed Spokane, Washington was just one hundred forty miles further north.

"Spokane?" she asked.

Aedan didn't answer.

"Huh," Sally said angrily. "Married five minutes and already getting the silent treatment."

Aedan turned to her in confusion.

"It's a joke," Sally explained. "When you work with dead people, you develop an odd sense of humor. They can be a stiff crowd."

Aedan returned his attention to the road. "We will get something to eat in Spokane."

"So it's just a pit stop?"

"Yes."

"And our final destination?"

Aedan went quiet again, but this time Sally welcomed the silence as her mind began to churn. *Spokane,* she thought, *phones, cars, people. Lots of people.* But first she needed more answers.

"Okay," Sally began, "since we're going to be spending time

together, I need to know what the hell all this has to do with the bodies at the funeral home? Did you write that spooky note on Mr. Higgins?"

"What note?"

Sally exhaled noisily. "He's here. Run!"

"I didn't write it, but this is promising."

Sally's forehead crinkled in concern. "Why?"

"I've followed many false leads in the past and my punishment has been severe. But this note you claim to have seen shows all has not been in vain. You may possess the gift we need. "

"What gift?"

"To speak for the dead."

Sally paused, her face frozen in shock.

"Speak for the dead?" Her voice was barely above a whisper; something about that phrase triggered a memory—her mother, eyes open but blind, arms dripping in fresh blood, a beatific smile upon her face.

"What did you see?" Aedan asked, his voice growing in excitement. "When you touched her?"

Realization began to sink in, and Sally felt sick to her stomach. "I don't know what you're talking about."

The man's dark eye glistened. "I needed to be sure. I studied you on the security tape from the bar. You traveled with her, didn't you?"

Sally shook her head, not wanting to believe this mad man's words. "Did you kill that woman?" Her voice was shaking. "As a way to... to test me?"

"How else could I know? You didn't react when I sent you the cleaning lady."

Sally gasped. "Mrs. Shoumatoff. You killed her, too?" Sally closed her eyes, trying not to let the floodgates of despair open.

"I suspect she had been dead too long before reaching you. I wasn't sure if it made a difference."

"So you killed Mrs. Higgins outside my office because you wanted me to touch a fresh corpse?"

"What did you see when you touched her mouth?"

Sally ignored the question. "And what about her husband? Why did you kill him?"

"It was necessary. I couldn't simply let him go. Not with what he knew. Besides," Aedan continued, "he needed to be punished for—"

Sally held up her hand. "I don't want to know." Tears pooled in her eyes and began streaming down her cheeks. "You're a monster, you know that?"

"No, you'll see. Once we're back home everything will be made clear."

Under her breath, Sally muttered, "I should have never stopped running."

29

Jersey entered Sally's apartment for the second time that day. There was no sign that she had ever returned.

With a despairing sigh, he entered the bathroom, rolled up his sleeve, and pulled the plug on the cold bathwater. As the drain gurgled, he opened her medicine cabinet and studied the contents. Along with the usual assortment of toiletries and feminine hygiene products, there was a small bottle of prescription sleeping pills and an over-the-counter bottle of ibuprofen.

He next entered the kitchen and found the cat food, which he poured into a spill-proof bowl beside the fridge. At the sound of the dry pellets hitting the plastic bowl, the calico cat poked its head around the corner and flashed Jersey a suspicious scowl.

Jersey lifted the second bowl and filled it with fresh water. After placing it on the floor beside the first, he backed out of the kitchen and turned his attention to the lone bedroom. As he opened the door, he could hear the cat crunching at its food.

In the bedroom, Jersey searched through Sally's strewn clothes and a small leather travel pouch he had noticed her wearing around her waist when they went for coffee. The pouch contained her wallet, cellphone, iPod, and keys to the apartment—all things one usually didn't leave behind.

Sitting on the unmade double bed, Jersey flipped through

Sally's wallet. It contained one credit card and one bankcard, a driver's license, and a customer loyalty card for a nearby coffee shop. Two more lattes and she would receive one for free.

He powered on the cellphone and opened its electronic address book. There wasn't a single stored entry. Next, he switched on the iPod and dug into its menu for a list of contacts that would have been synced from a computer's address book. Again, the list was empty.

Jersey scanned the room again. There was no sign of a desktop computer or portable laptop. He walked through the apartment once more, but if Sally owned a computer, it was also missing.

"Where are you, Sally?" he asked the room.

Despite knowing his partner would call him ridiculous, Jersey slipped Sally's driver's license and keys into his pocket before walking back through the living room to the front door. The cat stopped eating and followed him with her large green eyes. They reminded Jersey of her owner's.

"I'll check in tomorrow," he said and jangled the keys. "Maybe she'll be back by then."

The cat continued to stare as Jersey left the apartment and locked the door.

30

Home to less than two hundred thousand people, the city of Spokane spread itself across fifty-eight square miles on both sides of a once salmon-rich tributary of the Columbia River. From the freeway, however, it possessed all the bleak box-store charm of a discount mall.

When Aedan showed no sign of slowing down, Sally rattled her chains. "Are we getting something to eat?"

Aedan turned his dark eye upon her, but didn't speak.

"You promised," Sally pushed. "And I really have to pee again."

"We'll stop soon."

"I have to pee badly," Sally insisted, not wanting the lights of civilization to fade behind them. "It's been hours and I'm cramped up."

Aedan flicked on his signal light and veered the car off the freeway to a row of competing gas stations, all advertising the same price per gallon.

He picked the station furthest from the off-ramp and with the least amount of cars parked outside its small restaurant and smaller convenience store.

"I'll order us two salads with chicken," said Aedan.

"I'd prefer a cheeseburger," Sally said, "but I really need to pee first."

Aedan stepped out of the vehicle and looked around at the mostly empty lot. Three pick-up trucks and a rusted Honda were parked on the far side of the restaurant and none of the pumps were being used.

When he was satisfied, Aedan walked around to Sally's door and yanked it open. He knelt down until his singular gaze was level with hers.

"Don't do anything stupid," he said. "I don't want to harm you, but I'm not someone you mess with. Do you understand?"

Sally nodded and lifted her shackled hands.

Aedan stared at her for a moment longer before pulling a small silver key from his pocket and unlocking both cuffs.

Sally slipped out of the car with her head lowered to hide her excitement at finally being free of her bonds. She only wished she had her pearl-handled straight razor with her because with the anger she felt, she had no doubt she would use it.

Aedan wrapped one hand around her upper arm and squeezed. Sally flinched at the strength of his fingers as she felt her muscles being crushed under the iron grip. Aedan leaned in close to her.

"The washroom is outside," he said. "We'll get the key from the store. You won't say a word."

Before Sally could answer, Aedan forced her into step with him and they crossed the asphalt lot to the convenience store. A scattering of neglected streetlamps buzzed like hungry insects as though growing impatient with the day's dull light.

An electronic alert on the reinforced steel and heavy-glass door twittered their arrival. Looking up from a lightly thumbed copy of *US* magazine, a top-heavy woman in a red T-shirt greeted them with a gap-toothed smile. A pithy slogan on the shirt read, *Got Gas?*

The woman's smile faded when she saw Aedan's damaged face.

Sally tried to catch the woman's eye, but her attention was so focused on Aedan's deformity that Sally doubted she even noticed there was another person.

"Washroom," said Aedan.

"Uh-huh." The woman reached under the counter and produced a steel key attached by an eight-inch length of chain to a long wooden shoehorn. The horn had a generic image of leaping salmon etched on its smooth surface. "Jus' passin' through?"

Aedan accepted the key. "We'll also want food."

"Restaurant is jus' through that door." The woman indicated a second set of glass doors off to her right. "My Bobby's on tonight an' he makes a real nice burger with American cheese and a special Jack Daniels BBQ sauce. Our reg'lars love it."

"Mmmm, that sounds—"

Sally moaned as Aedan squeezed her arm with fingers of constricting steel.

"You okay, honey?" asked the woman, her attention suddenly focused where Sally wanted.

"She needs to pee," Aedan said abruptly. He spun and dragged Sally back through the glass door and outside.

"I'm sorry," Sally blurted. "I'm just hungry, and it did sound—" Sally squealed as Aedan's grip tightened even more, and she feared her bicep was about to be ripped from the bone.

"Don't!" Aedan hissed.

Sally was led to the side of the building opposite the restaurant where Aedan used the key to open the lone door.

"I'll be right here."

He tossed her inside and the door banged closed behind.

In the dim light of the cramped room, Sally rubbed her sore arm and quickly took in her surroundings. One toilet, one sink, one urinal, one mirror, and a disgusting stench. There was no wooden plunger or any caustic cleaning products that she could use as weapons, and the mirror was fastened to the wall with four large bolts. There wasn't even a window to escape through.

Crap! She said to herself. *Crap, crap, crap.*

There was a knock on the door.

"Everything okay?"

"Fine!" Sally shouted back. "It's just—" She had an idea. "It's my period. Could you get me pads or Tampax? I'm sure I saw some at the store."

A heavy silence followed by "I can't—"

"I'm bleeding here, Aedan," Sally whined. "I can't travel around with bloody jeans. You think people won't notice that? It's not like you gave me a chance to pack."

Another silence.

"Look," Sally continued, making her voice less angry in supplication. "It's light flow, so if you could get some pads that will be fine, but I need something."

"Don't move," Aedan warned. "If you move—"

"Lock me in if you don't trust me. You have the key."

A heavy hand slammed against the door and Sally jumped, her heart leaping into her throat. *Had she pushed him too far?* Her lungs stopped pumping and nervous sweat beaded on her forehead as she waited for the inevitable. But the door didn't open, and Aedan didn't enter.

Sally released her breath slowly as the sound of the lock turning in the door was followed by heavy footsteps walking away. Sally waited several seconds, her heart thumping in her chest, her breathing still faster than she wanted, then she simply turned the lock.

She didn't think Aedan had believed the lock couldn't be opened from the inside, but he must have trusted that she was too scared of him to bluff.

Pushing the door a crack, Sally hoped he wasn't calling her bluff, too. When nothing happened, she opened the door further and poked out her head. She spotted Aedan's back as he vanished into the store. At best, she would only have minutes before he returned. At worst, seconds.

She scanned the parking lot, desperate for anything that would help her escape. There were no people, no idling cars, and definitely no cops. Then she saw it. A short distance past the entrance to the store was a public telephone box. She would only have one chance.

Gathering up all her courage and strength, Sally ran for the telephone as fast as her legs would carry her. As she flew by the door to the convenience store, she prayed Aedan wasn't looking out. If he was, there was nothing she could do.

When she reached the telephone, she punched in zero.

"Operator," said an unexpected human voice. "How may I—"

"Reverse charges to the following number," Sally blurted, her voice on the edge of hysteria. "It's urgent. Vitally urgent." Sally read out the number and began to pray as she waited for the operator to connect her.

The phone started to ring. One ring. Two rings. Three ri—

The phone was picked up.

"Hello?"

"This is the operator call—"

"It's Sally," she broke in. "Listen."

"Excuse me, ma'am."

"Where are y—"

"Sister Fleur," Sally gasped. "Seattle. Hur—"

A knuckled fist slammed into the side of Sally's skull and sent her sprawling onto the tarmac. She hit the road with a heavy slap, her hands and knees stinging from the impact. Her head felt separated from her body.

With a groan, she rose onto skinned knees, her head spinning in a nausea-inducing cyclone. Her ears were ringing, her vision blurred, and her stomach churned. She had never been hit that hard before in her life.

As Sally fought against the nausea, a man's voice called out her name from a distance so far away it could have been a dream. She tried to shake her head, to bring her vision back into focus. She had been hit with a sledgehammer. Her tongue was bleeding; her teeth felt loose.

Sally looked up toward the sky and her vision was suddenly filled with Aedan's angry face. This was not the same face she thought she could escape, the face she could outrun. This was the terrifying visage of her nightmares.

Sally whimpered and raised her hands in pleading self-defense as Aedan drew back his arm. But there was nothing she could do as his fist drove forward in a blur. Sally's head snapped back and everything went black.

31

"**O**perator!" Jersey screamed as the sound of a one-sided scuffle sent shards of ice slicing through his veins. "What's happening there?"

"I assure you, sir, I don't—"

"I'm a cop," Jersey snapped. "I need to know where this call is originating from. Now!"

"Sir, I—"

"Now, goddammit!"

But by the time he was told the address of the truck stop in Spokane, it was too late.

Sally was gone.

32

Jersey frantically worked the phone and computer in a search for anything that could connect him with the woman from Sally's desperate plea: *Sister Fleur.* Why Sally wanted him to find a nun in Seattle, Jersey couldn't fathom. And with no last name or known religious order, it was proving difficult.

When no matches popped up on a large scale inter-agency database query, and even an Internet search came up empty, Jersey also worried that it was his own Catholic upbringing that made him instantly think of the church when Sally used the term sister. As his partner liked to remind him, he didn't know enough about Sally's background to understand her references. Sister could be a salutation for any number of things outside of the nunnery.

When the report arrived from the Spokane cops who had responded to his request and rushed to Sally's last known location, Jersey's fear deepened.

The only witness to her abduction—a convenience store clerk with a distrust of the police and a pending trial for drunk driving—hadn't noticed the make of vehicle. *"It was a big one, but not a four door"* or its plate *"I don't think it was from Washington if that helps,"* but her description of the disfigured man, *"He gave me the creeps let me tell you,"* with the shorter woman, *"She did look kinda scared, but I figured she jus' needed the toilet, you know?"* matched Sally's description of the mystery man in Higgins' car. The same man, Jersey suspected, who had left the disappearing message on the driver's corpse.

After coming up empty with the Catholic Archdiocese, Jersey began scrolling through online directories of various religious orders in the Pacific Northwest. Of the ones he managed to contact, no one had a Sister Fleur registered or had knowledge of a Sally Wilson.

Cursing his lack of progress, Jersey picked up the phone and dialed his partner.

Amarela answered with a sleepy, mumbled groan.

"Who do you know in Seattle?" Jersey asked without preamble.

"Jersey? That you? What time is it?"

"Don't you have a contact at the SPD?"

"Yeah. Kameelah Steele, she's working sex crimes up there. Why?"

"I need a favor."

"What's going on?"

"Sally's in trouble."

"You think or you know?"

"She called me. She's been abducted by the same man she saw in the car with Higgins when he drove over his wife."

"Abducted? Why?"

"I don't know. That's why I need a favor."

"Give me five. Where are you?"

He told her.

JERSEY'S DESK PHONE rang five minutes later.

"I've got Kameelah on conference," said Amarela. "Go ahead."

"Kameelah?" Jersey began, "I'm looking for someone, possibly a nun."

The voice that came on the line sounded alert and professional, but with the sultry, rhythmical hint of an educated South African accent.

"I'm sex crimes, detective, not missing persons, but I'll do what I can."

"Her name is Sister Fleur."

There was an audible intake of breath.

"Kameelah?" Amarela asked.

"I know where she is," said Kameelah.

"Holy crap!" gasped Amarela. "Am I good or what?"

"Where?" Jersey asked.

"If it's the same woman you're looking for, she's at Harborview Medical Center. Last I checked, she was in critical care but the doctors had high hopes."

"What happened?"

Kameelah took a breath. "Last week, two nuns were assaulted on the outskirts of the city. Sister Fleur had been selling religious knickknacks to passing tourists outside a country store with another member of the same order. They were attacked in the woods a half-mile from the Immaculate Heart Mission as they walked home. There were no witnesses and the attack was brutal. Both women were strangled into submission and beaten. The other nun didn't make it. Her rosary beads were embedded a full half-inch deep in her neck. Sister Fleur was luckier, but not by much."

"And you were called in because—"

"There were signs of rape," Kameelah finished. "Sister Fleur had been stripped naked and there were some very nasty contusions all around her pubic region, but the sadistic bastard stopped short of actual penetration. He wasn't interested in sex. I believe he tortured her. After killing the first nun, he took his time with Sister Fleur. There wasn't an inch of her body that wasn't bruised."

"He wanted information," Jersey said, his voice distant.

"About Sally?" Amarela asked.

"Who's Sally?" demanded Kameelah.

"I'll tell you when I get there," said Jersey.

AFTER JERSEY HUNG up the desk phone his cellphone rang.

"What the fuck?" Amarela asked. "You're going to Seattle?"

"This is the only clue I have to where Sally is being taken."

"*If* she's been taken, Jersey. You barely know her."

"I know fear."

"What if she's playing you?"

"She's not."

"Christ, Jersey, you're naive. It's one of the things I love about you, but—"

"She's not playing. This is real, and she needs me."

"Okay, pick me up. I'm not letting you do this on your own."

"No," Jersey said. "I need you to stay here and cover my ass with the lieutenant."

33

Sally awoke in a dark, cramped space, but this time she knew where she was. That knowledge, however, did nothing to quell her fear or quiet the terrifying voice that rang so loudly in her mind: *He's going to kill you.*

Her body rolled as the Cadillac rounded a sharp turn, and her restricted movements told her that Aedan had reattached the nylon straps around her wrists and ankles.

Sally reached up her bound hands to feel the side of her face. A painful bruise stretched from lower jaw to forehead, and from ear to nose. She touched her skin gently, the slightest contact making her flinch. The bastard had a powerful punch, and he hadn't even attempted to pull it. She could feel deep-tissue bruising in the shape of each knuckle.

Her fingers found her nose. It was numb and fragile, but not broken. A splash of blood had sprayed from the nostrils and dried on her cheek. Her right ear was still ringing and her eye was swollen half-shut. She checked her mouth and found her upper lip was split, but like her nose, the bleeding had stopped. Her jaw ached, and there was a clicking sound when she tried to move it, but it didn't feel like any teeth were missing.

Perhaps, worst of all, this time she really did need to pee.

Sally rolled onto her left side, being careful not to move too quickly as her brain felt balanced on a pin, pulled up her scraped knees and lashed out in an awkward mule kick.

A dull thump echoed from the barrier between seat and trunk. To Sally it sounded pathetically weak, but it did the job. Through a small rip in the carpet, the brake light flashed a bright red to briefly illuminate one corner of the otherwise empty space.

As the car slowed, Sally eased onto her back and tried to look as submissive and frightened as possible. It wasn't difficult.

When the trunk lid swung open, the outside sky was a dark blanket punctured by a thousand stars. Sally couldn't remember the last time she had seen so many stars. When the lid reached its apex, however, a bright light clicked on to kill the sky and reveal Aedan's misshapen face. He glared down at her with the same menacing scowl that had preceded her savage beating at the phone box.

"I-I need to pee," Sally stammered.

"You've tried that before."

"I know. I'm sorry. I… I really have to go."

"You can go in there."

A shuddering breath escaped Sally's lips as fresh tears filled her eyes. She didn't have the strength to argue, never mind fight or run. Her display of weakness annoyed her. Not the fact that she felt so powerless but that she couldn't hide it from the monster before her.

Aedan's dark eye narrowed as though contemplating his options. When he reached his decision, Sally couldn't help the trembling fear that overcame her. He leaned into the trunk, slipped his hands under her arms, and lifted her out.

As soon as her feet hit the ground, Aedan grabbed her hands and fastened a metal handcuff around her left wrist. He then attached the second cuff to a welded anchor point inside the trunk. The two cuffs were separated by a four-foot length of chain.

Sally decided any argument on her part could result in

something worse than four feet of freedom. Aedan backed out of the tiny circle of light spilling from the trunk.

"You have five minutes," he said from the darkness. "Don't waste it."

Sally looked down at her bound ankles and carefully shuffled her way around the car until its rear fender gave her partial privacy. She then unbuckled her jeans and wiggled her hips until they slid down to her knees. She felt foolish and angry and more scared than in all the years since the death of her parents.

Life hadn't been easy as she grew into a woman. There were so many times when Sister Fleur made her leave a town just as she was settling in, making friends and discovering who she was inside. The explanations for their sudden departures were never good enough, the secrecy as thick as lies, and when troubled adolescence turned to reckless adulthood, they became even less so. Sally had come to despise her guardian and when Sister Fleur finally settled in Seattle, Sally took off for Portland. The gulf between them, however, was much larger than a three-hour drive could bridge.

But now in the darkness, under a blanket of stars and the watchful eye of a brutal stranger, Sally wished with all her might that Sister Fleur was with her, whispering that everything would be all right. Just as she had done all those years ago when Sally would wake up screaming in the middle of the night, haunted by visions of her dead parents.

As Sally squatted beside the rear tire, she heard the strike of a match followed by the pungent aroma of loose tobacco blended with something much harsher, like vinegar. She glanced over her shoulder, staring into the darkness until she saw a crimson firefly blossom and die. The unpleasant vinegar smell carried on the wind.

"You finished?" Aedan's voice sounded strained as though he was holding his breath.

Sally stood and refastened her jeans. "Can I ride up front again?"

Aedan stepped into the circle of light with twin funnels of smoke trailing out of his nostrils. The effect made him appear demonic.

"I warned you, I'm not someone to mess with."

"I know. I'm sorry, but—"

Aedan lunged forward with the reflexes of a snake and grabbed Sally's arm.

"Okay, Okay," Sally whimpered as Aedan squeezed flesh and bruised muscle against bone.

As Aedan returned her to the trunk, more tears fell from her eyes, but they did nothing to soften his mask of stone.

He closed the lid, sealing her in darkness.

34

Jersey arrived at the front entrance to Harborview Medical Center on Seattle's First Hill after a frantic two-hour drive from Portland.

He had kept himself awake with a thermos of black coffee plus his entire music collection set on shuffle and blaring out of the car stereo via his attached iPod. The combination of strong coffee, sleep deprivation, and dead anarchist rebel songs had him feeling wired and punchy.

A tall, strikingly handsome woman with skin the color of bittersweet chocolate and curly hair so short it could have been a woolen skullcap, stood under the harsh lights of the hospital's art-deco inspired entrance. She was wearing skinny blue jeans tucked into dimpled ostrich-skin boots and a caramel-colored cashmere sweater under a light nylon windbreaker. She was also smoking a small, sweet-smelling cigar and under the fluorescent blue light, her flawless skin practically glowed.

As he moved closer, Jersey couldn't decide whether she would be best suited in the role of an untouchable runway model—all pouty lips and attitude—or a disemboweling Zulu warrior. Either way, she made him nervous.

Perhaps sensing his anxiety, the woman opened her lips to

reveal a blinding and utterly captivating smile. A bright pink tongue followed as she plucked a flake of tobacco off its tip.

"Kameelah?" Jersey asked.

The woman held out her hand. When Jersey accepted it, he discovered the Seattle detective had a very firm grip.

"Amarela says good things about you, which is rare for her when it comes to men."

"Yeah, she's not too fond of my gender. We all tend to—"

"Piss her off," Kameelah finished.

Jersey laughed. "So you do know her?"

"Indeed."

Kameelah took a final drag on her cigar before stubbing it out in a stone pedestal filled with sand that had been designed for just that purpose.

"I checked with the doctors and they've agreed to let us see the Sister, but they don't expect her to be responsive."

"Do they know when she might be up to answering questions?"

Kameelah shrugged. "The docs tell me it's out of their hands."

Jersey looked deep into Kameelah's eyes. They seemed bottomless and had the unsettling quality of making you want to dive in headfirst. "Let's hope she's a fighter."

"After the beating she received, she's had to fight for every breath."

SISTER FLEUR LOOKED as fragile as a child as she lay under a plain white blanket on the stiff hospital bed. Twin transparent tubes were taped to her nostrils and bags of clear liquid dripped into a catheter in her arm.

Her face was one massive and ugly bruise with both eyes bulging like overripe plums and her lips so swollen they seemed ready to burst.

A young nurse checked the intravenous drips. "She's breathing on her own now. That's always a good sign."

"Has she said anything?" Jersey asked.

The nurse shook her head. "Not a word, poor soul."

Jersey crossed to the bed and took the Sister's hand. Four of her fingers were in metal splints and her arms were mottled with yellow and purple bruises.

"Christ," he muttered.

"You should see the rest of her," said Kameelah. "This bastard didn't miss an inch."

"I'll take your word for it." Jersey released the woman's hand and stood back. "She's the key to where this animal has taken Sally."

"Then lets figure out where she fits," said Kameelah. "That's what we're good at, right?"

The confidence in her voice filled Jersey with hope. He liked this woman.

IN A DESERTED sitting area, Kameelah and Jersey sipped from paper cups of coffee and filled each other in on the missing details of each case.

"So you don't know how Sister Fleur connects with your missing mortician?" Kameelah asked.

"No idea. Sally called in a panic and gave me the name. She was cut off before…" His voice faded.

"Which means she trusted you could put the puzzle together," said Kameelah. "With Sister Fleur out of commission, we should run a deep background check and see where their paths cross."

Jersey pulled out Sally's driver's license and handed it over. "If you want to handle the computer work, I wouldn't mind taking a look at the Sister's room in the mission. Maybe there's something there that isn't on the grid."

"Tell you what." Kameelah parted her lips to show strong teeth. "Since we've just met, I'll let that slide. But when you're on my turf, you don't go solo. We'll both do the computer work and then we'll visit the mission together. Deal?"

Jersey couldn't help the grin that creased his face. He would have had the exact same reaction to a visiting detective coming onto his turf.

"You know," he said. "I can see why Amarela likes you."

Kameelah's eyes sparkled.

35

Sally was exhausted, stiff, and sore as the Cadillac slowed once more before finally coming to a rolling stop. Locked in the disorienting darkness of the trunk, she had lost all track of time, but the aching weariness in her bones told her they had been traveling for hours and across hundreds of miles.

Sleep had been impossible, despite the rhythmic rocking of the vehicle and the stifling warmth that radiated from beneath the floor. Every time she had tried to close her eyes, a wave of fear that she would never wake up washed over her. Despite knowing she was in a car, it still felt too much like a coffin and Sally now understood how people developed claustrophobia.

The driver's door opened and closed with a passive click rather than an angry clunk. That was a good sign. The man's anger had cooled. Sally waited for the trunk lid to be opened, the delay interminable. One part of her desperately wanted to see the sky again and to breathe fresh air. The trunk had become stale, and she was all too aware of the ripeness of her own body. Fear had turned her sweat sour.

Another part of her, however, felt reluctantly safe in the dark cocoon, and she feared what would happen once she was back in Aedan's hands. The pain inflicted by his fists had been both crippling and humiliating, each blow making her feel small, weak, and powerless. It wasn't something she ever wanted to repeat.

Voices.

Sally strained to listen. Aedan and at least two others, one of them female, but it was difficult to hear clearly. The only word that cut through the chatter was: *Salvation.*

When the trunk lid finally opened, Sally blinked up at the night sky and felt a wave of relief when she saw the stars still shone. The feeling was short-lived as the trunk light snapped on, and Aedan reached in to pull her out.

After she was on her feet, Aedan unfastened the metal cuff around her wrist and tossed the chain into the trunk.

"Can you walk?" he asked.

Sally nodded, too afraid to open her mouth in case all that came out was a blood-curdling scream or, worse, heart wrenching sobs.

"You'll be safe here." He bent to cut the bonds around her ankles.

"Safe?" Sally queried. Her voice was constricted, gravelly, as though she had been gargling dust and stones.

"We'll get you water and food, and Mother will see you get bathed and dressed in fresh clothes."

Aedan reached out his hand and tilted Sally's chin up until he was looking directly into her eyes. "You're home," he said, his mouth twitching. "You're finally home."

If Sally had managed to draw any moisture from her parched throat, she would have spat in his eye.

AEDAN TOOK HOLD of Sally's arm and turned her toward a formidable two-and-one-half-story wooden house on an imposing stone foundation fronted with river rocks. Painted white with black trim in a Tudor style, the house had a wide front porch and a solid front door painted a deep navy blue. The paint glistened as though still wet, and the door looked strong enough to secure a bank vault.

Most impressive of all was a large circular stained glass window in the attic that gazed down upon visitors like a giant eye. The center of the window was made from a kaleidoscope of green glass, while the etched outer rim glistened in reds, blues, and gold. Something about the window was familiar, but before Sally could process it, she was dragged up the front steps, across the porch and through the blue door.

Inside, the house was well used and tired, but also strangely familiar and oddly comforting. The air smelled of ginger muffins, boiled cabbage, and the rich aroma of strong coffee. But there was a scent missing that Sally couldn't quite place. A scent that should have been there. Something sweet, yet... *pipe tobacco*.

Sally inhaled the air around her and swore she could almost sense its ghostly presence: a blackened clay pipe smoldering with toasted Virginia tobacco laced with ripe cherry liqueur.

She turned to her left and saw a pot-bellied stove in the middle of a huge, open-plan kitchen complete with industrial-sized, stainless steel fixtures. The old-fashioned stove was still radiating warmth, but there was no one in the room to enjoy it. Sally turned to her right where an antique, barroom-style player piano sat by the porch window and made her think of summertime parties and people singing along to old songs they knew by heart.

I know this house, Sally thought.

Aedan led Sally to the foot of the stairs, and then waved her ahead. But as they rounded the top bend and stepped onto the landing, Sally froze. The door directly in front of her led to a bathroom. Sally knew this even though the door was closed. A flash of memory ignited in her brain, and Sally's knees went weak.

Run, Sally! Run!

The distant voice of her mother.

Sally swiveled her head in panic, but Aedan was behind her, barring any retreat.

"Go on," he said.

"I don't want to be here."

"You'll be fine."

Sally moved past the bathroom, her eyes growing in panic. The door to her mother's bedroom loomed at the far end of the narrow hallway. It was open a tiny crack and Sally could hear music playing from inside. The song was familiar—the ting, tinkle, ting of a wind-up music box—and Sally had an overwhelming urge to flee.

Aedan stopped in front of Sally's old bedroom door and pushed it open.

Sally shook her head aggressively. She didn't want to be here, she didn't want to return. Didn't they know that her mother had told her to run?

"You need rest," said Aedan. "Mother will see to you."

Before Sally could protest further, Aedan shoved her into the room and pulled the door closed.

Sally skidded on the floor and immediately rushed back. She grabbed the handle and pulled, but the door wouldn't budge. Then she heard a metal bolt sliding into its hasp and knew she had become a prisoner in the same house she fled as a child.

With her back pressed against the door, Sally took in the room. Nothing seemed familiar except... a hand-sewn patchwork quilt covered the single bed next to the lone window. Sally knew the quilt contained over two hundred separate pieces of fabric recycled from old clothes and blankets that had been important to her mother. Some of the pieces had come from Sally's own clothes as she outgrew them, while others had come from her grandmother's. Until this moment, Sally hadn't thought about the quilt in almost a quarter century.

Other memories awakened within—her mother tucking her

in at night with a lullaby on her lips. She was a beautiful woman with eyes the color of a Mediterranean sea, the color of Sally's eyes. Her mother's hair had been long and curly and a natural orange so bright it was like the setting sun on an autumn night.

Is that why Sally dreamed of being a redhead?

She had forgotten her mother's beauty and her gentle songs. Her violent death had blotted everything else out. Happiness scrubbed away by the pull of a trigger.

Sally crossed to the window and attempted to open it, but found it had been nailed shut from the outside; wide nail heads shiny from hurried blows. Frustrated, she sat on the bed and angrily brushed pointless tears from her eyes. She didn't know what these strangers expected of her, but she didn't want to return to a past where her only clear memory was so full of pain.

Laying her head on the pillow, Sally pulled her mother's quilt around her like a cocoon. Beneath the spicy fragrance of cedar from the trunk where it had been stored for all these years, the tattered squares of cloth held another scent, a secret perfume of childhood laughter, giggles and tears.

Sally inhaled deeply as she closed her eyes, too tired to think and too sore to move.

36

edan drove the Cadillac through the wide front gate that sat between the two main homes and guarded the vast compound beyond.

His tires crunched noisily along the circular gravel drive to the rear of the walled estate. There, he pulled into a one-car garage that had been designed for a much smaller vehicle. The interior of the garage was so tight; he could barely swing his door open far enough to squeeze out.

After side-shuffling his way to the overhead door, Aedan pulled it down and fastened a heavy-duty padlock on the hasp. In the morning, he would replace the Idaho license plates with the car's original North Dakota ones. He would also destroy the stolen plates with that week's garbage in the old oil drum they used as a burning barrel.

Aedan knew he was being overly cautious, but it only took one slip to bring down their fragile house of cards. For all its boasting about freedom, America was not a country that embraced difference. In his experience, the great melting pot was actually a sausage maker that ripped, chopped, and ground you down until you became part of the same quivering mass. Instead of a country of leaders, it had become a country of lambs. And lambs, as he knew all too well, were destined for the slaughterhouse.

Aedan walked across the courtyard designed by his grandfather after a medieval fortress in the north of England. The simple layout and elegant symmetry of it had always stayed with him.

Two matching and impenetrable homes dominated the front of the property as gatekeepers to the secret paradise within. On the far side of each house, eight-foot-tall stone walls jutted out at hard right angles and stretched for over sixty feet before turning ninety degrees and running the entire length of the perimeter to form a protected square. At the rear corners of the property, but inside the protected grounds, were two more stately homes, now in sad disrepair that had once belonged to two of the four founding families.

In the center of the square—surrounded by raised garden beds, a bounty of fruit trees, and crushed gravel pathways—a circular church dominated the enclosed two-acre spread.

The only entrance to the church and gardens for the families who lived outside the walls was the imposing stone and iron gateway that Aedan had passed through. And although the gate was rarely locked, as strangers were few, the community found it comforting that it would be a formidable obstacle to overcome if the need ever arose.

Aedan walked by the unlit church that doubled as the community's licensed school, his boots crunching on a groomed pathway that wound through the flower and vegetable gardens, until he came to the massive rear wall. Some of the families who helped build the wall had written their names in the mortar. Aedan's name was one of them, but he had been a younger and more carefree individual then.

Leaving the garden path, he continued beside the wall until he came to a steel door inset into the stone. It didn't have a handle or a lock. To open it, Aedan pushed one of the river rocks that made the wall. The rock clicked against a magnetic lock and swung out to reveal a computer keypad hidden inside. Aedan punched in his four-digit code and closed the stone lid as the sound of a heavy bolt being withdrawn from deep within the wall told him the door had unlocked.

Pushing through the steel door, Aedan entered a private wooded acreage the community had allowed to stay untamed as a further measure of privacy. It was here that he felt most comfortable.

After ensuring the door was locked behind him, Aedan made his way to a small, but pleasant, A-frame cabin tucked in the trees. The night was cold, but the sight of his home filled him with a comforting warmth. He had been on the road too long this time. The information that led him to Sister Fleur had turned into a ten-day excursion. Or more accurately, the ten-day conclusion to a twenty-five-year journey.

Inside the cabin, Aedan crossed to the stone hearth that dominated one wall and lit a wood fire that he had left prepared for his return. As the dry kindling caught, he peeled out of his rank clothing and left them in a heap to be added to the fire once it was strong enough.

Tired and dirty, sweaty and soiled, he entered his cedar-walled bathroom and turned the copper faucets to fill the six-and-one half-foot-long soaker tub. The long tub allowed him to stretch out completely with an inch to spare at both head and feet.

As the tub filled, Aedan studied himself in the mirror. He truly had a horrendous face. It was the kind of visage that people would remember even when they couldn't recall anything else. Ask for the length of his hair, the color of his eyes, or how tall he stood, and every potential witness would be dumbstruck. None were able to see beyond his deformity.

It also itched like hell.

Aedan reached into the medicine cabinet and retrieved a bottle of rubbing alcohol and a bag of cotton balls. He soaked the cotton with alcohol and rubbed the cold liquid against his scalp. After several passes, his ruined flesh began to pucker and peel away from his hairline like a snake shedding its skin.

He continued to swab the alcohol down the center of his face and around his nose until a distinct ridge of melting flesh appeared. When he was satisfied with the progress, Aedan dug his fingernails into the ridge and pulled.

The deformation tore under his grip and began to rip from his face in sheets of prosthetic rubber.

After the worst of it was removed, Aedan blinked his right eye several times. Having been hidden in the dark for so long, the pupil was taking its time shrinking back to normal. The tender skin around it was painful and raw. The eye drops had done little to soothe its near-fortnight confinement behind rubber, makeup, and glue.

Aedan looked in the mirror again and moved his lips into the shape of a smile. Beneath every mask, hid another, but at least he was almost back to the one most recognizable as his own.

Before submerging in the bath, Aedan returned to the medicine cabinet and removed a small square of tinfoil and a butane lighter. He smoothed the tinfoil on the bathroom counter before holding it shiny side down over the lighter. Once the foil had blackened slightly, he removed it from the flame. Next, he opened a plastic bottle of generic painkillers and reached inside to remove a small bag of brown powder. After spooning a hit of the powder on the foil, he placed a short glass tube between his lips.

When he returned the foil to the flame, the caffeinated heroin melted into a light maple liquid. White smoke curled skyward as the liquid ran freely across the squared foil. Aedan chased the dragon's tail with his glass tube, sucking the smoke deep into his lungs. The taste, a toxic mixture of bitter and sour, always made him think of what he would taste after death, a lick of the grave: wood, dirt, and decay.

As weariness from the long journey began to drain his body, Aedan glided over to the bathtub and slipped in. He closed his eyes and felt his legs and torso liquefy in the bath's warm and soothing embrace. He continued to melt until he was sunk up to his neck and the water lapped against his cheeks like a wave of velvet tongues.

Chuckling softly to himself, Aedan allowed his brain to dissolve into a pleasant state of euphoria.

37

"These women are ghosts." Kameelah's weary sigh filled the room as she looked up from her laptop. "Are you sure you don't have anything else?"

Jersey grunted from his prone position on Kameelah's white leather couch. He was too tired to think, but racing thoughts of Sally and the danger she was in made it impossible to sleep.

"That's it," he said. "And you know more about the Sister than I do."

"Well according to her driver's license, Sally didn't exist until ten years ago. And Sister Fleur still doesn't. She draws a blank on every databank I have access to. Like I said, ghosts."

"Ghosts that somebody wants to hurt."

Kameelah closed her laptop and yawned. Jersey followed suit, his jaw aching from the power of it.

"We need to catch a couple hours," Kameelah said through another yawn. "I'm beat."

"We should go to the mission."

"It's the middle of the night and even nuns need sleep. What good are you to Sally if you're dead on your feet? If we had a clue, we'd follow it, but we don't."

Jersey relented. "Just a couple hours."

Kameelah rose to her feet and stretched, her fingers reaching to the plastered ceiling. From Jersey's vantage point on the couch she looked eight-feet tall.

"I don't make a habit of allowing strange men to sleep over."

"But?" Jersey allowed his eyes to drift into narrow slits, his eyelids struggling to remain at half-mast.

"But Amarela says you're just a big ol' teddy bear."

Jersey snorted, "So does that mean we're not gonna share a bed?"

"Not at all. I like teddy bears."

Jersey's eyes sprang open and Kameelah burst into laughter.

"Gotcha!"

Grunting again, Jersey rolled onto his side with his back to her. "You don't know what you're missing," he mumbled.

If Kameelah responded, Jersey missed it. He was already snoring.

WHEN JERSEY OPENED his eyes a few hours later, Kameelah was crossing the hallway between bedroom and bathroom. Wearing mint green bikini briefs and a matching full-coverage bra, she was positively stunning.

With generous hips and breasts, a tight stomach, long legs and skin as silky as melted chocolate, she was an ebony goddess. A goddess with a gun close to hand, but still.

Kameelah caught him looking and came to a halt with one hand resting on the bathroom door. Her bicep bulged, the curve of the muscle surprisingly sexy, while her toned legs radiated power. A thoroughbred, Jersey thought as he rubbed the sleep out of his eyes, the kind that could kick your ass without breathing heavy.

"You always spy on your friends?" she asked.

"You always look this good in the morning?"

The compliment caught her off guard, causing her to smirk. "I work at it."

"Me, too, but we must have different trainers."

"Good genes help, too."

"Oh, goody," said Jersey. "I can blame my folks."

Kameelah laughed. "Wash up, we'll grab a bite on the way."

BREAKFAST CONSISTED OF a large coffee and a sticky cinnamon bun from a local bakery.

"You eat like this all the time?" Jersey sucked cinnamon, sugar, melted butter, and honey off his fingers. It was ridiculously messy but absolutely delicious. Served warm out of the oven in a little cardboard box with melting cream-cheese icing spread on top.

"I treat myself once a week. Can't be good all the time. Too boring."

"Yeah, that's why I'm fat," said Jersey. "Cause I'm so darn exciting."

"You're not fat," said Kameelah. "More husky. Besides, women prefer a little meat on their men."

"Is that so?"

"We secretly fear that all skinny men are gay."

"I think you're right," said Jersey with a smirk. "Oprah did a special on it."

"Don't be dissin' my girl."

"Wouldn't dream of it."

38

The Mission of the Immaculate Heart sat in a clearing surrounded by thick woods at the top of a country road that had more ruts and bumps than an antique washboard. Kameelah drove slowly, not wanting to overtax the suspension in her definitely-not-department-issue Jaguar XK convertible.

When Jersey raised his eyebrows at the sporty two-seater with its aluminum-alloy shell gleaming in a metallic shade he later learned was called Emerald Fire, Kameelah had grinned and pointed at the custom license plate. It read: BabyGrl.

"Nobody loves a baby girl like her rich daddy," she explained.

Three-quarters of the way up the winding road, Kameelah slowed even further and pointed to a dirt path that vanished into dense, dark woods.

"The Sisters were attacked down there," she said. "Less than a mile from the Mission."

"He must have stalked them."

"Or lay in wait," said Kameelah. "He knew exactly what he was doing."

"He leave anything behind?"

"Nothing that offered any leads."

When the car rounded a corner and broke from the tunnel of trees, the Mission came into view. A circular driveway made of crushed white rock led to a series of simple, boxcar-style buildings connected end-to-end like a game of dominoes. Each building was painted a gleaming white and had the flat roof and boxy architecture of a Spanish pueblo. With small windows and monochromatic paint job, it reminded Jersey of a D.I.Y. building kit that was still in a state of construction.

Kameelah parked the Jag in front of a wooden door that announced its importance by being sheltered beneath the only canopy in sight. Kameelah walked to the door and knocked as Jersey scanned the exterior for any sign of religious affiliation. He didn't see any.

"Where are all the crosses?" he said aloud. "I thought these places loved their symbols."

"This isn't your typical Mission," said Kameelah. "The sisters broke away from the Catholic church to form their own order. This was a couple decades ago, right after the Pope at the time publicly chastised them about their methods."

"Methods?" Jersey asked.

"I've brought a few women here myself," Kameelah explained, "when other avenues failed. The nun who runs the order specializes in helping the most vulnerable among us. Nearly all of her recruits are survivors of one kind or another, and some of their stories would rip your heart to shreds."

She locked eyes with Jersey and continued, "It's difficult to work sex crimes and still enjoy being in the presence of men. Some of the women within these walls have been subjected to such heinous acts of abuse that the total eradication of your gender wouldn't be enough to slack their thirst. Most women discover the Mission after they've hit their lowest point. Some decide to stay, but many try to return to the same fucked-up world that stomped on their soul. The rate of suicide among abused women would shock you. The sisters here can only do so much."

"And now some bastard has struck at their heart," Jersey said.

Kameelah nodded grimly. "You better stick close. I don't want to find you buried out in the woods. The paperwork would be a nightmare."

Jersey's stomach jumped when the door opened suddenly behind Kameelah and a woman with a face like a stewed apple beamed out at them. She was dressed in a flowing, long-sleeved dress the color of a robin's egg with a white habit and matching bib collar. Apart from her wrinkled face, the only exposed flesh was a pair of hands with skin so transparent that blue veins and the outline of bones could be seen within.

"Sister Gillian," said Kameelah. "We're here about Sister Fleur."

"And Sister Emily," the nun answered with a sad shake of her head. "A terrible, terrible tragedy. One soul in Heaven, the other fighting to stay on Earth."

"If it's possible, we would like to see Sister Fleur's room."

"Of course, dear. Come inside." She opened the door wider and reached out to squeeze the woman's arm. "It's good to see you again, Kameelah. Pity it's always under such horrible circumstances."

As Jersey caught up to them, the nun released Kameelah and turned to him. "To answer your question, detective, the entire building is our cross. If you were to view us through God's eyes, you would see this."

"Ahhh." Jersey had no other response.

They walked the long, narrow hallway toward the sisters' living area. As they did so, the elderly nun hooked her arm around Jersey's. She smelled of cigarettes and peppermint, and her energy belied her age.

"I don't know what Kameelah has told you," said Sister Gillian with a husky growl, "but I still like men. Not all of them mind. Heck, not even most of the selfish buggers. But a few. I still like a few."

"Ahhh, that's good to know," he said awkwardly.

The nun's eyes sparkled with mischief and she squeezed his arm tighter. "And you don't have to worry, it's only the evil ones we bury in the woods."

Walking in front, Kameelah turned her neck and winked back at them. The delight on her face showed she was enjoying Jersey's discomfort.

The hallway led to a central hub that branched off in three directions. The hub was designed as a central meeting and reading area with assorted, over-stuffed chairs scattered around in singles and pairs. The focus, however, was a large three-quarter-circle couch that faced a well-used, wood-burning fireplace. The conversation couch could comfortably seat twelve.

Glancing up, Jersey saw the ceiling was slightly pyramidal in shape and constructed mostly of glass. On a clear day, the room would be bathed in sunlight, and on a rainy one, the fire would offer cozy comfort.

Sister Gillian led Jersey through the empty hub to the hallway on their left.

"You're Catholic," she said.

"Lapsed," said Jersey.

"No such thing. You either believe or you don't."

"I lost faith in the church."

"Then we have something in common."

SISTER FLEUR'S ROOM was a cozy cell with a small window that looked out on a rose garden. It also contained more modern conveniences than either Kameelah or Jersey expected.

The single bed was utilitarian, but it was dressed in a colorful quilt and complementary pillowcase. A small nightstand beside it contained a collection of books and an adjustable reading lamp. A pair of wireless headphones rested on the bedpost. Jersey suspected they were tuned to a small flat-screen LCD television mounted on the wall at the perfect height for watching in bed. The room also contained a portable microwave oven, a small bar fridge, and a corner table that boasted a shiny aluminum iMac computer.

"You have Internet access?" Jersey asked the nun.

"Oh, yes. We run wireless broadband throughout the Mission. There are so many troubled souls out there, we try to spread the word as far as we can. Our podcasts are proving very popular."

Jersey tried to hide his surprise, but Sister Gillian caught it.

"We're very modern now, detective," she said. "God's word—the true word—is needed more than ever. What kind of messengers would we be if we ignored the latest advances in communication?"

"Makes sense," Jersey agreed, but then a troubling thought flashed through his mind. "Was Sister Fleur involved in your podcasts?"

"Why, yes." The nun beamed. "She has a perfect speaking voice. Not too fast, not too slow. It's almost hypnotic in its cadence, like waves on a beach. I could listen to her all day."

Jersey turned to Kameelah. "Maybe that's how her assailant found her. Her voice led him straight here."

The nun gasped. "Our podcasts are messages of peace and hope. We deliberately try not to antagonize—"

"I'm sure they are," said Jersey. "But it wasn't the message our attacker was listening for."

"Do you mind if we look through her computer?" Kameelah asked. "It may have some answers."

"Of course," said the nun. "We have nothing to hide."

39

Sally awoke to the knowledge that she was not alone in the room.

She bolted upright. "Who's there?"

A dark figure stood by the window. The morning light shining brightly through the glass created a two-dimensional silhouette with all the curves of a brick: solid and stocky with broad shoulders, strong back, and wide hips.

"It's only me, child."

The figure turned from the window and approached the bed. As the silhouette drew nearer, it blossomed into a heavyset woman in her mid-sixties with lifeless shoulder-length hair the color of decaying chestnuts. Her face was round and plain with a wide, upturned nose, and a double chin. Makeup might have brought some life back to her slack, colorless skin, but there was little she could do about a large port-wine birthmark that spread in a teardrop shape from below her left eye to encompass all of her left cheek and part of her chin.

Her clothes reflected a definite need for order and control with a matronly dress in unflattering blue checkers, pulled in at the waist by the thick straps of a white baker's apron, similar to the one Mrs. Shoumatoff had worn back in Portland.

Sally's gaze returned to the woman's face. Her eyes were a surprisingly arresting shade of violet.

"Who are you?" Sally asked.

"Most of the family calls me Mother." Her voice was warm, welcoming. "But I know that may sound strange on your tongue having lost your own at such a tender age. So 'til we get to know each other better, you call me Helen. That okay?"

"Where exactly am I, Helen?"

The woman smiled. "Why, you're home, child."

Sally swallowed the acrid taste of fear invoked by those words. None of it had been a dream.

"I'm sure," Helen continued, "you'd like a bath, breakfast, and a clean change of clothes. That always makes a person feel better, doesn't it?"

Sally nodded.

"I'll start the bath, then. Back soon."

The moment the woman left the room, Sally leapt out of bed and rushed to the door. She turned the handle and pulled, but it was locked from the outside.

No matter how pleasant the woman seemed, Sally reminded herself, she was still a prisoner.

WHEN HELEN RETURNED, she took Sally by the arm and led her into the hallway.

"Your bath is nice and toasty," she said. "I've laid out clean towels and fresh clothes. There are just a few ground rules…"

Sally stopped listening as they approached the bathroom. It was the same room where her father had stood with a shotgun in his mouth. The same gun he used to kill her mother.

Sally wrenched her arm free from Helen's grasp. "I can't."

Before the woman could react, Sally bolted for the stairs, running past the bathroom without looking, taking the corner and—

She slammed straight into a burly man with a shaved head.

He was dressed in black pants and shirt, but with a priest's white collar cinched around his thick neck. Sally bounced off his barrel chest and tumbled backwards before finding herself unexpectedly snatched up in strong arms and pulled into the man's coarse embrace.

"Is this little Salvation Blue?" the man chortled. "Come to give her old uncle a hug at last."

Sally squirmed against the stranger, but his arms were too powerful. With her face squashed against his chest, she could hear his heart thumping loudly beneath a heavy layer of pectoral muscle.

"My we've missed you," continued the man. "It was like losing a lung when you disappeared, half the oxygen just seemed to leave the place."

The man pushed Sally out to arm's length, hands the size of catcher's mitts still gripping her tight. She tried to break free, but the man didn't seem to notice. He beamed at her, his oval face lit up like a Jack O'Lantern.

"You're the spitting image of your parents," he said. "The beauty of your mother and the stubbornness of your dad. Ach, we miss them so."

Tears formed in the burly man's amber eyes as Sally stared at him in horror.

Helen approached to take hold of Sally's arm. The man, with a tinge of sadness in his voice, said, "She looks at me as if she doesn't know me."

"She was only six when she left us, Father. You've changed a bit since."

"Me?" Father chortled again and winked at Sally. "I can't believe that."

"I was taking her to the bath," said Helen. "But she got startled, poor dear. Could you help me?"

Sally opened her mouth to scream out her frustration—*she didn't want to be here, she had been kidnapped, didn't anybody notice... or care*—but a rippling shadow, like a snake swimming in a jar of cream, beneath the man's skin caused her to hold her anger inside.

"You'll want to listen to Mother," he said, all warmth gone from his voice. "Her kindness is great, but her temper can curdle your blood. I ought to know."

"Don't frighten the girl, Father."

"She's already that, Mother. I just want her to understand her options."

The icy calmness of the man's voice frightened Sally more than Aedan's fists.

When he released his grip on her, Sally allowed Helen to escort her into the bathroom without further trouble.

40

Her father's ghost wasn't waiting in the tub when Sally lowered herself into the warm, sweet-smelling water.

Despite the steam rising into the air, it took five minutes for Sally to stop shaking and finally uncurl her body from its tight rigor. Helen had left her alone in the room at least and for that Sally was grateful.

As her tension unwound, Sally soaped her body, her fingers massaging deep into sore and tired muscles. None of this made sense to her: a family she had forgotten existed; a house she had never desired to see again; a husband promised at birth; and the vision that started it all, a gift or a curse that she never knew she possessed.

After she finished soaping, Sally dunked herself under the water. Her eyes remained closed, not wanting to look up at the ceiling, just in case there loomed a shadow that she had no desire to see.

Next, she shampooed her hair and dunked under again. This time she stayed submerged longer; holding her breath, testing herself. The silence was bliss.

When she finally emerged, Helen was sitting on the toilet, lid closed, watching her.

Sally gasped and covered her breasts; protective, embarrassed.

"What do you see down there?" Helen asked, her violet eyes twinkling. "In the darkness."

"N-nothing," Sally stammered.

"But that's not the truth." The woman's voice was dark, edgy. "Is it, child?"

Sally straightened her back, refusing to play the victim. "Can you hand me a towel?"

The woman stood and a strange blue halo appeared around her head, created by the sunlight streaming through a small lead-paned window behind her. Despite the beauty of the light, however, the unreadable face hidden in the shadows beneath it remained an enigma. Helen handed Sally a towel. It was thick, fresh, and fragrant.

"Breakfast is on the table downstairs. When you're ready."

When the door closed, leaving her alone once more, Sally released a long breath that she hadn't realized she was holding.

After drying off, Sally looked around for her clothes. Her jeans and T-shirt were gone, as was her dainty undergarments. In their place was a simple white dress with buttons running up the bodice and a pair of pedestrian, plain white granny panties. Flat-soled, white leather slip-ons lay on the floor to finish the virginal look.

Neat trick, she thought to herself. Either dress like they want or go naked.

Sally slipped into the dress and studied herself in the mirror. With her shock white hair, pale complexion, and white dress, she looked like a ghost.

Not surprisingly, she felt like one, too.

BREAKFAST CONSISTED OF a bowl of powerfully chewy oatmeal with a miserly sprinkle of brown sugar and raisins, fresh orange juice, a soft-boiled egg served in an eggcup, and multigrain toast. The toast was buttered and sliced into fingers just the right size to dip into the egg yolk.

Sally tried to hide her enthusiasm for the food, but she was too famished.

Helen beamed at her as she ate.

"That's the spirit," she said. "You'll need your strength."

"Why?" Sally asked between bites of crunchy, yolk-soaked toast.

"We're having a special ceremony this afternoon. The first of its kind since your mother passed."

Sally stopped eating and wiped her mouth. "You knew my mother?"

"Of course, she was my sister-in-law. Your father was my husband's brother."

"What was she like?"

Helen's mouth formed a tight line. "I'm sure you knew her as well as anyone."

"But I didn't," Sally blurted. "I mean… I don't remember. My entire childhood is a blur." Sally's eyes narrowed. "Didn't you like her?"

Helen bristled. "Your mother was very likable, dear. Everyone misses her greatly as we do your father."

"Why did he do it?" Sally asked in a small voice. "Why did he kill my mother?"

Helen busied herself at the sink, turning her back in an effort to hide the flush that burned her cheeks.

"We'll never know," she answered curtly. "Now finish your breakfast before it gets cold."

Sally dipped another bread soldier into the soft yolk and changed tactics. "What kind of ceremony are you planning?"

Helen turned back around. Her eyes were closed in reverential memory, and her mouth had formed a beatific smile.

"You'll speak for the dead, Salvation. You'll lead them through death's door, and you'll bring back the word of God."

41

Kameelah called Jersey over to the computer to look at several news pages Sister Fleur had bookmarked in her web browser.

"She viewed these articles numerous times over the last few months," Kameelah explained.

Jersey pulled over a small wooden stool and scooted close to the screen. The first page contained a short article published in the *Spokesman-Review* that was a follow-up to an earlier story about the body of a young woman discovered on the banks of the Spokane River. There were few details except the woman's identification being officially released, and a disturbing passage that read:

> Spokane investigators are still refus-
> ing to verify one witness's report that
> the victim was missing both eyes and her
> throat had been torn open, "Like she was
> attacked by a wolf. A human wolf."

"This reporter's working for the wrong paper," said Jersey. "National Enquirer should pick him up."

Kameelah switched to a second page. This one was a news story published in the *Idaho Statesman*. It was dated eight weeks ago. Another young woman had been murdered and her body dumped on the banks of Snake River in Idaho Falls.

Kameelah pointed to the relevant section:

> Police are refusing to speculate at this
> time on a possible connection with the
> unsolved murder of a woman discovered on
> the banks of Spokane River six months
> earlier.
>
> When confronted by this reporter about
> grisly similarities in the two cases,
> Chief Sydney Charles did admit he was
> very concerned "by the removal of the
> victim's eyes. That tells us we're deal-
> ing with a real animal here."

"Same reporter?" Jersey asked.

Kameelah scrolled up to check the byline and nodded. "Must have switched papers."

"Which means there could easily be other victims with the same M.O. The only reason there's a connection between these two is because our boy was on the scene to see the damage or interview witnesses who did. Cops in other jurisdictions could be keeping the eye removal quiet."

"Standard procedure," said Kameelah. "Keep something back to rule out false confessions."

"But why was a nun so interested in these two cases?"

"The victims are both females in their early thirties," said Kameelah. "Same as Sally."

Jersey paled. "If this killer has been searching for Sally, maybe these women were false leads. He could have been fumbling in the dark until Sister Fleur's voice led him here. She was the missing key."

"But why remove the eyes?"

Jersey pinched the bridge of flesh between his eyebrows. "Did I tell you about Sally's..." He paused. "What Sally claimed she saw after touching the victim in the alley?"

"Claimed she saw?"

Jersey squirmed. "She said it was like a vision, or a dream or something. She saw the murder through the victim's eyes as if it was happening *to* her. That's how she knew the car's license plate."

"Like a psychic?"

"I guess. It's tough for me to digest, but I… well, I know that she believed…"

Kameelah knit her brow, the unexpected wrinkles like ripples on a calm lake of unfathomable depth. "Okay" she said after a few moments. "What if Sally's ability is the reason she's been kidnapped. If these two dead women were false leads like you said, removing their eyes could be a form of punishment for *not* having the gift."

Jersey took it to its logical conclusion. "Which means if Sally can't repeat her vision trick, she could be next."

42

Sally stood by the window and watched through a gap in the curtains as a steady procession of some two dozen cars and minivans drove down the long gravel driveway to park side by side in a small meadow in front of the compound. The meadow was separated from the main road beyond by a thick copse of red cedar and occasional silver maple.

The maples were beginning to lose some of their leaves, flashes of fishing-lure silver as they lost their grip, spun and fell; a sure sign of the oncoming winter.

Smiling faces, young and old, emerged from the cars to greet one another. The children laughed and ran around with friends from other vehicles as though they had been trapped inside for days; the men shook hands and shared jokes; the women hugged and showed off baked goods they had brought on best china plates and covered in clear plastic.

The men wore suits in dark shades. The women wore long-sleeve dresses with high collars and sensible shoes; older women added hand-knit or crocheted shawls to ward off the chill. All the children were in their Sunday best with teeth brushed, hair combed, and shoes polished.

Sally watched them through the glass, wondering if they knew she had been brought here against her will, if one of them might help her return to her own life.

"They know who you are," said Helen softly as she approached from the kitchen. "They've been waiting for you a long, long time."

Sally turned from the window. "I don't understand. This isn't my home, it isn't my church, and it's not my life."

"Of course it is, child. You were chosen by God to house this gift, just as your mother before you and her mother before her."

"But I've tried to tell you, I don't have a gift," Sally protested. "And my mother—"

"You were too young to remember," interrupted Helen. "But your mother was *very* gifted. She delivered to us great news and great joy."

Sally's frustration bubbled to the surface. "I work with the dead every day in the funeral home, and I've never received a single vision."

Helen's smile never faltered. "Of course not. Their souls were long gone by the time their bodies reached you. How can you follow a soul if it's not there? It's like answering the phone after the caller has hung up."

"Are you listening to yourself?" Sally stomped her foot like a frustrated toddler. "I don't want any part of this, don't you understand that?"

Helen lost her smile and her face grew dark. "It's your destiny, child."

"Screw my destiny." Sally jammed her fists against her hips and glared at the woman in petulant defiance.

"That," said the booming voice of the barrel-chested priest as he rounded the corner to join them, "is not an option."

Sally stared into the priest's stern face and raw honey-amber eyes. She saw the snake slither within his flesh, and she recoiled.

The priest held out his hand. "Come. The congregation is waiting."

SALLY WAS LED through the kitchen, out the back door, and into a large courtyard that spread itself around the uniquely shaped church in its center.

The building had the appearance of a funnel turned upside down but with its erect tail snipped short. The main circular base was painted white like the large homes that dominated each corner of the acreage, but every few feet a curved rib of smooth red cedar flowed from the ground to the edge of the roof. The walls between each rib were constructed from dozens of angled slats, like window shutters, that would allow light and air to enter while maintaining complete privacy from anyone trying to look in from more than a couple of feet away.

The distinctive roof had a hand-woven quality to it and sat atop the base like a bamboo Chinese peasant hat, but with its peak cut open to form a chimney. White smoke puffed from the opening.

As Sally was escorted across the courtyard, she noticed the well-tended gardens and peaceful calm of the walled commune. Each house had its own garage, garden shed, and private patio surrounded by a small patch of lawn and flower garden. The open areas between the houses were dotted with communal vegetable beds, large greenhouses, and multiple flower gardens designed with a commercial, rather than esthetic, purpose.

The sound of grinding metal caused Sally to glance behind her. The two massive doors that led into the courtyard from the meadow shuddered slightly under mechanical pressure and began to swing closed.

A man operating the machinery looked in her direction and waved, but Sally didn't believe the gesture was intended for her.

The burly priest holding Sally's arm tightened his grip and steered her away from the church's front doors. Helen followed obediently behind as they skirted around the side of the building to an unobtrusive opening set into the concrete foundation at the rear.

The priest led Sally down a short flight of steps and through a wooden door into a brightly lit cellar. Apart from a few boxes pushed to the sides and assorted junk hanging from the curved walls, the basement was bare. On the floor, however, were two circular platforms of polished wood.

The priest led Sally to the circle positioned in the epicenter of the room and helped her step onto the shallow platform.

"Don't move," he said. "Mother will tell you what to expect."

The priest then moved to the smaller circle closer to the rear of the basement and pressed a button on the wall. His platform rose upon a silent steel pedestal until he vanished through a hole in the ceiling.

43

Father Black ascended from a hole in the floor and studied his audience gathered in the round.

Spread out in a horseshoe around him, faces were beaming as excitement buzzed like a swarm of caffeinated bees.

These were his children, his followers, his family. And they were hungry for the Word.

Father Black stared at the burning wood fire contained within a massive cast-iron bowl in front of him. He grinned wide; the cat with the newborn bunny, milk-fed and blind.

They had been waiting twenty-five years for this moment. Twenty-five years of fumbling in the dark, praying for the guiding light.

It was time to tell his congregation that the long wait was over.

A LOUD ROAR of whistles, cheers, and thunderous applause filtered through the floorboards, making Sally look up in confusion. She had never heard such excited noise in a church before. The feel of cold steel against her ankle, however, made her quickly look down again.

"What are you doing?"

Helen rose from her knees where she had fastened a steel cuff around Sally's ankle. The cuff was anchored to an iron ring embedded in the wooden platform.

"It's for your own safety," said Helen.

"Bullshit!" Sally gave her ankle a shake. "I don't know what you expect from me, but I damn well don't plan to cooperate."

"That would be unfortunate. Father has waited a long time for your return." Helen paused, and her violet eyes sparkled crimson in the basement light. "I, on the other hand, rather wish you'd never been found."

Sally froze, the woman's about-turn making her mind reel. "W-what do you mean by that?" she stammered.

But Helen just smiled innocently, her birthmark a dark stain upon her face, as Sally's platform shuddered and began to rise.

Above, voices sang out in welcoming jubilation.

44

Kameelah parked the Jaguar outside Harborview Medical Center. The car's smooth lines and shimmering green skin glistened in the sunlight, causing even the sick and injured hobbling toward Emergency to turn and stare.

Kameelah didn't seem to notice, but Jersey felt a pang of embarrassment over the unsolicited attention as he climbed out of the butter-soft leather seat. He had never known spendable wealth, and although he often imagined it, he wondered that if he was ever suddenly blessed with riches, he could get over the guilt. With a little more thought, he decided he wouldn't mind finding out.

The trip to the Mission of the Immaculate Heart had uncovered nothing beyond conjecture to point to Sister Fleur's attacker or her connection with Sally. Feeling frustrated, Jersey had suggested they revisit their only solid lead.

Kameelah and Jersey rode the elevator to the recovery ward on the fifth floor where Sister Fleur had been moved to a semi-private room.

Inside the room, the same young nurse from their first visit was tucking the sheets around her unconscious patient. The Sister's hair had been combed and appeared much softer, but the bruising in her face had turned murky, and her swollen eyes were only slightly less bulbous. She still wore oxygen tubes taped beneath her nose, and two I.V. bottles dripped clear fluids into her veins.

The nurse smiled at the two detectives as they entered.

"She's just had her bath," said the nurse. "That always makes one feel better, doesn't it?"

"Has she said anything?" asked Jersey.

"Nothing, I'm afraid."

"But she's been awake?" asked Kameelah.

"No," said the nurse. "I gave her the bath by sponge, but we think it's just a matter of time now. We've got her on Dilantin to prevent seizures from the head trauma and anticoagulants to make sure unexpected clots don't form from the other injuries, but it's up to her now. She'll open her eyes when she's ready."

An elderly woman in the next bed sat up. "How come the cops are here? Is she a felon?"

"No, no, Mrs. Potter," said the nurse as she moved around the bed. "Sister Fleur was the one who was attacked."

"Well what if he comes back to finish the job?" screeched the woman. "I don't want to be here if…"

Jersey tuned the woman out and turned to Kameelah. "I'm going to make a few phone calls. You okay here for a while?"

"Sure." Kameelah pulled up a chair beside the Sister's bed and stroked her hand. "But bring back coffee. Black, no sugar."

Jersey grinned. "I could have guessed."

IN THE HALLWAY, Jersey found an uncomfortable chair in an out-of-the-way corner and discreetly slipped out his cellphone.

Hospitals didn't like visitors using cellphones because the possibility existed they could interfere with monitoring equipment, but Jersey believed the real reason was when the darn things rang, it scared the patients half to death. And some of them were nearly there, already.

His first call was to his partner. Amarela picked up on the third ring.

"About time you called," she said without preamble. "The lieutenant has been flipping, and I've run out of excuses. By now you've had the shits so long you should only weigh twenty pounds."

"Tell him I'm taking some personal time."

"You're not coming back?"

"I'm still looking for Sally."

"Hmmm."

Jersey knew Amarela had mixed feelings about his attachment to a woman he had only just met, but he still wished she wouldn't make it so obvious.

"She's in trouble," he said. "I need to find her."

"Okay," Amarela sighed, "I get it. How's Kameelah?"

"Black, no sugar."

Amarela laughed. "Ain't she just."

"Anything new on Peter Higgins or his dead parents?"

"Nada. I've got the lab running a tox screen on the dad, but the lieutenant has reminded me twice today that, unless I get a positive result pronto, the case is closed."

"He's probably right."

"What?" Amarela's voice was practically a shriek.

"I don't think this has anything to do with the Higgins' family anymore. It all points to Sally. She was the target."

"So we harassed the son for nothing?"

"No, we harassed the son because he was an ass and because the evidence pointed his way. Now it points in a different direction."

"Oh." Sarcasm dripped from her tongue. "That's alright, then."

"Can you do me a favor?"

"Another one?"

Jersey chewed his lip and waited, not wanting to get into a debate about who owed whom and where the current tally stood.

Finally, Amarela broke the silence. "Okay, what?"

"I left Sally's apartment keys in my desk drawer. Can you check on her cat. Give it food and—"

"Seriously!" Amarela protested. "A cat?"

"You love cats."

"I never said that. There's a big difference between cats and pus—"

"Gotta go," Jersey interrupted. "Give my love to Clarissa."

"We broke up again."

Jersey bit his tongue, but his partner still heard his lack of surprise in the pause.

"Don't be a bastard," she said.

"Wha—"

Amarela hung up.

Jersey rolled his eyes. Women had long been a mystery to him, but lesbians took it to a whole other level. He dialed information and asked for the news desk of the *Idaho Statesman.*

When the phone was answered in Boise, Jersey asked to speak to reporter John Underwood. The voice that came on the line a few seconds later sounded all of twenty.

"John here. Wha's up?"

"You wrote the stories about the dead women missing their eyes."

"Yeah, that's right." His voice broke in pitch, excited, but trying not to sound it. "Who's this?"

"An interested party. Can we talk off the record?"

"Sure. Are you the killer?"

Jersey chuckled. The kid had seen too many movies.

"No, I'm a cop."

"Based where?"

"Portland."

"No shit."

"You sound like my partner."

"Huh?"

"Inside joke."

"Oh… What can I do for you?"

"Have you heard of any other cases that match your two victims?"

The reporter laughed. "Is this a joke? Who put you up to this?"

"I'm being serious, John."

"You really a cop?"

"Yes," Jersey snapped. "Portland Homicide. Detective Jersey Castle. You want my badge number?"

"No, no, tha's cool. It's just some people think I have an obsession, you know? Nobody else believes these cases are linked, but I saw the second vic at the morgue, and I can't see two different people doing something this sick, you know?"

"So what about it, you heard of any others?"

"You got one in Portland?"

"No."

"Oh… why the interest then?"

"Answer my question first."

The reporter sighed. "The paper didn't let me run with it, but eighteen months ago there was a woman found in Calgary. That's about seven hundred miles north of here in Canada. Her body was found by the Bow River, and she was missing her eyes. The case is still unsolved."

"And what's the link? Apart from the eyes."

"All of the victims were in their early thirties with a similar body shape: slim, athletic build, and none of them were known sex workers."

"Any connection between them?"

"None that I've found. One worked in a bank. Another ran a small gym. And the third, the one in Calgary, was a television reporter. Two were blondes, one was brunette. I haven't found anything that indicated they ever knew one another."

"What about witnesses?" Jersey asked.

"Nothing the cops will share with me, but I doubt it. I would've heard."

"Any theories?"

Jersey could almost hear the shrug over the phone.

"Sick bastard on the prowl," John said with a heavy sigh. "Someone who travels on business, maybe. What's your interest?"

"Just fishing right now, but if I come up with anything I'll let you know."

"You think they're connected?"

Jersey hesitated, then, "I do."

"Serious?" John practically squeaked with delight.

"Deadly."

Jersey hung up and shambled back to the Sister's room with a cloud over his head. Kameelah looked up at him as he crossed the threshold.

She frowned. Those wrinkles again.

"Where's the coffee?"

Jersey slapped his forehead and turned to fetch it.

WHEN JERSEY RETURNED with two lukewarm coffees and two sadly deflated doughnuts on a grease-stained paper plate, Kameelah stood up and unexpectedly wrapped him in a hug.

"What was that for?" he asked.

"You looked like you needed it."

"I always look like this."

Kameelah laughed. "Okay, maybe I needed it, too."

They both looked over at Sister Fleur lying unconscious in her bed.

"Yeah," said Jersey softly, "I guess we did."

Kameelah accepted her coffee and took a sip. She managed not to shudder.

"How did your calls go?"

"Amarela sends her love." This brought a smile to Kameelah's lips. "And our reporter found a third woman with missing eyes. Same age range as the other two."

Kameelah's brow furrowed. "Any leads?"

"Nothing."

"So where does that leave us?"

Jersey stared down at the hospital bed. With pain in his voice, he said, "Unless our only eye witness wakes up, we've just hit a fucking dead end."

45

Sally's platform ascended to the church sanctuary from directly beneath the massive wood-burning fire that dominated its center. As her platform rose, the circular cast-iron hearth was automatically pulled skyward on four coiled strands of tensile steel.

The bottom of the thick pan glowed red from the heat to cast a warm velvety glow while the flickering shadows of the flames above grew in intensity to prance across the conical ceiling like frenzied ghosts.

The effect was mesmerizing, but Sally noticed that few people were looking up. All of their attention was on her.

Eager faces were glued to her ascension from the cellar. Men, women, and children looked upon her with such delight, it was as though she was a Las Vegas magician rather than a kidnapped beautician. And despite her adamant refusal to show weakness, her body shook with such a cocktail of fear that her virginal white dress quivered in the light of the rising flames.

When her platform finally locked into place, the fire loomed high above. The smoke that blanketed the ceiling and crawled down the walls in whispery fingers was sweet and soothing to the mind, but as the wooden ceiling began to warm, the temperature inside the building climbed toward stifling.

"Behold the Seer," bellowed Father Black from his raised podium several feet behind Sally. "Let us pray."

Sweat beaded on Sally's brow as she looked helplessly across a curved sea of bowed heads and muttering lips. She wondered if this was what it was like to go insane. You were still you, thinking you were sane and holding onto logic, but the world had somehow shifted and left you the odd one out.

Sally wanted to scream and run for the doors, but the weight of the priest's eyes on her back kept her silent and the chain around her ankle kept her still.

"Bring out the Travelers." Father Black clapped his hands together with a thunderclap of flesh.

All heads swiveled in their pews as two elderly people were ushered forth from the rear of the church.

The first, a man in a wheelchair and wearing a red, oversized shirt, was in his late eighties with white hair and a sunken, toothless mouth. His skin was the blotchy color of over-ripe banana and his throat was a mass of scar tissue. He sported a breathing tube in his trachea that had also robbed him of voice, but his sky blue eyes burned with intelligence.

He was clearly afraid.

The second was an elderly woman being led down the aisle by a younger congregant who looked enough like her to be her daughter. The older woman didn't seem to know where she was. Her eyes drifted around the room and her mouth moved in rhythm to a conversation only she could hear. She was dressed similar to Sally, but in red rather than white, and her thin hair had been freshly washed and curled.

Both of them were brought to a large altar that stood less than two feet from Sally's podium. The altar was nearly five feet long and thirty inches wide. Made of intricately carved wood and polished stone, its top was hollowed into a basin and lined with smooth granite.

The elderly woman was made to kneel before the altar and her arms placed on top so that she could rest her head on her forearms. The man in the wheelchair was moved beside her. He placed his arms in the same position without any aid.

As Sally looked upon them, too afraid to breathe, never mind speak, the elderly woman looked up and smiled with all the wonder of a child.

"We're going on holidays," she said, her voice lilting in a sing-song cadence. "To the seaside. Oh, I do love the seaside, don't you?"

Father Black's voice boomed again. "Let us sign Hymn number seven, while the children are led outside. The ritual of the Journey is not for those too young to comprehend."

While the congregation sang a familiar church hymn, Sally watched the children being gathered in the aisle and herded toward the front door. A cool finger of breeze entered from the doorway, but it was quickly snapped off by the heat from the overhead fire. Once the church doors closed again, the youngest member of the congregation was a rake-thin boy of around seventeen who was so excited to be included that he could barely sit still.

The hymn ended, and Father Black clapped his hands together once more.

"Bring out the Deliverer."

A door opened at the rear of the hall, and Sally gasped as a tall man dressed from head to toe in black robes stepped out. His face was hidden beneath a silk hangman's hood with a white cross stitched down its center. Dark eyes burned behind slits in the crossbar.

The audience began to murmur another prayer, the noise level rising as the members found a common beat.

Sally pivoted on the spot to catch the priest's hot gaze behind her. His eyes were practically glowing with anticipation.

"What are you doing?" she yelled to be heard above the prayer. "This is madness."

The priest didn't hear. His attention was riveted on the hooded man whose steps fell into rhythm with the chant as he approached the stone alter.

The congregation's prayers built in intensity, the voices becoming a buzzing drone. Sally spun to face them. All eyes were raised to the smoke-covered rafters in reverence.

"Stop this," Sally yelled. "Please."

No one seemed to hear her plea.

The Deliverer stopped beside Sally and inclined his head at the two people kneeling by the altar. The woman's eyes became less glassy in the presence of the black-clad hangman. She suddenly began to look from side to side in panic as though awakening from a dream and not knowing where she was.

The congregation's chant continued to build, the noise almost deafening.

Father Black called out. "Why have these two souls been chosen for the Journey?"

The younger woman who had walked her mother down the aisle stepped forward and raised her hands to the ceiling. The chanting diminished as her voice increased in volume to be heard.

"My mother's mind is lost. She doesn't know her children or her grandchild. She soils herself and weeps for no reason. Her spirit is trapped in a maze of confusion. It needs to be free."

The congregation rewarded her with a rousing *Hallelujah*.

A man in a two-piece suit and dark tie stepped forward to stand behind the elderly man's wheelchair.

"My uncle is a proud man," he announced in a loud, clear voice. "But his body is broken and cannot be mended. Although his mind is clear, his dignity has been soiled and his soul yearns for the Journey."

Another eruption of Hallelujahs was followed by the stomping of feet and a return to the loud chanting of prayer.

A voice whispered in Sally's ear, "You'll want to watch this."

Sally spun to face the Deliverer, his frightening hood inflating and contracting in time to heavy breathing. She recognized his voice, although the words were no longer slurred.

"Aedan? This is insane. I can't—"

Sally gasped as Aedan pulled a long knife from a leather sheaf on his hip. The blade was nearly eight inches long, its hilt guard a glistening gold.

"What are you—"

Sally halted in mid-sentence as the prayers ended and the church became as silent as a tomb. She turned to the audience, but all eyes were on—

Aedan strode behind the two kneeling parishioners and raised the knife above his head. The sharp steel reflected the blood-red glow of the crackling fire overhead.

Father Black raised his hands to the ceiling in capitulation as Aedan grabbed the toothless old man by what was left of his hair, yanked back his head and gamely slit his throat.

Sally screamed so loud her lungs threatened to burst as a fountain of blood splashed over the altar and across her white dress.

Members of the congregation leapt to their feet in celebration, their communal prayer erupting into an even louder chant than before.

Aedan grabbed the arm of the terrified elderly woman before she could run. Foaming saliva spilled from the woman's mouth as she stared up at the monster in black.

"We're going on holidays," she sobbed.

As Aedan repeated his gruesome task, a chorus of "Hallelujah" and "Praise God" erupted from the congregation.

Sally vomited her breakfast across the floor as she struggled to get away from the flow of blood, but her ankle was cuffed tight to the floor and the chain only stretched a short way.

After laying the bodies across the altar, Aedan whipped off his hangman's mask and returned to Sally. He grabbed her by the arms.

"It's your turn."

Sally squirmed and cried and—

She looked at Aedan's face; his deformity was gone. Somehow, he had been miraculously cured and, yet, he looked more horrifying than ever.

Sally pleaded, "Let me go."

Ignoring her pleas, Aedan forced Sally down to her knees in front of the altar. The floor was awash in blood, the victims' slit throats having filled the basin to overflowing.

"Follow the souls," Aedan said. "Tell us what you find."

Sally screamed again as Aedan plunged her hands into the trough of warm, fresh blood.

46

In the basin of blood, Sally's hands entangled with the dead and a blinding light flared in her mind.

She felt the knife blade slicing across her throat; the sharp agony of ripping muscle and sinew; the suffocating loss of blood rushing from her body; the sleepiness of death; the longing to hold on; to never let go...

Two minds merged with her own... two journeys... one path... the light began to clear and beyond it she saw...

WHEN SALLY OPENED her eyes, Helen was cradling her head in her lap. They were still in the church and the bloodthirsty congregation was watching in rapt silence.

Sally tried to push herself up from the floor, but the wood was slick with blood and Helen's grip was too strong. She groaned. "What's wrong with you people?"

Helen stroked Sally's hair. "What did you see, dear? Tell us what you learned."

"It was horrible," Sally gasped. "I felt you murder them. Don't you people understand? You cut their—"

"What did you see in the light?" Helen hissed. "Did The Almighty speak to you? Did He impart a secret?"

Sally lurched into a sitting position and angrily shook off

Helen's grip. "There's nothing there! Okay? Nothing but death and pain and—"

Helen slapped her across the face as a female member of the congregation screamed and fainted. Sally's eyes burned with hatred as she recognized the woman who had led her own mother down the aisle to an execution.

"Concentrate, child," urged Helen. "You were with them as they traveled to the light. Tell us what you saw."

But Sally refused to say another word.

47

Jersey poured himself a fresh coffee and gazed out a smog-streaked window at the blocky, faceless buildings that made up Virginia Street. A good ten blocks from the scenic Puget Sound waterfront, Seattle's West Precinct was a glass-sided rowboat stuck in a turbulent sea of concrete and tarmac.

Serving a downtown population of around seventy-six thousand spread over twelve square miles, the busy police bunker felt sadly too much like home. Even the posters and notices stuck on the wall beside the coffee pot bore an uncanny resemblance to the ones back in Portland.

One notice in particular made him laugh. It was a candid snap of a young, rebellious looking character cradling a camera and sticking out his tongue. He was identified as Tom Hackett and the word *Prick* was scribbled over his face in red pen. Next to it was a newspaper clipping showing a photograph of a police officer being elbowed in the face by a protester at a recent rally. The photographer had perfectly captured the moment of agony as sharp bone broke the officer's nose in a spray of blood. Jersey leaned closer to read the photo credit and grinned when he saw Hackett's name. *Prick indeed.*

Kameelah pushed open the glass door to the lunchroom, a puzzled frown creasing her otherwise flawless face.

"I just received a phone call."

"The nurse?"

"No," said Kameelah. "The nun."

THE NUN WITH the face like Seventies corduroy opened the front door to the Mission of the Immaculate Heart and ushered the two detectives inside.

"Thank you for returning," said Sister Gillian. "Sister Mary Theresa has received an unusual email that appears to have been sent by Sister Fleur."

"The unconscious Sister Fleur?" Jersey clarified.

"Mmmm, precisely."

The nun led them down the narrow corridor to the intersecting hub of the cross-shaped building, and then right to a long row of offices.

As they passed open doors, Jersey saw groups of nuns, both young and old, dressed in casual clothing and busy typing on computers. Each of them wore a headscarf of robin egg blue.

At the end of the hallway, they came to a closed office door. Sister Gillian knocked, waited a moment, and then ushered them inside.

Sitting behind a desk, practically hidden by an impressive widescreen computer monitor and backlit by a large picture window overlooking a spacious garden, Sister Mary Theresa beamed at the detectives with such voltage, Jersey wondered if she was under the impression they had brought her a cake.

"Ah, welcome, welcome."

The nun leapt from her chair and came around the desk to greet them. Her energy was electric.

Dressed in full habit, bib collar, and impenetrable blue dress, Sister Mary Theresa grabbed Jersey's hand in a firm grip and gave it a powerful shake. She then moved to Kameelah and said, "Do you mind?" as she opened her arms.

Kameelah shook her head, though her eyes grew wide as the nun lunged forward to give her a big hug.

When the nun stepped back, she said to Kameelah, "You are so very pretty. How did you ever get into this violent business?"

"I could ask the same of you," said Kameelah.

Sister Mary Theresa brushed away the rejoinder. "You're a helper. I can tell by your soul. So kind and full and generous." She turned to Jersey. "And you. You're just too gentle for this work. I can see right past your armor to the very heart of you, and it's devouring you. Right..." she stepped closer and laid a hand over his soft stomach "... there."

"U-uh." Jersey stammered.

"You need to exercise more and watch your diet—especially salt," continued the nun. "The stress will kill you. Do you have hobbies?"

Jersey nodded as the nun rested her hip on the edge of the desk and folded her arms. A small curl of unusually vibrant yellow hair had escaped her white headscarf.

"Hobbies are good. They help us put life in perspective. I like to grow tomatoes. Don't I, Sister Gillian?"

The wrinkled nun who had escorted them to the office nodded vigorously.

"I love tomatoes," Sister Mary Theresa continued. "Beefsteak, Cherry, Plum, Marmande, Oxheart... have you ever tasted a Cherokee Purple? I love them raw, in pasta and salads, on toasted bread with aged white cheddar, but I especially love them in soup. Do you know how I make the most wonderful tomato soup?"

"We were told you had an email," said Kameelah.

The nun's eyes twinkled and her lips twitched in an amused grin.

"So pretty," she said, "but so sad."

"Can we see the email?" Jersey asked.

"Of course."

Sister Mary Theresa led them around the desk to look over her shoulder at an iMac with a twenty-seven inch screen.

"It appears to have come from an automated Internet relay service," explained the nun. "Probably triggered when Sister Fleur failed to log onto their site to reset the countdown. I'm guessing she had to log in once a week."

She called up the email and the detectives read:

Dear Sister Mary Theresa:

If you are reading this, then I am either missing, dead, or injured in such a way that I can no longer communicate.

I have always feared this day would come, and I only pray this reaches you in time to save the woman under my protection.

The attached file will give you everything you need to find her. Please take her to one of our sister missions and hide her from those who wish to use her for purposes our Lord would never condone.

Yours in spiritual devotion,

Sister Fleur.

"Can you print off the attachment?" asked Jersey.

The nun turned to a printer on the desk beside her and pulled out a sheaf of papers. "Already done."

Jersey took the papers from her hand and looked at the top sheet. It contained a candid black-and-white photo of a young woman with a troubled smile.

"That who you're looking for?" asked Kameelah.

Jersey nodded. "She's younger in this photo, but it's definitely Sally."

Sister Mary Theresa looked up from her computer. "The report says her birth name is Salvation Blue and she was raised in a small community outside New Town, North Dakota. However, it appears she was living…"

The nun continued to speak, but Jersey was no longer listening. He was too busy heading for the door.

"HOLD UP!" KAMEELAH grabbed onto Jersey's arm in the long hallway of the mission that led to the main doors. "Where are you going?"

"North Dakota."

"Why? What makes you think she's there?"

"When she called me, she was in Spokane. It makes sense that whoever took her is taking her back home. You read the email. Sister Fleur said she's in danger. Sally wanted me to know where she was."

"I'm coming with you."

"This isn't your case."

Kameelah bristled. "Some son-of-a-bitch murders a nun and batters another on my patch. Damn rights it's my case."

Jersey squeezed the knot of flesh between his eyebrows. "Sally's safety comes first and…" He hesitated. "And I can't promise I'll do everything by the book."

Kameelah raised her eyebrows. "You mean you're making this personal?"

"Yes."

"Well, good. That makes two of us."

48

ather Black stormed around the kitchen, kicking chairs and denting table legs as he fumed.

"You made me look a fool," he yelled at Aedan. "You swore she had the sight."

"She does," Aedan challenged. "You saw for yourself at the altar. She blanked out for at least five minutes. She was with them on the Journey. She saw—"

"How could she have walked the path?" Father Black argued. "How could she bathe in the Lord's light and then refuse to tell us?"

"She's scared," said Helen. She stood on the other side of the heavy kitchen table, keeping it between herself and her husband's temper. "It was too soon."

"Too soon?" White foam flew from the corners of the preacher's mouth. "I've waited twenty-five years for—"

"We need to win her over," said Helen. "Show her we're family. She didn't even know she had the gift. I told you that, but oh, no, you—"

"Win her over?" Father Black tore at his hair, his eyes bulging. "Win her over?" He yanked the white collar from around his throat and threw it on the floor. "Florence just about had a heart attack in her seat when that witch said there was nothing. Nothing! She sacrificed her mother for the Journey because she believed in our ways, believed in *my* sermons."

"Her belief hasn't ... changed," soothed Helen. "She'll understand—"

Father Black took another swing at a toppled wooden chair, sending it soaring across the kitchen floor to smash into an industrial-sized baker's oven. It missed Aedan's leg by inches, but he didn't flinch in the slightest.

"We've told the congregation we're bringing them proof of the Word. Proof that the Journey leads to a better life. We live by that faith. And if this witch is going to rebel like her whore of a mother did, then we'll need to find another way."

"I've sent her cousin up—" Helen was cut off.

"There is no other way." Aedan stepped forward to face his father. "Salvation is our only link to the Journey. We need to make her tell us what she saw."

"And how do we do that?" asked Father Black.

Aedan's eyes narrowed. "We don't give her any other choice."

49

Sally lay curled in a bloody ball beneath her bedroom window, sobbing. Her captors hadn't allowed her to stop and wash when they dragged her back to the house and locked her in the upstairs room.

Her white dress was such a mess of congealing gore she could barely find enough clean material to wipe her bloody hands, arms, and face. The cloying smell was so overwhelming it was making her head spin, but after vomiting at the church, her stomach was empty.

She heard the lock in the door being turned and, fearing a beating, curled into a tighter ball. The door opened and closed almost instantly, the lock quickly re-engaged.

Curious, Sally opened one eye to see a girl of no more than fifteen. She was standing by the door, studying the room behind glasses so thick and round they made her eyes bulge. Her face was a near perfect oval except for a flat chin. She also had a tiny button nose, dark bushy eyebrows, and a flush of pink in each chubby cheek. Her lips were thin and her mouth looked too large for her face. Someone had made her wear an unflatteringly plain white dress.

When the girl noticed Sally's one-eyed gaze, her mouth opened in a wide grin that curved higher on one side than the other.

"Hel…lo," she said.

Her speech was slightly garbled and as she walked closer, the distinct signs of Down Syndrome became more apparent.

"What ha… ha… happened to you?" The girl's words were spoken carefully, each one formed and released before the next left her lips. "You are… dir… dir… messy."

Sally slowly uncurled her limbs and sat up. She brushed a matt of tangled hair from in front of her eyes, blanching at the sight of her fingers stained with dried blood.

"I had an accident," she said carefully. "Who are you?"

The girl moved closer, but became distracted by the window.

"You can see… see… the gardens," she said as she moved beside Sally and looked out. "That is… nice."

"Yes," said Sally. "What's your name?"

The girl turned her back to the window and plunked herself down on the floor beside Sally where she began to smooth the wrinkles out of her white dress.

"I am April," she said. "I have a friend… May… and I have a friend… June. Isn'atfunny?" She laughed at her own joke.

"That is funny," said Sally. "Do you live here?"

"No. Just… visit."

"Who sent you in here to talk to me?"

"Mother told me… your name is Sally. You lived here a loooong time ago… whenyouwere… little." April scrunched up her nose. "Mother isn' my mom, but I… I… tol'to call her Mo… Mother. Isn'atfunny?"

"That is," agreed Sally. "Why did Mother send you?"

April shrugged. "I was playing in the garden. I saw… carrots. Baby ones. Doyoulike… carrots?"

Sally nodded.

April wrinkled her nose again. "Your dress is stinky."

Despite herself, Sally laughed. "It is. I'm sorry."

"That okay." April turned her head and looked into Sally's

eyes. She frowned and tilted her head slightly to one side. Then she beamed. "There you are." She lifted her finger to point. "You were... hiding."

Sally was taken aback. "What do you—"

The lock turned and the door swung open to reveal Helen. She had her arms crossed firmly over her bosom and the crimson flush in her face was a disturbingly mottled hue. Her eyes were red, too, as though she had been crying.

"Hel... lo, Mother," said April in a sing-song chant.

"Hello, April. Should we take Sally for a bath now?"

"Oh, yes." April clipped two fingers onto her nose. "Stinky."

WHILE APRIL SAT on the toilet lid, looking out the small window and humming a familiar church hymn, Sally filled the bathtub and stripped off her ruined dress. Her pale skin was a canvas of blotchy pink and red from the blood that had soaked through. Her left arm was also noticeably bruised in the shape of fingers from Aedan's grip as he dragged her from the church.

Helen took the soiled dress without a word and closed the bathroom door behind her.

"Bye, bye," said April before returning to her hymn. Sally recognized it as *Jesus Loves Me.*

When the bath was ready, Sally dumped her granny panties into a wicker hamper and climbed into the tub. The water was scalding, but Sally relished the heat.

She began to scrub herself clean, using a loofa the size of a rolled-up magazine and a thick bar of unscented soap that appeared to be homemade by someone with no passion or joy for the art. Her skin protested the rough treatment, but Sally wanted every molecule of the blood removed.

Tears began to flow again as she thought of the madness in the church and recalled the feel of the knife blade against her throat, the sharp edge slicing through her skin, muscles tearing, her windpipe...

But it wasn't her throat, Sally reminded herself. It felt like hers, but the pain was reflected. The knife had been used to butcher two innocent people while she stood by. She felt what they felt, saw what they saw, traveled beyond pain... toward death... to...

Sally lowered herself onto her back and sunk under the water. Behind closed eyes, red sparks danced across her eyelids like a miniature cosmos. *What had she seen? Could she describe it in words?* Her lungs started to ache, and she sat up to take in a deep cleansing breath.

When she opened her eyes, April had moved to the side of the tub and was watching her.

"I can wash... hair," she said with a bright smile. "I wash... baby brother's and... M... M... Mom says I am... help... f... f... ful."

"Thank you, April." Sally tried to compose herself, to push the memory behind a concrete dam, to stay strong. "That would be lovely."

Sally grabbed the shampoo bottle and squeezed a green blob into April's outstretched palm. April grinned and mixed the sticky-smooth balm with her short fingers before placing her hands on Sally's head. As Sally closed her eyes, April spread the shampoo across Sally's wet hair and began to work it into a thick lather. Her blunt fingernails worked away at the matted patches of dried blood until they dissolved, and soon her fingers began to knead at Sally's skull. The massage was so gentle and so soothing Sally actually began to relax.

The reprieve was short-lived.

The bathroom door opened and a male voice barked, "Leave us."

Sally tried to open her eyes, but the shampoo had flowed across her face in a foaming curtain.

"I... I... I am washing... Sal—"

"Get out!" the voice growled. "Now!"

Sally splashed her face with water and swept away the blinding shampoo. When she could finally see, April was being forcibly shoved out of the bathroom, her voice rising in a hysterical scream. Helen appeared in the hallway, her chest heaving as though she had rushed up the stairs, to comfort the girl just as the door slammed shut and the latch was thrown.

With his back to the door, Aedan's face was a burst blister of rage.

"You have no right!" Sally yelled and angrily covered her bare breasts with crossed arms.

Aedan rushed forward, dropped to his knees, and grabbed Sally's hair in a firm grip. Sally squealed as pain shot deep into her scalp.

"What did you see?" Aedan demanded. "You made a fool of us. The whole congregation watching, and you wouldn't speak the truth."

"You murdered those people. They needed care—"

"They were travelers." Hot spit flew from Aedan's mouth to land on Sally's face. "You were their guide."

Aedan pulled on Sally's hair until the back of her neck felt near the breaking point. He ran a finger of his free hand across her tight throat and the coldness of it made her shudder.

"You'll tell me what you saw."

As Sally struggled to shake her head, Aedan grabbed a washcloth from the side of the tub, dunked it into the bath water, and then jammed it into her mouth.

Sally tried to fight, but she couldn't close her mouth, and her tongue wasn't strong enough to dislodge the gag. As her eyes grew wide with fear, Aedan slammed his open hand against her forehead and shoved her under water.

Sally flailed her arms, any thoughts of modesty lost to survival as she clawed and scratched at the arm holding her down. Her lungs quickly started to burn from the exertion and stars exploded in her eyes.

Then, suddenly, she was yanked out of the water. She tried to breathe, to inflate her lungs, but with the gagging wet cloth still in her mouth she could only manage to inhale a small amount of air through her nose.

Aedan plunged her under the water again and the agony that coursed through her body was unbearable. Every muscle and organ screamed for oxygen.

She endured two more dunkings before blacking out.

50

Sister Mary Theresa finished reading the printed attachment for the third time before turning to Sister Gillian who was inhaling a hand-rolled cigarette beside the open window overlooking the garden.

"I fear I misjudged our Sister Fleur," she said with sadness in her voice. "She was such a broken angel when she came through our doors, I never saw her true strength."

Sister Gillian sucked the burning tobacco down beyond her fingertips before flicking the nicotine-soaked nub out the window.

"She needed time to meditate and heal," said Sister Gillian, exhaling a lungful of smoke. "It wasn't until her recent involvement in our sermons that she truly began to climb out of her shell. She has a rare gift for reaching people and you could feel that fire reigniting within her."

Sister Mary Theresa tilted her head in contemplation. "I should have embraced her more fully. I believe she would have found great comfort in our mission, and the strength she shows in this report would have made her a natural. She did so much on her own, imagine what—"

"She's not dead yet," said Sister Gillian.

Sister Mary Theresa sighed heavily. "I mistakenly believed this attack on our sisters was made by a random beast. Another feral animal ripped from the womb to destroy Creation's true sex." She inhaled. "His disappearance troubled me... the trail growing so cold, so quickly... I've been blind—"

"But now we see," Sister Gillian finished solemnly.

Sister Mary Theresa smiled grimly. "Set up a guard rotor. I want one of us by Sister Fleur's bedside 24/7. I need to know the moment she's awake."

51

Kameelah glanced over as Jersey flipped through Sister Fleur's report for the umpteenth time.

Neither of them had the resources to book a private plane, and Jersey couldn't face the possibility of sitting still while they waited for a standby seat on one of the few mule-train flights to Fargo.

Instead, they were traveling east on the I-90, which would lead them eight hundred miles through Spokane, Coeur D'Alene, Missoula, and Butte until they hit Billings, Montana, a popular tourist spot for those who wanted to watch a reenactment of *Battle of the Little Big Horn*.

From there, the I-94 snaked northeast for two hundred miles. Once they crossed into North Dakota, it was a further one-hundred-fifty miles on crappy back roads before they reached New Town.

With over seventeen hours of driving in front of them, Kameelah allowed her speed gauge to creep above the posted limit. The Jaguar purred its appreciation. It wasn't good to keep a thoroughbred cooped up in the stables too long.

"Anything?" Kameelah asked.

Jersey placed the report on his lap.

"The nun and Sally have a long history," he said. "The report is pretty cryptic, but it seems Sister Fleur discovered Sally when she was six years old after a violent incident in her home that claimed both parents. She doesn't go into specifics, but Fleur took Sally out of the state."

"Kidnapped?"

Jersey shrugged. "Sister Fleur calls it protection. They had a falling out when Sally became an adult, but the Sister still kept track of her from a distance."

"She mention anything about the eyeless dead girls?"

Jersey nodded. "When the woman's body was found in Spokane, Fleur started to worry, and I'll quote here..." Jersey picked up the report and flipped through. "...'the church has awakened from its long slumber to go in search of the Seer.'"

"The Seer?" Kameelah asked. "Is she talking about Sally's visions?"

"That'd be my guess," Jersey agreed. "The second dead woman rattled her even further. She wrote..." Jersey glanced down at the report again, "... 'perhaps I was wrong to hide the secret of her inheritance from her, to downplay the danger of her gift and the people who wanted to use her.'"

"So Sally didn't know she was being hunted?" Kameelah said.

"And Sister Fleur didn't know about the third victim in Calgary, which shows whoever was looking for her had been hunting far longer than she suspected."

"Why didn't she warn Sally?" Kameelah asked. "If she cared that much about her, why did—"

"Maybe she was planning to," injected Jersey. "But the hunter got here first."

Jersey's cellphone rang before Kameelah could respond.

52

Sally coughed awake on the bathroom floor. She was naked, wet, and shivering, but relieved to be alive.

She drew in a deep breath and instantly regretted it as her lungs went into spasm and another staccato burst of coughing wracked her chest. She spat up water as she struggled to control her breathing.

When the coughing stopped, the tears began. Each drop burned like acid against her bloodshot eyes.

She cursed her own weakness and brought her emotions under control, wiping eyes and runny nose on her bare arm.

The lock turned in the bathroom door.

Sally pulled herself into a crouch, preparing for the worst. The only weapons at her disposal were teeth and nails, but if she had the strength, she was prepared to use them.

The door swung open.

April stood in the doorway with Helen glowering behind her. In April's arms was a neat bundle of white cloth. Upon seeing Sally alive, Helen gave April a gentle push to move her inside and closed the door again.

"Are you... okay?" April asked. "That man pushed me away. I did... did... didn't want to go."

Sally unfurled her lips over bared teeth and uncurled from

her crouch. As she stood up, April placed her bundle on top of the hamper and grabbed a large white towel.

She handed it to Sally with a smile.

"Iamglad… you're okay. That man was scary angry."

Sally wrapped the towel around herself and fought off another wave of tears.

"I'm glad you're okay, too," she said, and meant it.

53

"It's Amarela," Jersey told Kameelah as he answered the phone.

"Jesus, Jersey," Amarela began before Jersey could say hello. "You've landed me right in it."

"I told you to tell the lieutenant—"

"Yeah, yeah, you're taking personal time, but he's not buying it and he's dumping the shit on me."

"What shit?"

"The Peter Higgins shit."

"Is he still complaining? What have we done now?"

"No, he's not complaining, and that's the problem."

"What do you mean?" Jersey was confused.

"He's gone missing." Amarela sighed. "His wife says he hasn't been home in twenty-four hours."

"So? Maybe he went on a bender to grieve for his folks. Twenty-four hours isn't a—"

"With his daughter?" Amarela snapped.

"You're not making sense."

"Exactly! Morrell is all up in my ass, telling me to make this top priority, but—"

"Start at the beginning." Jersey recalled the family photos on the mantle at the Higgins' residence in Maywood Park. Peter had a teenage daughter and a newborn son. "What's this about the daughter?"

"Okay." Amarela took a deep breath. "The lieutenant sent me to talk to Harriet, Peter's wife. It seems that Peter disappeared shortly after we talked to him at his house. Maybe he didn't appreciate the joke about me wanting to shoot him, I don't know. But when he disappeared, he took his daughter with him. He didn't leave a note, he isn't answering his cell, and he hasn't called home. Harriet is positive something bad has happened."

"Why would he take his daughter?" Jersey asked.

"Well that's the question, isn't it? I asked the wife and she tried to hide it, but I got the distinct impression that he didn't have much affection for her."

"The daughter?"

"Yes. You know she has Down Syndrome, right? Well, she was their first child, but the two of them were barely out of their teens at the time." Amarela paused. "Reading between the lines, I would say Peter held some resentment that the unplanned pregnancy forced him to leave college and get married much sooner than he planned. Harriet didn't come right out and say it, but I gather fatherhood—especially the challenges of fatherhood to a Down's child—wasn't something Peter embraced."

"How are their finances?" Jersey asked.

"The money from his parents' estate will definitely help, but they don't appear to be in crisis."

Jersey scratched his nose, thinking. "We're back to the beginning," he said. "I believed this was all about Sally, but if Peter was involved in the deaths of his parents, maybe he went to pay off the hitman. He took his daughter along to show... what? That he's a family man with a lot to lose if he doesn't keep his mouth shut about the sordid arrangement."

"But the hitman," added Amarela, "didn't give a damn and killed them both?"

"It's one possibility."

"Shit! You have to get back here. I can't do all this on my own. Where the hell are you anyway?"

"Kameelah and I are following a lead."

"To Sally?"

"Yes."

"And where is this lead taking you?"

"North Dakota."

"Oh, fuck me!" Amarela exploded. "How long is that going to take?"

"I don't know. As long as it does."

Amarela's voice grew taut. "This case is breaking open down *here*, partner, not in fuck-knows-where North Dakota. I need you back."

"I understand," Jersey soothed. "But Sally is part of this, too, and her trail leads east." Jersey allowed a silence to fill the airwaves before he added, "Did you ask Peter's wife about a connection with Sally?"

"No!" Amarela sulked. "Why?"

"Because the message was left on his father's body. If Peter's involved in his death, then they have to be connected."

"Maybe they ran away together?" Amarela sounded pleased by the possibility.

Jersey was taken aback. He hadn't considered that.

Amarela's tone verged on gloating. "Peter could have called her after we left his house and told her to leave the apartment and run away with him."

"Along with his daughter?" Jersey retaliated. "The one who you just said he didn't like very much."

"Maybe I got that part wrong."

"If that was the case," Jersey said brusquely, "why did Sally call me in a panic from a phone box in bloody Spokane?"

"I don't know," Amarela admitted in a small voice, "but that's why we work better as a team, right?"

Jersey exhaled, allowing his sudden balloon of anger to deflate. "We are a team, Amarela, and we're working this together. Peter and Sally are connected, somehow. I need you to go back to the wife and try to find that connection. You should also post an all-points on his car and track his credit cards. Meanwhile, I need to pursue this lead on Sally. We'll compare notes later, okay?"

Sally grudgingly agreed.

After hanging up, Jersey turned to Kameelah and suggested she pull into the next gas station. He needed coffee; strong, black, fully-caffeinated coffee.

54

Sally unfolded the bundle of clothes and slipped into a fresh white dress and a laundered pair of sensible underwear. When she turned to the mirror, April handed her a wood-handled brush.

Sally pulled the flat brush through her damp hair, any chance of rebellion among the follicles abolished by the unyielding bristles. In the mirror, she had difficulty recognizing her own reflection. In a matter of one day, her face had become hollow, almost skeletal, and her skin had lost what little radiance it ever possessed.

Despite being an expert in its application, Sally had never been one for wearing makeup—a reflection she thought now of her childhood guardian's disdain for what she called 'the war paint of troublesome youth.' And, if Sally was being honest, she had been trouble, but makeup was not the source. If she had a date, of which there were few, she endured the penciling of eyeliner and smudge of lipstick in an understated shade. But as she studied her face now, she understood the value of cosmetic disguise. Her skin was that of a battered wife, a bruised canvas of abuse.

"You look sad," said April in her quiet voice.

Sally placed the brush on the side of the sink and turned to face the girl.

"I am sad," she said.

"Why?"

"I don't want to be here. I want to go home."

"Me, too," said April, her eyes widening. "I miss… miss my mom. We should go."

Sally tried to smile, but her heart wasn't in it. "The people who brought me here won't let me."

"Why?"

Sally thought about the ceremony. "They want me to do something at their church. Something… " Sally hesitated. "Something I don't have the power to do."

"Oh?"

April picked up the brush and attempted to pull it through her own hair, but the bristles hurt, and she quickly put it back. "I… I saw the church. It's in the garden."

"Yes, it is." Sally hesitated again. She wasn't sure if she wanted to hear the answer even as she asked, "Did you see me in the church?"

Before April could answer, the door opened. Helen stood in the hallway and beckoned them forth.

April bounded ahead of Sally and when she reached Helen, the woman bent and whispered in her ear. April glanced back at Sally. She looked upset.

"What's going on?" Sally asked.

"Nothing," assured Helen. "Father wants to see you downstairs. Alone."

55

The phone on Sister Mary Theresa's desk rang.

When she picked it up, the voice on the other end said just two words.

Sister Mary Theresa thanked the caller and disconnected the call. She punched a button for an internal line that connected to Sister Gillian's office.

"Sister Fleur is awake," she said when the phone was answered. "Tell the Angels to prepare."

56

Father Black sat at one end of the kitchen table with a mug of steaming coffee cradled in his large hands. Aedan sat on his right with his back to the heavy wooden shutters that blocked most of the light from the front window.

Aedan's eyes were dark and unflinching beneath hooded lids as Sally entered the room, and she could sense a murderous rage bubbling just beneath the surface like a cancer of the blood.

When Sally crossed the threshold, the priest gestured to an empty seat at the opposite end of the table.

Helen joined them as Sally sat.

"Would you like coffee?" Helen asked. "It's fresh brewed."

Sally's first reaction was to scream: *You kidnap me, beat me, and try to fucking drown me...* but she controlled it.

Despite her anger, Sally realized she wanted a cup.

She nodded and an unpleasant tremor rippled through her flesh. It took sheer force of will to stay strong and not collapse into a blubbering heap... to beg for mercy... to throw a fit. She pressed her weight into the seat, thankful for its solidity, and faced the priest.

She refused to make eye contact with Aedan.

Father Black took a long, slow sip of coffee and waited in silence while his wife placed a steaming mug in front of Sally.

"Milk?" Helen acted as though it was a pleasant tea party on a lazy Sunday afternoon.

"Black is fine."

Sally curled her hands around the mug, absorbing its warmth before bringing it to her lips. Her hands trembled, but only slightly.

"Careful," warned Helen, "I percolate it on the stove. Father likes it strong."

Sally sipped a small amount into her mouth, relishing the scorching, bitter heat.

Then—with a vicious snap of her wrist— she flung the hot liquid at Aedan.

Aedan's eyes widened in the millisecond it took for the scorching liquid to splash the right side of his face. He roared and leapt backwards, his feet becoming entangled in the wooden chair.

Helen screamed, "Don't touch it!"

Aedan kicked the chair away, his hands hovering a fraction above his melting skin. He gasped through the pain, his eyes aflame with anger, his face already beginning to blister.

"You fucking bitch!"

Aedan slapped Sally hard across the mouth, knocking her out of the chair and onto the floor. The empty coffee mug flew from her grasp and smashed in shards nearby.

Aedan groaned and bared his teeth as he stomped around the table and drew back his foot to kick the vulnerable woman.

"Enough!" bellowed Father Black.

Aedan spun to face his father, but his anger was too raw to be stopped. He kicked Sally in the stomach with such force she was lifted from the floor.

"We have to treat this," Helen yelled. She rushed forward to grab her son's arm.

Aedan lifted his foot again, this time to stomp.

Father Black stood up. "I said enough."

Father and son stared at each other until Aedan slammed his foot down with enough force to crush bone—

His foot landed less than an inch from Sally's head.

Sally gasped, her chest wheezing like a burst accordion, and curled into a protective ball.

Aedan spat on her before allowing himself to be dragged to the sink where his mother splashed his scolded face with cold water.

"I'll call the doctor," Helen said. "I think he's still in the meadow."

Sally felt Father Black looming over her as she lay in the fetal position. She was perfectly still and perfectly quiet. No tears, no whimpers, just the wheezing as she struggled to catch her breath.

"Get up," he barked. "We need to talk."

Sally slowly lifted her head and looked around, assessing the danger. When she was satisfied that Aedan's mother had him under control, she unfurled and stood. Returning to her seat, her movements were cautious. Her stomach ached like someone had tried to gut her with a dull spade, and her mouth was bleeding, but she wasn't about to let Aedan see any more of her pain.

Father Black eyed her with newfound respect.

"Your mother was a fighter," he said, his voice flat. "My brother used to talk about how stubborn she could become when she set her mind to something. 'Course, your father was too damn soft for his own good. She wouldn't have treated me that way."

Sally settled at the table and wiped blood from her mouth onto the back of her hand.

"I don't remember them," she said. Then, her voice turned hard, "Except for the way they died."

Father Black took another sip of coffee. "That was unfortunate."

"Why did my father kill my mother?" Sally asked.

Aedan jerked his head from the sink, the right side of his face scarlet. "Because she was a witch," he spat. "Like you."

Helen shushed her son and pulled him by the arm again. The two of them disappeared out the rear door to find the doctor.

Father Black sipped his coffee and watched them leave.

"Who knows what happens behind closed doors," he said after a moment. "Your mother rode him to the edge and when he finally fought back, it took them both over."

"I have no memory of them arguing."

"You have no memory," Father Black corrected. "They could have fought like jackals." He paused. "Maybe you were lucky to get out alive."

"I don't believe that."

Father Black shrugged. "Can you prove otherwise?"

Sally looked away and saw the coffee pot still percolating on the stove. She tilted her chin in its direction. "Do you mind?"

Father Black's mouth formed a thin, wary smile. "So long as you drink it this time."

SALLY CROSSED TO the stove, wincing slightly at the pain in her stomach, more bruises for her growing collection. She washed the blood off her hands at the sink and found a new mug. She filled it with hot coffee, then crossed to the fridge and added a small drop of milk.

She turned to the priest. "Spoons?"

"Next to the stove."

With her back to the priest, Sally opened the cutlery drawer and discreetly removed two pieces of stainless steel. She placed the teaspoon in her cup and stirred. The metal collided with the side of the mug with a sharp tinkle before Sally dropped it with a clang into the metal sink. With the familiar noises distracting the priest, Sally slipped the second piece, a heavy butter knife, up her dress sleeve and out of sight.

To calm her nerves, she took a sip of coffee. It was strong, syrupy, and delicious.

Keeping her back to the priest, Sally took a quick assessment of her situation. The front door was likely locked, but the back door wasn't. Unfortunately, it led to the enclosed gardens and unless the large doors were open to the outside, it was a dead end. Even if she did escape, she needed transportation…

With her stomach and face still aching, Sally put on a brave face and returned to the table, mug in hand. She held her left arm down by her side, protecting the dull knife.

Father Black steepled his hands. "I fear we started on the wrong foot. You're family, but—"

"You murder people. You're not my family." The words slipped out before she could stop them, her anger too close to the surface.

"It's not murder—"

"You slit their thro—"

"Silence!" Father Black slammed both hands onto the table. The force of the blow made the table jump. "Listen to my words, or I will make your stay more unpleasant." His eyes burrowed into Sally's skull. "You don't want to know what I'm capable of."

Sally believed him. She nodded sheepishly for him to continue.

Father Black inhaled deeply through his nose. "You have a gift," he began. "The same gift as your mother. It is the ability to travel with a departed soul in the journey of death. You walk beside them as they seek out the light. You see the dangers; the wrong turns. You can guide them to the portal and into our Lord's embrace. But unlike those souls, you can return. You can bring back His message. You can enlighten, educate, inform." He paused. "And yet you refuse to tell us what you saw."

Sally stared at the priest over her coffee cup, her jaw unhinged, her expression disbelieving.

"You make it sound so natural," she said in a restrained voice. "But I watched Aedan cut those people open and then force my hands into their blood—"

"It was their time."

"Their time?" Sally's voice trembled. "You sacrificed them. It wasn't—"

"Their lives were in ruin," Father Black argued, "their families in crisis. These were bright, eager souls trapped in prisons of broken and disturbed flesh. Medical science is a soulless machine. We are not meant to live with such crippling burdens simply because science allows it. How many people are crying out in pain, begging for release but being refused because our government wants to control what is morally right? How dare they! That is not their mandate. Would you rather choose stronger and more experimental drugs or eternal peace and salvation? With the blessing of those souls, we freed them for the Journey. You must have seen that once you broke through the veil."

"I felt their fear and their pain," Sally said coldly. "I didn't feel their blessing."

Father Black waved that off. "You know the Journey exists. You've traveled and returned. You can offer people guidance through the dark unknown. You can quell their fears." He wiped a prickling of perspiration from his brow and licked his lips like a junkie with a fresh needle, all loaded and ready. "What else did you feel when you crossed over? Was there a message?"

Sally stared into her coffee. "What messages did my mother bring back?"

Father Black sighed. "Your mother was a servant of our Lord who—"

"Why did Aedan call her a witch?" Sally interrupted.

"Aedan is angry."

"Why?"

"You've been missing a long time, Sally. Our church is built on our belief in the Journey, but without a Seer to assure our congregation..." He paused, his face revealing strain. "Faith can weaken."

"If my mother was so important to you," Sally said carefully, "why wasn't she protected?"

Father Black closed his eyes and folded his hands in prayer. "Your father loved you."

"That's not what I asked."

He opened his eyes again. "You were too young to understand, but that's why we need you now. The answers you seek are available to you. Your mother knew so much of the world and she learned it all on the Journey. If I could travel—"

"I'm sure that could be arranged," Sally quipped, but instantly regretted it.

Father Black slammed his hands on the table again and his face flushed red.

"Don't ever!" he blustered, spittle spraying from his lips. "The punishment for blaspheme—" he struggled to finish the sentence as the back door opened, and Helen entered the kitchen.

Father Black turned to her in annoyance. "Where's Aedan?"

Helen instantly bowed her head in supplication. "He returned to his cabin. The doctor gave him—"

Father Black's fists hit the table. "Return this... this... *woman* to her room. Her lesson has not been learned."

Helen hurried to Sally's side and took hold of her arm. Sally shook her off and pushed away from the table. She would leave of her own choosing.

The priest's eyes burned into her back as she did so.

57

edan slammed an open hand against the bathroom mirror and cursed as the glass spidered in long, silvery tracks.

The right side of his face, shiny with antiseptic gel, had erupted with a half-dozen unsightly blisters. All he needed was for his eye to start sliding down his face and he would look as gruesome as his earlier disguise.

He tossed two more useless painkillers into his mouth, crunched them between his teeth, and dry swallowed the bitter white mess. The taste of it made him shudder, but he had never been any damn good at swallowing pills whole.

He gave the pills a full five seconds. When they did nothing to alleviate his pain, he opened the medicine cabinet and withdrew his bottle of generic painkillers and the small bag of brown powder inside.

He twitched with anticipation as he spooned a generous hit on a square of foil and shoved the glass tube between his lips. The right side of his mouth was dry and his lips were cracked. The doctor had told him to drink lots of water as burns caused dehydration, but he also said Tylenol #3s would help his pain.

Fuck that!

Aedan was an expert at hiding pain. He touched flame to foil and waited for the heroin to melt, bubble, and smoke. Using the glass tube, he sucked the curling white smoke deep into his lungs.

By the time he exhaled, the pain had shifted to a different part of his brain. It stuffed itself inside a small cupboard with a windowless door that he could wedge closed and rest his back against. The pain didn't disappear, but it became so muffled, trapped in its own dark space, he could ignore its existence.

The tube fell from his lips to clatter in the sink as he straightened his back and faced the cracked mirror again. The watery blisters on his face looked like alien incubators, the cloudy pus expanding and contracting in a rhythm only it could feel.

He had an urge to pop them, to feel the sharp prick of pain and the melting sensation of his own hot juices running down his scalded face. But he didn't want to bare the scars for everyone to see. It was better to carry them inside, tucked away, private.

He thought about the unexpected assault at the kitchen table. The bitch had fought back and actually scored a hit. The idea of it was unfathomable. He had nearly drowned her, sent her hurtling to glimpse death's door, and yet she came back fighting.

If he could know love, he would have to agree that his parents had selected the perfect wife. But love was an unrealistic emotion, and there was no way he could allow this witch to gain power over him.

He had only been a child, but he witnessed how that mistake destroyed his uncle. The congregation revered his wife, while he shrunk in insignificance. Every mistake, of which there were many, was magnified to the point that he was vilified. Aedan had pitied his uncle until his father explained that it was weakness that brought him low, cowardice that had allowed his role to be twisted and destroyed by the powerful witch in their midst. His uncle wasn't to be pitied for the failing was his own.

Aedan sure as hell wasn't going to let that same thing happen to him.

Once she delivered the healing message that would make their congregation strong again, Sally would have to go. She already knew how to make the Journey, but next time he would make sure she didn't return.

58

Dust.

That was all the Angels left in their wake when they roared out of the yard in response to the call.

In the hospital, Sister Mary Theresa hung up the phone and returned to Sister Fleur's side. The battered nun's body was broken and bruised, but the fire in her eyes burned so brightly it could set the ceiling alight. She had told her friend and mentor everything that was missing from her email report.

"We'll find her," assured Sister Mary Theresa. "And we'll bring her home."

Sister Fleur blinked away tears. "She's still so angry with me." The words were a struggle; her mouth and lips still badly swollen. "I failed as a mother, and I couldn't be a friend. I tried—" She choked and began to cough. The involuntary action made her eyes squeeze tight, and she cradled her chest as if to hold the bones in place.

Sister Mary Theresa took her hand and squeezed in an effort to share the pain. "You did what was necessary at the time," she said. "You were her protector."

"If only I could have explained," Sister Fleur wheezed. "Her gift... she didn't know. I... I—"

"Shhh. It's alright. There's still time."

"But is there?" Sister Fleur asked. "How long have I been here, unable to help? That monster—"

"Won't touch you ever again."

Sister Fleur winced. "It's not me I'm scared for."

Sister Mary Theresa released the patient's hand and stood. Her shapeless nun's habit had been replaced by head-to-toe black leather and her vibrant yellow hair poked out in errant tufts beneath a Stars & Stripes bandanna. She picked up a black motorcycle helmet and tucked it under her arm.

"Leave this to us."

IN THE HOSPITAL parking lot, Sister Mary Theresa straddled a powerful Harley Davidson Fat Boy and affixed her helmet. She would meet her six deadly angels on the road, and God help anyone who stood in their way.

59

"Do you still want to go home?"

April nodded.

Sally had brought April to sit beside her on the bed. They were alone in the room.

"Does your dad have a car?"

April nodded again.

"Can you get the keys without him noticing?"

A look of panic flooded April's face.

"It's okay," Sally assured. "It would just be until we got home. Nothing will happen to it, I promise."

"Daddy will be very... up... up... angry."

Sally squeezed the girl's hand. "It'll be okay. Once we're home, he'll understand that you just wanted to see your mom. He won't be angry after that."

"He... he's angry a... a lot."

"But this is special, April. This time you're helping me, and I'll explain everything to him once I'm back home."

"Maybe he will help—"

"No!" Sally's voice was too sharp and April recoiled. "I'm sorry, April. It's just... remember when I said the people here didn't want me to leave? Well, your father might be one of those people, and

I don't want him telling anyone. This needs to be our secret. Can you keep a secret?"

April nodded. "Mom and I have secrets."

"Good, good, that's good. Well, this would be the same. I need you to get your father's keys without him knowing. Do you think you could do that?"

April shrugged. "I can try."

Sally hugged the girl tight to her bosom. "That's all I ask."

WHEN HELEN RETURNED, she beckoned April with her finger. "I need you to take supper to your father."

"Can I comebackto… to see Sally?"

Sally turned away to look out the bedroom window. She could feel Helen's eyes on her back, but she continued to feign indifference, not wanting her captors to know how attached she was becoming to the sweet teenage girl.

"After supper you can come back for a little while," Helen said. "But then Sally will need to rest. She has a big day tomorrow."

Sally abruptly turned around. "What do you mean?"

"Father needs to hear the message." Helen smiled coldly and Sally could sense the predatory wolf that lurked within her grandmotherly shell. "And you'll travel the Journey until you bring it back."

"But—"

Helen held up a hand and her eyes turned hard. "Save your excuses for Father and the others. I never believed your mother had the sight, and I don't believe you do either." Helen's smile grew at the irony. "I guess that means I'm the only one who believes you. Pity that doesn't mean anything."

Sally leapt from the bed. "But you have to tell them or they'll keep killing innocent people."

Helen snorted and locked her hands on her hips in a menacing pose. The furrows around her eyes knit tighter together and the birthmark on her face seemed to deepen in color as though suddenly flushed with bile.

"I don't have to do anything," she snapped. "You're the one who's so damn special. Do you think the men would have listened to a word your mother said if she wasn't so pretty? Men are like bulls, all cock and balls but so easily led by the ring through their nose. Is it any wonder she drove your father insane?"

Helen shook her head as though trying to knock a disturbing image out of her mind. "Unless you tell them what they want to hear, dear, all that blood will be on your hands. And yours alone."

Sally stood in stunned silence as Helen pulled April out of the room and slammed the door.

AFTER A FEW moments, Sally shook herself out of the trance.

The only true thing she knew was the killing would never stop. The church's whole basis for being was the Journey, and they would keep killing no matter what she told them. History had taught her that sacrifice was like an addiction. The ancient Aztecs spilled blood to thank the gods when times were good. And when times were bad, they spilled more blood to appease them.

Sally tugged at her dress sleeve and the butter knife slid into her hand.

There was only one option.

60

Jersey and Kameelah swapped places after stopping for a bathroom break and caffeine top-up at a roadside gas station. After showing Jersey how to adjust the Jaguar's seat and mirrors, Kameelah reclined the passenger seat and produced her web-enabled cellphone.

"So what's the name of the church in Sister Fleur's letter?" she asked.

Jersey brought the Jaguar to 10 mph above the speed limit. He couldn't keep the pleased smile off his face as the car responded to his touch. This was the type of vehicle he had been destined to drive. Unfortunately, he had been born into a blue-collar family with a budget that couldn't climb past a used Dodge, and his cop's salary was no better.

"The name?" Kameelah prompted, her touch-screen phone at the ready.

"Oh, sorry." Jersey set the speed control and relaxed into the seat's soft grain leather. "Ermmm… Sabbath Day's Journey."

"Sounds like a rock band."

"It's from the Bible, but definitely a strange choice. If I remember my Sunday School lessons, a Sabbath day's journey was the distance Israelites were allowed to travel on the seventh day. About one thousand yards. In other words, stick close to home, except for a short walk to attend Mass."

Kameelah grinned. "And this was before televised Sunday afternoon football and pizza delivery?"

Jersey smiled back. "Who knew the NFL was so religious."

Kameelah typed the name into the search engine on her phone and began to sort through the results. Most of the hits referred to the Bible quote, *"Then they returned to Jerusalem from the Mount called Olivet, which is from Jerusalem a Sabbath day's journey."*

"The Bible doesn't actually explain it," Kameelah mused as she read a few entries. "The rabbis interpreted it as a limit to travel, but this church could have a different idea."

She returned to the home page and ran the same search on Blogs. A lone entry caught her eye. "Listen to this. A girl claiming to be a member of the Church of a Sabbath Day's Journey says her grandmother was murdered at the altar."

"Murdered?"

"That's what she says, but the whole blog is written in over-dramatic teen speak. Here, I'll read this part. 'As usual, all the kids — *yes, I said kids, sheesh, I'm fifteen*—were sent outside when Father Black got to the good part. We all know about the *Journey*, they keep telling us about the friggin' *Journey*, but they keep the ceremony so damn secret. We don't even have a *Seer*. Like, how can we trust it even works? Mom and Dad say we have to believe, but… well, anyways, that's a whole *other* story.

" 'We were outside, but the guardians weren't watching 'cause, like, they've deff got the hots for each other. It's soooo obvious, like, duh! Well, Lydia and I snuck around the far side and peeked through the shutters. Mom and Dad were walking down the aisle with Gramma, who hasn't been well. She's been, like, peeing the bed and stuff. *Yuck, like, Gross, I know!* But she's still my Gramma. Then, and I still can't believe it, a man wearing a black hood grabs my Gramma and, like, right there in front of everyone, cuts her throat.

" 'Oh, My God!! I totally freaked, it was *so* gross, I know. Lydia and I ran, but, like, there's no place to go. I tried to ask mom about it later, but, like, she just said Gramma got sick and died on the way to hospital. She must think I'm *soooo* stupid. There was no ambulance or nothing. Her funeral is this weekend, and, like, I don't know what to do.' "

"Any other entries?" Jersey asked.

"None. All the links are dead, too. This entry was caught in Google's archive. It was written nearly ten months ago and nothing since."

"She mentioned the Seer." Jersey scrunched his face as a disturbing thought rose to the surface. "Sally works with corpses, but she was surprised when she had her…" he still found it difficult to digest, "… vision."

"When she touched the hit-and-run victim?"

"Yes. That woman died only moments before Sally touched her."

"So?"

"What if Sally's trick only works on fresh kill?"

"Hold on." Kameelah turned in her chair. "Are you thinking this church deliberately kills people so Sally can have a vision?"

"It's a possibility. Two people were killed in Portland just to get her attention."

"But this girl's grandmother was killed months before Sally was kidnapped. Why do that if you don't—"

"Maybe they had someone before," Jersey interrupted. "A Seer who could do the same thing as Sally, but they lost her somehow. Instead of stopping, they continued the ceremony without her. But, like the girl's blog says, without the Seer's visions, the congregation is losing its faith. They need a new one."

"How did they know Sally had the gift?"

Jersey snapped his fingers. "Because she had a vision when she was a child. She started to tell me about it at the funeral home. It must have happened before she left the church with Sister Fleur."

Kameelah pinched the pocket of flesh at the bridge of her nose. "If the church needs to kill people to kick-start a vision, what's the upside?"

Jersey thought about it. "Maybe Sally can see more than just the moment of death."

"See more?" Kameelah was incredulous.

"Hey, I'm an old Catholic boy, I was brought up to believe in life after death. But for all that preaching, there's never been proof to back it up, that's why they call it faith. But what if Sally can cross over and glimpse what lies beyond? That would be worth worshipping, don't you think?"

"At what price? An incontinent grandmother?"

"I'm not condoning it. I'm just saying it's the one question we all want answered, isn't it?"

"I prefer ignorance," said Kameelah. "If paradise awaits, why should I bother with the everyday shit of this world? And if it's the opposite, then remind me to cancel my DNR declaration."

Jersey stared straight ahead, his mind whirling. "The trouble is," he said after a moment, "what happens if the church doesn't like the vision Sally brings back? What if, as the atheists preach, there's nothing there?"

"Well that's simple," Kameelah said offhandedly. "If you don't like the message, you—"

Jersey's cellphone rang. Before he could answer it, Kameelah snatched it out of his hand.

"You watch the road." She flipped open the phone. "Detective Castle's phone."

"Kameelah, is that you?" It was Amarela.

"Hey, girlfriend. Jersey's driving. Can I help?"

"I just talked to Peter Higgins' wife again."

"Uh-huh."

"Have you guys come across any reference to the Church of a Sabbath Day's Journey?"

Kameelah arched her eyebrows. "We were just talking about it. Why?"

"Harriet says Peter and his parents were members once, but they left and moved to Portland before Peter was in his teens. She said it was odd, but Peter had been talking about it before he disappeared, as though trying to get her interested. She said it sounded like a cult and—"

"We think that's where Sally's been taken," Kameelah interrupted.

There was a pause. "That's our connection," said Amarela. "Peter and his daughter must be heading there, too."

61

Sally dropped to her knees in front of the bedroom window and stuck the knife into the crease between window and sill. The window had been nailed shut from the outside, but that was where her captors made a mistake. If they had used screws, she wouldn't have had a prayer.

There wasn't much leverage, and she was afraid the knife could snap at any moment, but by taking her time and focusing her efforts on the three points where the nails had pierced the sill, she began to see progress. It wasn't much, barely a sliver, but she felt the anchors begin to loosen. When the right edge lifted a fraction, she turned her attention to the center, forcing the knife deep into the narrow slit. When she felt it respond, she quickly moved to the left edge and repeated the action.

She had been working for over an hour when she heard the lock being turned. She quickly moved to the bed and slid the knife under her pillow.

The door opened and April entered with two plates of food on a tray. Helen stood behind, keys jangling in her hand. She stared at Sally with suspicion.

"Are you feeling okay?"

"I'm fine," said Sally. "The food smells good."

"Why are you flushed? You're perspiring."

"I got scared when I heard the door," Sally said quickly. "I keep expecting Aedan."

"You have a right to be scared," Helen said flatly. "Father doesn't want you dead, but there are far worse things a man can do to a woman."

Sally opened her mouth but decided to remain silent. What could she say to a woman who not only allowed, but accepted, the inherent brutality of her son?

"Eat your supper and rest. I'll be back to collect April. She has work tomorrow as well."

AS SOON AS they were alone, Sally turned to April. "Did you get the keys?"

April looked down at her plate. "D-daddy didn't have his coat."

Sally bit back her disappointment. "That's okay. I'll think of something else."

"Daddy was in the church," April continued. "He said there is a special cer... cer... service tomorrow, and I can be in it."

Sally was only half-listening. She had retrieved the knife from under her pillow and turned her attention to the window. She dropped to her knees and forced the knife into the narrow groove.

"Daddy says I... I get a new dress."

"That'll be nice," said Sally absently.

April wrinkled her nose. "I like dresses, but... but Daddy says it's red. Idon'likethat."

Sally turned, her face pale. "Your dress is red?"

April nodded. "You like red?"

"No." Sally's voice broke as she thought of the last two people who wore red before their throats were cut and her hands were plunged into a pool of their blood.

April's eyes filled with tears. "I w... w... won't wear it... if... if you d... d... don't want me to."

Sally squeezed the girl's arm in reassurance, but she didn't know what to say. She tried to smile. "You eat your supper. It looks good."

While April picked at her ham steak, mashed potatoes, boiled peas, and carrots, Sally returned to the window. She jammed the knife deep into the spot where the middle nail had been hammered, gouging the wood with renewed effort. She pulled and strained to increase her leverage, but just as she felt a tremor of movement, the knife blade snapped.

Sally's hands banged against the wood and she jumped back with a squeal. But it wasn't the pain of scraped knuckles that made her want to weep, it was the useless stub of broken steel attached to a handle too thick to fit into the crack.

The remainder of the knife was jammed in the crevice, sealing the window even tighter than before.

62

Sally threw the broken knife under the bed in frustration and squeezed her eyes to scream silent obscenities in her mind.

April moved in close and laid her head on Sally's shoulder to offer comfort.

"Th-there's another window," April said quietly.

Even though she fought against it, Sally's tone was full of frustration. She snapped, "Where?"

April blinked and lifted her head off Sally's shoulder. Her eyes began to fill with tears again, and Sally's heart melted.

"I'm sorry, April. I was angry at the situation, not at you. I know you're trying to help. Please, where's the other window?"

April's tears dried up instantly. "Bathroom. I looked at garden when you were in... in bath."

Sally pictured the bathroom in her mind, mentally measuring the window that offered ventilation beside the toilet.

It was small, but so was she.

She immediately crossed to the door and hammered it with her fist.

HELEN OPENED THE door and stared at the two occupants. "Tired of each other already?"

"I need to use the washroom," said Sally. "And thought I would get ready for bed."

Helen glanced over at her untouched plate. "You weren't hungry?"

Sally went on the attack. "Being slapped around by your son can do that."

Helen shrugged. "Suit yourself." She stepped back from the door to allow Sally to pass.

"C-can I go, too?" April asked.

"Looks like you've made a real friend, there," Helen said to Sally. "Did you know you are related?"

Sally stopped in the doorway. "How?"

"You're cousins." Helen paused to think. "Well, technically, second cousins. April's grandfather and your father were brothers. April's family is one of the four founding cornerstones of our church."

"So good seeds can grow from bad fruit," said Sally.

Helen's mouth twisted into a sneer. "Her father wouldn't agree."

HELEN ESCORTED THE two women to the washroom and locked them inside. She promised to return with a nightgown for Sally after she took care of the supper plates.

"We don't have much time," Sally told April when they were alone. "You listen at the door and warn me if anyone comes."

Sally turned on the taps to the bath to provide some busy noise, while she rushed to the window, slid open the lock and shoved upward. Despite her fear that the window would also be nailed, it slid open a full fourteen inches before jamming in its tracks.

She stuck her head out the window and inhaled the cool night air. She looked down. The drop to the ground was a good twelve to fourteen feet. Dangerous, but possible, so long as she didn't break an ankle on landing.

Then she glanced to her right. The large stone wall that ran the entire perimeter of the grounds was only two feet away from the window. If she could swing her feet over to it, she could drop down to the outside and be gone before anyone thought to look.

Sally retreated back inside to review her options. April looked at her with bright innocent eyes, and Sally knew she wouldn't be able to take her. The odds of making it were already slim, but April would make them impossible.

Sally crossed the room and knelt down to eye-level. She took the girl's round face in her hands and put a steel cage around her emotions.

"April," she began. "I need you to listen carefully. I'm going out that window and I'm going to find help. I will be back for you. Do you understand?"

"Y-you want me to stay?"

"I need you to stay, April. The window is too high for you, but I will be back to take you home. Do you trust me?"

April nodded and Sally felt a chasm opening in her chest.

"Stay by the door," Sally continued. "And don't let anyone in until you have no other choice, okay?"

April stared at her with large, doe-like eyes.

Sally turned her back.

She couldn't delay any longer.

63

The sight of seven leather-clad bikers filling their gas tanks was not an uncommon sight at the twenty-four-hour Crossroads Truck Center in Missoula, Montana. But when all seven were female, the mustached clerk took notice.

"Uh, you some kinda gospel group?" he asked.

He had noticed the large red crosses adorning the backs of their black jackets. The intricate stitching made it look as though the crosses were bleeding. Beneath each cross, stitched in heavy white thread, were two words in Latin: *Angelus Domini.*

Sister Mary Theresa handed over a credit card to pay for the fuel on all seven bikes. "Something like that."

The clerk rolled up his left sleeve—the white T-shirt turned gray from dust, sweat, and poor laundry habits—to expose a stringy bicep sporting a crude, hand-drawn, blue-ink tattoo. If it hadn't been bought in prison, he had visited the worst tattoo artist in the state.

The tattoo was of a circular Celtic cross with the motto scrawled beneath: *Joy shall be in Heaven.*

Sister Mary Theresa smiled and recited, "Joy shall be in Heaven over one sinner that repenteth."

The clerk grinned, showing a set of badly fitted false teeth. "You know your stuff, sister." He handed her back the credit card. "Careful on these roads. The devil rides at night."

"True," said the nun, "but he doesn't want to mess with us."

64

Sally returned to the window and struggled for the best method of escape. The opening was too small for her to straddle the sill, and she couldn't go headfirst.

She started to panic.

If she had managed to open the bedroom window she would have had all night to escape, but now she might only have minutes—or less.

She turned her back to the window, laid her chest on the toilet lid and walked her bare feet up the wall. When her feet reached the opening, she eased backwards and felt herself slide out into open space. Her dress snagged against the rough wood and began to rise up her thighs, but now was not the time to worry about modesty. When her hips crossed the vertex, her legs dropped, and gravity came to her aid.

Her dress rode up past her hips and became snagged on the ledge. It threatened to smother her as she grasped hold of the windowsill and took one last look at April.

The girl waved just as a key turned in the lock behind her.

Sally cursed and started to swing her legs, aiming for the top of the wall, but the damn dress was blocking her view. She slid further out, the dress ripping, her fingertips screaming from the effort of holding her weight.

She heard April protest that Sally was in the bath, but the words must have fallen on deaf ears.

Helen burst into the room and instantly yelled for help. "Father! She's escaping."

Sally swung her legs faster, trying to feel the top of the stone wall with her feet, but there didn't seem to be anything out there but air.

Hands grabbed hold of her wrists and attempted to pull her back inside, but hoisting a dead weight is entirely different from pushing someone around.

With staunch determination, Sally swung her legs as hard as she could and when they reached the apex of their arc, she released her grip on the ledge.

Her wrists popped free of Helen's grasp, and Sally went twisting into the night air.

SALLY'S FEET HIT the top of the stone wall, and for a brief moment she thought her hips and torso would follow for a perfect ten-point landing. Unfortunately, she didn't have the necessary momentum to disobey gravity.

She fell backwards, her hands stretched out in disbelief, fingers reaching for the rock ledge that was too far away.

She landed in a patch of newly-toiled garden with soft dirt and horse manure as cushioning. Despite the fortune of her landing, Sally's breath was forced out of her lungs by a double-barreled punch in the back.

She gasped and wheezed, the immobilizing pain greater than when Aedan had tried to drown her.

Her brain was on fire, telling her to move, *move*, *MOVE*, but her body was useless. She wheezed, desperate to fill her lungs with oxygen, but they stubbornly refused to expand.

Stars danced in her eyes until she was on the brink of darkness.

And then, with a sudden jolt, a lock was turned in her chest and her lungs inflated with a deep, agonizing breath.

Sally rolled onto her front and pushed up on her knees. Her eyesight was still blurry, her breathing was pained, but her strength was returning.

She staggered to her feet, free of the house, but still trapped behind stone walls.

65

A edan stood and waited.

When Sally finally made it to her feet, he waited still. A garden statue made of flesh turned stone.

He watched the agonized red and blue hues retreat from her pale skin and imagined the fog dissipating from her incredible green eyes.

He waited until she raised her chin in defiance and prepared to make good her escape. Then, he moved just enough to catch her eye.

She gasped and tried to run, but he was far too quick. He grabbed her arm and pulled her close.

She struggled against him, the heat and friction of her lithe body warming his own.

He grabbed her hair and yanked backwards, exposing her full face to him. She was scared, but still resistant, and its combination excited him.

With a cruel smile, he leaned down to kiss her. He wanted to crush his mouth against hers, bruise her lips like ripe berries, and suck the last breath from her body. But as his lips neared hers, Sally lunged forward, her teeth snapping like a wolf.

Aedan yanked his head back, but too slowly. Sally's teeth sunk into his lower lip and held on.

Aedan yelled in panic and tried to push her away, but a low growl escaped Sally's throat and she began to shake her head, her teeth sinking deeper into his soft, plump lip.

Aedan groaned as he wrapped his hands around the mad woman's throat and squeezed. Sally's eyes bulged, but her teeth remained embedded in his lip. Aedan could feel his flesh starting to rip as he squeezed harder until Sally's eyes rolled back in her head.

He could feel her losing the battle, slipping away, when—

Her right knee jerked up and slammed into his groin with such force that it made his eyes spin in their sockets.

Aedan lost his grip and staggered backwards, temporarily blinded by pain. Sally pushed him aside and turned to run.

She didn't get far.

Father Black and several elders were waiting. By the time she reached them, Sally was too exhausted to fight.

66

Father Black sat in the living room and waited for his five guests to settle into their chairs. Their unexpected foray into the garden had woken everyone and splashed a spot of color onto their cheeks.

Sally's last attempt at resistance was weak, and it had taken little effort to return her to her room behind lock and key. Quieting April down had been more problematic, but Mother had managed, with the help of Aedan, to remove her from the house.

Once Father Black was satisfied his guests' attention was refocused, he began.

"Our church is in crisis," he said. "I know this is not a surprise to those members who have endured the storms over the years that have seen the four founding families reduced to one." Father Black locked his gaze on each guest. "It is not the erosion of these families that is to blame, for this church was founded by one man, one family. As it began, so shall it continue."

A hand was raised. Peter Higgins, the youngest member of their cabal, and one not yet house trained. Father Black ignored it.

He said, "When my father built this church, he asked his three eldest sons to become corner posts in its foundation. To this end, they were each given a house and a new name. The House of Blue represented the ocean and sky; Green was for the land and new growth; White symbolized light and air. Upon my father's death, I inherited the mantle of Black, the keeper of shadows and the mortar upon which all others are built."

The hand was raised again, a nuisance, but Father Black continued to ignore it.

"My father was more than a man of faith, he was also a visionary. He believed that by building a church on four equal footings, it could continue beyond the collapse of any one house. He could not have foreseen the weakness and cowardice of my brothers that would leave everything upon my shoulders. I have been blessed with the duty of carrying this church for more than two decades, but with the return of the Seer, I believe it may be time to rebuild and expand."

Four of the five men nodded their heads in agreement, while Peter glanced around in confusion.

"Tomorrow, the Seer will walk the path once more and bring to us the answers needed to reignite the faith of those followers who have grown weak. During that glorious ceremony, I shall announce that my son Aedan will take on the mantle and full control of the House of Blue. He will move into this house and restore its name, while Mother and I mark our return to the remodeled guardianship next door. It has been a difficult journey, and this house has offered safe sanctuary, but I finally feel ready to reclaim my father's house, the founding House of Black."

All five men applauded as Father Black turned his attention to Peter.

"I shall also announce that Peter will re-open the House of Green that has been handed down from my brother Nicholas. Nicholas and his wife died in a recent tragedy in Portland with no one to guide their way. Fortunately, it was not before their son had the foresight to return to his roots and his one true family, the church."

The other four men applauded loudly at this announcement, and Peter beamed at the attention.

Father Black continued, "To cement his return and prove his faith, Peter has also chosen a traveler for tomorrow's ceremony. It is our hope that this traveler will help guide the Seer to a wiser course of action."

One of the older men cleared his throat. "The Seer is clearly troubled by her role. How do you plan to change that?"

A murmur erupted between the men, but Father Black silenced it by raising his hands in a calming gesture. "The Seer *is* troubled. Just as her mother was troubled before her. It is part of their nature, which is why they need a strong hand to guide them. My son has assured me, he will be that hand."

"He didn't look so strong in the garden when she was trying to escape," said the same man who had spoken earlier.

"That was unfortunate," said Father Black. "But—"

"It won't happen again." Aedan entered the room from the kitchen. His lower lip was swollen and bruised, its unhealthy color matching the burned side of his face. "She is clearly disturbed, and I have treated her too gently. The gift can be a curse to those who possess it. My uncle paid with his life to keep the Seer under control. I vow to you that I will do no less."

"Can we be sure she'll bring us the message tomorrow?" asked the man. "Today's ceremony was a disaster. The look on Florence's face. She sent her mother on the Journey, only to have that... that..." He sputtered, unable to find the right words.

"She will deliver the message," said Aedan. "I will make sure of it."

"Well, you better," said the man. "I fear our congregation will not survive another calamity."

Another man spoke up. He had ginger hair and a smartly trimmed goatee. "You speak of rebuilding, but I hear no mention of the House of White."

Father Black's eyes glistened darkly. "The House of White shall not be resurrected." He absently touched a faded six-inch scar that ran across his throat. "My brother's betrayal had deep roots that left no heirs. The House of Black shall absorb the House of White, unifying both corners into one."

Father Black noticed there was no applause for this decree, but neither was there dissent.

67

Kameelah gunned the Jaguar along the empty interstate and Jersey thought she appeared relieved to be back in control. Giving her pride and joy over to another person, never mind to a member of the untrustworthy male species, had been, in Jersey's mind, a huge compliment to the trust they had built in such a short period of time.

Kameelah rolled down the window to get some air blowing in her face, and Jersey worried that neither of them was as alert as they ought to be for traveling at high speeds in the middle of the night.

He was about to say something when his cellphone rang. He answered it with a yawn.

"Sorry," said a young male voice, "did I wake you?"

"Hardly," said Jersey. "Who's this?"

"John Underwood, *Idaho Statesman*."

"Isn't it past your bedtime, John?"

"Definitely, but your call earlier inspired me to go over some old ground."

"Three blinded women?"

"I believe there may be more."

Jersey stifled another yawn. "Sorry," he apologized, "it's been a long day. Go on, I'm listening."

"I phoned the parents of the two women whose murders I originally looked into. Neither of them appreciated my serial killer angle at the time, but they were at least grateful that I was doing something, unlike the police. We got to talking and I discovered a link I never knew before."

"Which was?" Jersey encouraged.

"Both women were adopted when they were young girls."

"Coincidence," said Jersey.

"Possibly, but I managed to track down the parents of the third victim, the one up in Canada, and it turns out she was adopted, too."

"It's still slim," said Jersey, although his tone betrayed an increased interest.

"The Canadian family is expat American," said the reporter. "When I dug further, I discovered all three girls were adopted from the same state agency in Bismarck."

"That's an odd connection," Jersey agreed.

"I would have called you earlier, but I had difficulty gaining access to the agency's computer records. There are at least two more unsolved murders of young women in this general area that match those first three. The police reports make no mention of missing eyes, but I've managed to link their names to the agency. Those victims were adopted as children, too."

"So what's your theory?" Jersey asked.

"Someone's hunting these girls using their adoption records."

"Why?"

"Beats the hell out of me. Maybe the killer abused them when they were kids and is now trying to cover it up before they come forward. It could be anything."

"Or," Jersey said, thinking aloud, "he could be searching for one specific girl. He kills the ones who turn out to be false leads just to scratch their names off his list."

"Now that's twisted," said the reporter.

"You've done good work, John."

"Thanks. Now, any chance of a quote so I can build a story from facts rather than theory?"

Jersey laughed. He liked the kid's spunk. "Give me twenty-four hours. Then, I'll give you all the quotes you need."

68

Sally lay on the bed, her mother's patchwork quilt clutched tightly in her hands.

Fear was gone. In its place was rage.

It wasn't just adrenaline, it was some primal need to punish. Twenty-five years of running. Running from a nightmare, running from the blood and the fear and the agonizing pain of the night that destroyed everything.

She couldn't, wouldn't, run anymore. It was time to plant her feet and make a stand.

Father Black had been firm but not overly rough when he dragged her back to her room and locked her inside. He hadn't berated or beaten her. He had simply uttered a chilling warning: "Your spirit shall be broken."

Her biggest danger was Aedan. Twice she had bested him; both times by surprise. He wouldn't take that lightly.

She rolled off the bed and crawled underneath, her arm stretching to its full extension until her fingers found what she was looking for: the broken knife. The handle was heavy and what was left of the blade was barely a nub, but its snapped tip had a ragged edge sharper than its blade ever did.

Sally returned to the bed and slipped the weapon under her pillow. Its presence gave her a momentary feeling of comfort.

69

Aedan, his head lowered in supplication, stood before his father. Despite his meek posture, rage coursed through his body and made the veins in his neck vibrate like high-tensile cables.

"The future of this church is in your hands," Father Black said. "I've told the elders of my plans for both you and the church, but unless the Seer can deliver, I fear it will be all for naught."

"I *will* make her talk," said Aedan.

"But how?"

Father Black walked to the fireplace where photos of his dead brothers and their families stared out at the desolate room. He picked up one photo that showed Sally as a child of no more than four. Her arms were wrapped tightly around her mother's neck, her eyes peeking out from between the long curls of her mother's red hair, while her father looked on. Only the mother was smiling, and in her eyes there glistened something akin to madness.

Father Black said, "Until shortly before the end, her mother was a true believer. A Seer of extraordinary talent, she guided our followers to the other side with such enthusiastic relish that… " he chuckled, "that I often felt jealous it wasn't my turn." He turned to his son. "Salvation's years away from the church have made her blind to her gift. How do you plan to make her see?"

Aedan bared his teeth. "I will plunge her neck deep in blood until she—"

"But," Father Black interrupted, "violence isn't working. She isn't afraid of you."

Aedan bristled. "I will step up—"

"She's a Seer," Father Black interrupted again. "She knows the path, she's seen the Journey. How do you threaten someone who doesn't fear death?"

Aedan stayed silent, knowing his father's question was meant as rhetorical, something for him to think upon while he slept. But in his mind, he already knew the answer: *Make her fear living.*

70

When his mother and father were asleep, each in their separate bedrooms on the second floor, Aedan returned from his cabin.

He crept up the stairs to Sally's bedroom, unlocked the door, and slid inside. A labored whine emanated from the bed as though the sleeper was wrestling with demons.

Walking softly, he crossed to stand beside her bed. She had kicked the blankets off and was lying on her stomach, bare except for a pair of white panties, her torn and mud-splattered dress tossed in a heap on the floor.

With the dim light disguising the bruising on her face, she actually looked quite beautiful. Her lips trembled in sleep as though struggling to speak, but the only noise that escaped was the undecipherable whine.

Aedan slipped one hand over her mouth as he climbed onto the bed and sat on her buttocks. She instantly arched her body in protest and began to struggle, but Aedan simply leaned forward until his full weight was pressed along her bare back. His stubbled cheek brushed against her smooth skin and her lungs wheezed, his dead weight making it difficult for her to breathe.

He pressed his lips against her ear. "Killing you is not difficult.

We could simply lie here in this embrace, not moving, and before the sun rose in the morning, your body would be cold."

Sally tried to move her arms, but Aedan had them pinned to her sides with his knees.

He continued, "I could sodomize you and then slit your throat, or do any number of unspeakable things to your flesh both before and after death."

Sally tried to bite his fingers, but his hand was clamped too tightly across her mouth.

"The pain I can inflict is great," he said. "But I fear you don't believe me." Aedan lifted his head and sucked in a deep, cleansing breath. He released it in a hiss as he returned his mouth to Sally's ear. "It's time to believe."

Aedan yanked his hand away from Sally's mouth and sat up, releasing the pressure in her chest. She only had time to gulp a quick lungful of air before Aedan snatched up her left arm and pulled it tight.

Gripping it above the wrist and below the elbow, Aedan dug in his thumbs and bent her arm to the breaking point.

Sally groaned in pain and begged him to release her.

Her whine hit notes of glass-shattering proportions as Aedan bent the arm over his knee, and then—

Sally screamed as the large bone snapped.

MOTHER RUSHED INTO the unlocked bedroom to find Sally sobbing on the bed, her face white with shock, her left arm cradled against her chest.

There was no one else in the room.

AEDAN RETURNED TO his cabin and headed straight to the bathroom. His eyes were spinning in his head as he struggled to control the rate of his breathing.

Everything was moving too fast. He could see air molecules flying around him, too large to enter his lungs.

He pulled open the medicine cabinet and flattened a square of foil. He wished he had a needle; something faster, more efficient.

His head was going to explode.

The heroin melted and bubbled and began to smoke. He inhaled deeply, greedily, wanting to turn his lungs inside out so he could wrap them around the smoke and swallow it in thick, white chunks.

Had the bitch learned her lesson? He didn't know. There was too much pressure. The church, his father, his obsession... the weight of it was becoming unbearable. He had been searching for Sally for most of his life and now, after all his effort, she was refusing to help.

The bitch deserved to feel pain; mountains of it.

His eyes rolled in his head until he could see the back of his skull. There was something back there, hiding behind his brain. It had mustard yellow eyes and tiny, sharp teeth... Aedan's thoughts drifted as though commanded by the creature. It didn't want to be seen. Aedan staggered out of the bathroom, his limbs rubbery and ethereal, and down the short hallway to his bedroom.

He found his bed and crawled on top of the covers, clutching the corners of the mattress so it wouldn't fly away without him.

In his dreams, he would build four mountains, and upon each peak he would build a house, and within each house he would raise a family, and everyone would worship him as Father.

71

Jersey opened his eyes to a red dawn.

The car wasn't moving. Kameelah had parked in a wooded rest area beside the road and reclined her seat as far as it would go. The awkward position of her neck caused her to snore, and the nasally rumble was so grating that Jersey wondered how he had possibly managed to sleep through it.

Jersey opened his door and stepped out to take a leak in a copse of scraggly pine. The air was crisp and his breath rolled from his mouth in ghostly, near-transparent puffs. Winter was approaching fast; the threat of snow ominous. When he was done, he zipped up and returned to the car.

Kameelah blinked open her eyes at the sound of his door closing. She wiped drool from her lips and wrinkled her nose as if she was about to sneeze.

"Sorry." She rubbed her eyes. "I couldn't stay awake."

"Better to pull over than end up in a ditch."

Kameelah grinned. "That was my thinking." She started the engine. "New Town isn't far. We can get coffee, directions, and splash some water on our faces before heading to the church." She hesitated, then asked, "Do you have a plan?"

Jersey shrugged. "We knock on the front door and ask if Sally's there."

"And if they say 'No'?"

"We'll insist they look again."

Kameelah pulled onto the highway and brought the car up to cruising speed. "Not much of a plan."

"No," said Jersey, "but since we don't have any jurisdiction, the harder we insist, the more pissed off they might become."

"And if they become violent?"

Jersey grinned. "Then that gives us enough probable cause to get the local cops to kick the door down and see what they're hiding."

"And what if Sally isn't there?"

Jersey's grin faded. "Then I better hope *The Rotten Johnnys* get more gigs, because my cop career will be in the toilet."

72

Sally sat in the bathtub with her back to the taps and washed herself one-handed. Her left arm hung over the side, the broken bone set in fresh plaster.

The doctor who arrived in the middle of the night had been a short man with sickly, jaundiced eyes beneath thick-rimmed glasses. Despite the lateness of the hour, he wore a western-cut suit adorned with a ridiculously colorful bowtie. The garish tie gave Sally hope that he wasn't a church member and that she could use him to get a message to Jersey.

Her hopes were dashed the moment he examined her arm and told her how privileged he was to be of service to the Seer. When he moved her arm, Sally's face drained of all color and she struggled not to either faint or vomit.

"It's definitely broken," the doctor murmured. "But I suspect it's a clean break." He smiled at her. "No sharp bones sticking out of the skin, so that's a good thing."

Sally opened her mouth to spit back a reply, but the menacing look on Father Black's face, as he loomed in the doorway, made her reconsider.

Without an X-Ray, the doctor said he had no option other than to wrap her arm in wet plaster and hand over two Tylenol #3s for the pain. When he finished setting the plaster, he told her to keep the limb elevated to bring down the swelling and that he would check on her later in the day to make sure the cast wasn't too loose. The fast-drying plaster hardened into a smooth white shell by the time the doctor had washed his hands and been escorted out of the house.

The pills had helped Sally gain a few more hours of sleep, but as she sat in the bathtub and clumsily splashed warm water on herself, she felt a raw weariness deep in the marrow of her bones.

Her escape plan had done nothing but cause her more pain, and she worried for April. She had asked to have the girl visit this morning, but Mother had refused.

"You'll see her in church," Mother said as she filled the bath. "You both have a big day ahead of you."

Sally pulled the plug and listened to the water gurgling down the drain. She wished she could join it; hold her breath and slide into the sewers; float to the river and away.

She climbed out of the bath and toweled herself dry, then slipped into fresh underwear and a new white dress. She wondered if the church bought the dresses in bulk, since all three had been identical, or if each time she wrecked one, Mother had to go begging to another church family for one in the right size. She hoped it was the latter; maybe someone would question why.

When she finished dressing, Sally crossed to the bathroom door, knocked and waited.

73

There was a knock on the front door as Sally dipped her fingers of buttered toast into the bright orange yolk of a soft-boiled egg.

Father Black crossed the room and stopped in front of the door. He casually flicked aside a small disc of metal that covered a glass peephole and peered out.

There was a second knock as he turned to face the kitchen. His eyes were flat and cold; rocks in a glacier runoff.

"Take her upstairs," he ordered. "Now!"

Mother instantly grabbed Sally's arm and pulled her from the table. Sally yelped, but before she could protest further, Father Black stormed across the room and clamped his hand over her mouth. He squeezed, hard, fingernails digging into her cheeks.

"No noise," he hissed. Then, to his wife, "Keep her quiet."

Mother's hand replaced Father's across Sally's mouth as she pulled Sally to the stairs and up to the second floor.

There was a third knock before Father Black removed a brass key from his pocket and unlocked the formidable front door.

JERSEY SQUARED HIS shoulders and subconsciously sucked in his stomach as the blue door opened. He didn't know what he was expecting, but the broad-shouldered man with a shaved head and clerical collar, wasn't it.

Jersey flashed his credentials, trying to make the movement quick yet perfectly innocent.

The man's eyes glistened amber in the morning light. "Sorry," he said, "I didn't catch that. You're police?"

The man held his palm out flat, forcing Jersey to hand over his I.D. The man read it carefully before looking down at Kameelah. "Do you have a card, too?"

Kameelah handed over her credentials.

"Interesting," said the man, "you work in different cities." He studied Jersey's face. "You're Portland Homicide and... " he turned to Kameelah, "you're Seattle Sex Crimes."

Jersey bristled. "We know who we are."

"And now so do I." The man smiled, but there was no warmth in it. "What can I do for you, detectives?"

"We're looking for a missing woman. Her name is Sally Wilson."

"I'm afraid I've never heard of her."

"You might know her as Salvation Blue," said Kameelah.

The man's eyes narrowed, crow's feet deepening into troughs as though he spent a lot of time outdoors squinting at the sun.

"Salvation Blue was my niece," he said. "She disappeared almost twenty-five years ago. Surely you can't be looking into her disappearance after all this time?"

"Your niece was living in Portland until two days ago," said Jersey. "We think she may have been brought here."

A full smile lit up the man's face. "That would be wonderful. I never dreamed I would ever see her again. I... we all assumed the worst, but to hear she's alive."

"Is she here?" asked Jersey.

The man shook his head. "No, no, I wish she was. I haven't seen Salvation since she was six years old. She vanished the same night my brother, Salvation's father, died in a tragic accident."

"Her mother, too," said Jersey.

The man's face twitched. "Yes, yes, it was a terrible blow." He shook his head, the movement much slower than before as though his skull had suddenly grown heavy. "I fear we'll never know exactly what that poor girl witnessed that night. I'm sure that's why she ran away."

"Could we come inside?" Kameelah interjected. "We've been driving a lot of hours."

The man seemed to consider it for a moment, but then he fastened a friendly smile on his face and stepped aside to grant them access.

"I'm Father Black," he said as Jersey crossed the threshold. "The spiritual leader of the federally-recognized Church of a Sabbath Day's Journey. Would you care for coffee?"

The two detectives followed Father Black into the large kitchen. When Father Black moved ahead of them to fetch the coffee, Jersey turned to Kameelah and whispered, "Federally-recognized?"

"He's letting us know that he's got a whole army of religious-rights lawyers ready to stomp all over us if we get out of line."

"And why tell us that?" Jersey asked.

"Pre-emptive strike," whispered Kameelah. "He's got something to hide."

74

Sally could hear voices drifting up through the floorboards, but they were so distant they might as well have been echoes of long-forgotten conversations.

Helen sat beside her on the bed, one hand clamped on her plastered arm, the other sealed across her mouth. Sally strained to listen, hoping for anything that might identify the unexpected guests. She didn't want to risk more pain unless it was a viable bid for escape.

JERSEY TOOK A gulp of strong coffee and felt the blood vessels open in his brain.

"Good coffee," he said.

Father Black accepted the compliment with a nod. "It's one of the few things we can't grow ourselves, but we make do."

"How did Sally's parents die?" Kameelah asked. She hadn't touched her coffee.

Father Black moved to the far end of the kitchen table and sat down. "As I said before, it was a tragedy. We don't like to talk about it."

"But Sally witnessed it," Kameelah pressed.

"Yes, she was in the house when it happened."

"And then she disappeared?"

"That's correct." Father Black lifted his mug to his lips but didn't drink. "I'm sure she was frightened, but I'm also sure she didn't mean to become lost and disappear. We searched for her but came up empty. The police, I might add, were not helpful."

"And she's never come back? Never visited?"

Father Black blew across the top of his cup and took a sip. "Not to my knowledge."

"Could she have visited without your knowledge?" Jersey asked.

Father Black's lips creased into a thin smile. "No."

"Have any members of your church been to Seattle or Portland lately?"

"No."

"You sound awfully sure," said Jersey.

"I am. We are a close-knit community. We don't keep secrets from one another."

"And why would a trip to Seattle be a secret?" Kameelah asked.

"It wouldn't," said Father Black. "But unlike your world, we look out for one another here. If a member of our church were planning a trip to a major city, he would make sure everyone knew in case something was needed that couldn't be acquired locally. No one has planned any such trips in recent memory."

"Did you ever stop looking?" Jersey asked. "For Sally, that is?"

Father Black placed his mug on the table and rubbed his face in a blatant display of weariness. "Yes. We gave up and moved on with our lives. Is that a crime?"

"Not at all, I was just—" Jersey stopped as the back door opened and a younger man walked into the kitchen. Like Father Black, he was dressed in black pants and a collarless black shirt. The only thing missing was the white collar.

The man didn't lift his head until he had fully entered the room. When he did look up, he was startled by the sight of the two strangers sitting at the table.

Jersey stared at his face. Beneath a mop of wavy, jet-black hair, the right side of the man's face was blistered and raw.

"Uh, sorry," the man stammered, "I didn't know you had company."

Father Black pushed back from the table and stood. "That's okay, son. The detectives were just leaving."

Jersey took another swallow of coffee, making no show of getting up from the table.

"Tell me," he said to the newcomer, "you been to Spokane lately?"

75

The younger man glanced at his father, then quickly shook his head. "I haven't left home in months."

"You sure?" Jersey asked.

"Yes. Positive."

"Only, we received a report of a man with facial scars matching yours from a gas station in Spokane. He had a woman with him. A very frightened woman."

"My son," Father Black interrupted, "burned his face only yesterday. It was an accident with a cup of coffee. You can ask our doctor."

"Strange accident," said Kameelah.

"Indeed, but there you are. These things happen."

"And what happened to your lip?" asked Jersey. "It looks like—"

"Being clumsy is not a crime, detective," Father Black boomed. "I would like you to leave now."

"I still have questions."

"But no jurisdiction, am I correct?"

Jersey shrugged. "It's a gray area."

"I think not."

Father Black moved forward until he loomed over the sitting detective. On the other side of the table, Kameelah got to her feet, her body language tense. Growing uncomfortable beneath the man's unflinching glare, Jersey finally pushed back his chair and rose to his full height. Without giving any ground, he stared into the minister's flat eyes.

"I'll be phoning our lawyer," Father Black said. "We have a special church ceremony happening today, and your presence will be disturbing to our congregation."

"Why?" Jersey tilted his head forward, closing the gap until their noses almost touched. "You got something to hide?"

Father Black took a step back, the muscles in his face pulsating as if something underneath the skin was struggling to break out. His words had to squeeze through clenched teeth. "We have nothing to hide, but our rituals can be misunderstood by non-believers."

"You quoting Jim Jones now?" Jersey quipped.

"How dare you!" The son rushed forward and stood shoulder to shoulder with his father. Despite their similar attire, they actually looked nothing alike except, Jersey thought, for the eyes. Their eyes were soulless. "I suggest you leave before my father is forced to take this matter to a higher authority."

Kameelah placed a hand on Jersey's shoulder and gave it a squeeze.

Jersey remained stiff, unyielding. He focused his attention on the younger man.

"Forget Spokane," he said. "How about a clearing in the woods outside Seattle, near the Mission of the Immaculate Heart? Ring any bells?"

"I demand that you leave," Father Black insisted.

Jersey kept his gaze locked on the younger man. "Two nuns were attacked by some cowardly son-of-a-bitch. He stripped them and beat them until they were barely recognizable as human beings."

"I-I don't—"

Father Black shut down his son with a look.

"There was DNA," Jersey lied. "This bastard was vicious, but he wasn't as careful as he should've been. Plus, he made one very,

very big mistake." Jersey waited, his eyes scanning the younger man's scarred face.

"Get out NOW!" Father Black's face was near crimson.

Kameelah squeezed Jersey's shoulder again. Her grip was strong, her fingers like pincers.

"Do you know what that mistake was?" Jersey asked.

Jersey watched the son attempt to look away, but he followed him, eyes boring deep. Jersey's lips curled in a cruel sneer. "His big mistake was one any amateur could make." He took a breath, drawing it out. "He left one of his victim's alive."

The man blanched, and in that brief, flickering moment Jersey knew for certain, he was the one.

FATHER BLACK FOLLOWED Jersey to the front door, his hands vibrating by his side as he struggled to refrain from wrapping them around the detective's neck and using his thumbs to crush the cop's vertebrae to powder.

Kameelah exited the house first, but just as Jersey stepped over the threshold, he unexpectedly spun back around. Father Black stumbled, caught off-guard by the surprise move.

Jersey opened his mouth and yelled one word at the top of his lungs: "Sally!"

UPSTAIRS, SALLY HEARD her name and, though she couldn't be positive, recognized the caller: *Jersey.*

Instantly, she struggled to break free of Helen's grasp. The old woman was caught by surprise, but Father Black had trained her well. As Sally squirmed, Helen used the weight of her body to hold her captive still. And when Sally scratched at her hand to loosen her fingers, Helen clamped her other hand on top, sealing Sally's mouth further and making it impossible for any noise to escape.

But Sally had more in her arsenal than her mouth. With a frantic lurch, she flung herself off the bed.

Their two bodies hit the floor with a heavy thump. And before Helen could readjust her grip, Sally started to bang her heels.

JERSEY GLANCED UP at the sound of something heavy hitting the floor above, but before he could react, Father Black placed both hands on his chest and shoved him out the door.

Jersey stumbled backwards off the porch and over the lip of the steps, unable to find his balance until he was caught in Kameelah's surprisingly strong arms.

"She's in there," he yelled before breaking free and rushing back.

Jersey pounded on the door and twisted the handle, but the door was locked and no one was answering.

76

Jersey pounded on the door with one fist and reached for his weapon with the other. Before he could pull the Glock from its holster, Kameelah rushed up the stairs and latched onto his arm.

"She's inside," Jersey rasped, emotion torturing his throat.

"How do you know?" Kameelah kept a firm grip on his arm.

"I heard… " he hesitated, knowing it sounded weak even as the words left his lips. "It was a thump. A loud thump. Sally's upstairs."

"That's not enough, Jersey, you know that. If you didn't hear a voice or a cry for help… that thump could've been anything."

Jersey stopped pounding on the door and turned to Kameelah. His face was flushed; his eyes crazed.

"You saw that man's face, he matches the description from the gas station. You also saw his reaction when I mentioned Sister Fleur was alive."

"I did," Kameelah said carefully, "but we can't break the door down based on assumption."

"Fuck the law," Jersey seethed. "I just want Sally."

Kameelah moved closer to him and stroked his other arm. The move was so intimate, it was almost a hug.

"Then let's make sure we get her out safely. You don't know

what room she's in or what the level of threat is. They could be armed and now they're frightened. We have to think like cops, it's what we're best at."

"She might not have time for us to act like cops."

"They need her, Jersey. If she's in there, she's alive. Why else would they be holding a ceremony they don't want us to see?"

Jersey inhaled sharply through his nose, inflating his lungs to their maximum, before releasing it through his mouth. He did this three more times, before asking, "So what's your plan?"

77

The back of Father Black's hand struck his son's cheek with the force of a shovel striking stone.

Aedan was knocked to his knees, his shoulder colliding painfully with the kitchen doorframe. Stunned, he barely had time to raise his hands in defense before two more knuckled blows glanced off his ears and scalp.

"You led them here," screamed Father Black, spittle flying from his lips. "How could you be so careless?"

"I didn't, I wasn't," squealed Aedan. He cradled his head in his hands in an effort to ward off another attack. "They're guessing."

"Guessing? Guessing?" Father Black lashed out again at his cowering son. This time he used his feet and landed a heavy blow against Aedan's exposed hip. "They said you attacked two nuns. Who were they?"

Aedan peeked out from behind the protective shelter of his arms. "I heard her on the Internet. A radio podcast."

"Who?"

"Fleur."

Father Black gasped and staggered back a step as though his son had struck a retaliatory blow. The rage drained from his face to be replaced with confusion. "Fleur White?"

Aedan blinked. "She was preaching at a mission in Seattle. I heard one of her messages on the Internet. I recognized her voice, she always had that distinct—"

"I remember." Father Black shook his head in disbelief. "Fleur White is alive."

"You always suspected an insider was involved with Salvation's disappearance, and you were right…" Aedan looked up at his father's rigid face, "but it wasn't the Greens. I tracked Fleur down and made her talk."

"You had no right to keep this from me," hissed Father Black.

Aedan shook off his words, leaving only the oldest, most hurtful to maintain their grip.

"Everything is a lie with you, father. You never told me the truth about what happened to the House of White, but I understand." Aedan stared into his father's eyes, struggling to express his emotions. "I don't know what the Seer told you before she died, but I do know you had to consolidate the church. I know you had to save us, that it was ordained."

Father Black rubbed at his eyes, but remained mute. He waited for his son to continue.

"The House of White was wiped out a whole month before the Seer was killed. Fleur didn't know why, only that you and your brothers argued, and then the death squad came for her family. She said you had a mass grave dug in the forest behind our walls. She remembered being marched into the woods, but little else. When she regained consciousness, she was actually buried under fresh dirt and had to claw her way out, climbing over the dead bodies of her husband and children. Your soldiers' bullets missed her vital organs, father. A careless mistake."

Father Black didn't move or blink, and his breathing was so shallow, he barely looked alive.

Aedan said, "She went into hiding, but it was only a short time before Uncle Blue lost his mind and killed the Seer, then himself. Fleur suspected you had something to do with that, too."

Father Black offered no response.

"Fleur found Salvation before we did," Aedan said, "and she's been hiding her ever since. It took a long time, and a lot of pain, before she told me that Salvation was working at a funeral parlor in Portland. Can you believe that? Surrounded by the dead and no clue about who she really was."

Father Black narrowed his eyes into piercing slits. "They said you left one of the nuns alive. Was it Fleur?"

Aedan looked away, hurt by his father's focus on his only mistake. "I thought they were both dead. I-I was sure…" His voice drifted.

Father Black's eyes softened and his mouth curled into the semblance of a smile. "The last of the Whites…"

He held out his hand and helped his son to his feet. "Go help your mother."

When Aedan reluctantly started to move, Father Black seemed to reconsider and clamped a hand on his son's shoulder to stop him. He leaned in close.

"When today's ceremony is over, you will return to Seattle and make sure the White lineage is ended once and for all. No more mistakes."

78

Sally wanted to weep when the bedroom door opened and, instead of Jersey, Aedan stormed in. Several large blisters had burst open on the burned side of his face and a sickeningly yellow puss oozed down his rubescent cheek.

Mother released her grip as soon as reinforcements arrived, and Sally quickly scrambled onto her bed and backed into the far corner. Aedan strode forward, his eyes burning coal, nostrils flaring.

"Don't you dare touch me," Sally warned. "I'll scream so loud, they'll hear me from two counties away."

Aedan stopped at the foot of her bed, his hands clenching and unclenching by his side. He began chewing the inside of his cheek as he struggled to form words.

"Who was here?" Sally asked in defiance of the danger. "Was it Jersey?"

"It was the sheriff," Aedan snapped. "*Our* sheriff. He's a member of the church and wanted to make sure you weren't going to disappoint us at the ceremony."

Sally's face fell. "Why did he shout my name?"

Aedan snorted. "He didn't, that was me. I ran into a cupboard door, and your name was the first curse that sprang to mind."

Sally didn't believe him and told him so.

"Like I care," Aedan snarled. "The only thing you need to

believe is the amount of pain I will cause if you don't do as you're told at the ceremony."

Sally pulled her mother's quilt around her legs. She tried to be strong, but her lips formed a trembling pout and her voice cracked. "I don't know what message you want to hear."

"You will," said Aedan, "even if I have to force it down your damn throat myself."

MOTHER FOUND FATHER Black sitting at the kitchen table with a mug of hot coffee in his hand. He smiled and beckoned her over beside him.

Mother was so taken aback by his sudden change of mood that she almost bolted from the room in panic. His failure to notice her rumpled dress, or the terrible mess her hair was in from wrestling with Sally, was troubling, but her place was to obey. Flattening the front of her dress as best she could and ignoring her wayward hair, she crossed to him.

"Fleur White is alive," he said, his eyes glistening with delight.

Mother gasped. "Impossible."

"No, no, don't you see?" Father Black laughed. "This explains everything."

"I don't understand." Mother pulled out a chair and sat.

"The Seer's prophecy," Father Black explained, "said the House of White would be our downfall. I believed I had taken care of that, but now to discover that Fleur survived explains all our troubles. Once she's truly dead, our church will rise from the ashes and be reborn in a glorious light."

Father Black's face lit up like a thousand watt bulb. "Don't you see? Everything is finally coming together. The return of the Seer, reopening the Houses, and soon the final destruction of the Whites. Our church will be stronger than ever."

Father Black leaned forward and kissed his wife full on the lips. Mother was so surprised, she almost fainted.

79

Jersey watched a steady parade of gleaming, hand-washed and Sunday-waxed, cars glide down the gravel driveway to park in the small meadow that fronted the gated entrance to the church courtyard. None of the families who climbed from the cars paid him or Kameelah any attention, nor did they seem to find it odd that four large men in black suits had taken up position beside the open gates.

Jersey leaned his hip against the Jaguar. "You think they've been told to avoid us?"

"Either that," said Kameelah, "or they just naturally distrust anyone who isn't a member of the congregation."

"They look so normal," Jersey mused.

"What were you expecting?"

"Well, if that girl's blog is to be believed, they're a bunch of granny killers. I expected something more gothic."

"My, what big teeth you have," teased Kameelah.

"Yeah, okay," Jersey agreed. "But you have to admit, ritual sacrifice usually doesn't go hand-in-hand with your best Sunday suit."

"Maybe they dress in costumes once the children are sent outside. That's when they'll bring in Sally and the real ceremony begins."

Jersey nodded grimly. "I could see that."

THE PRODIGIOUS HOUSE on the right side of the gate was where Jersey believed Sally was being held. The house to the left of the gate was a near mirror image, except its front door was painted black instead of blue and the circular stained glass window in the attic resembled the sharp-toothed terror of a gaping maw rather than an all-seeing eye. There was no sign of life inside. No lights, no smoke, no movement.

Before the congregation started to arrive, Jersey had attempted to walk the outside perimeter of the sizeable property to get a lay of the land. The woods at the rear proved too thick to allow an easy circuit, and he had to twice double back.

In the rear corners, however, he had been able to view the upper floors of two more stately homes, both secured behind the high wall. Unlike the two homes in the front, neither house had access to the outside world except via the large gateway.

Like the house with the black door, those two homes also appeared empty. Despite the chill in the air, no smoke drifted from their chimneys and every window was sealed behind heavy wooden shutters as though the owners had been expecting an unlikely hurricane to suddenly rip through the area.

When he returned to the car, Jersey had borrowed Kameelah's touch-screen cellphone to launch Google Earth and call up a satellite map of the compound. From the overhead map, he was able to see that the original design of the compound was obviously for four families to tend the impressive gardens around a centrally located, circular church.

Unfortunately, the satellite image also confirmed his own observation that the place was a veritable fortress.

He turned to ask Kameelah a question, but she was busy working the phone, trying to get local police and county courts to give them any excuse to enter the church before somebody else's grandmother had her throat slit. So far, she wasn't having any luck.

As Kameelah explained it, everyone was frightened of messing with religion after the Branch Davidian and Yearning for Zion disasters that had blown up in the faces of law-enforcement agencies in recent years. A teen's blog and a cop's suspicion, the detective was told, wasn't nearly enough to justify a warrant.

Jersey was watching another clean-cut family of four walk through the compound gates when his cellphone rang. He flipped it open and held it to his ear.

"Don't answer your phone." It was his partner, Amarela.

"What?" The phone beeped, indicating a second call. "Hold on." Jersey switched to the second call.

"Where the hell are you, detective?" barked Lieutenant Morrell. "I've just had a phone call from the Commander, who has received calls from both the Mayor and the Director of the fucking F.B.I. The Commander does not like receiving phone calls from the F.B.I., and I certainly don't like—"

"I'm following a case, sir. I'm sure my partner—"

"Don't bullshit me," Morrell snapped. "I have the biggest and best bullshit detector in the entire northern hemisphere, do I make myself clear?"

"Crystal, sir." Jersey thought quickly and his earlier conversation with Amarela suddenly snapped into focus. He launched an attack. "But you should know I was informed that Peter Higgins went missing along with his daughter. You wanted us to find them. My partner said it was a priority."

Morrell hesitated. "Uh… yes, but—"

"I believe they're here," Jersey said quickly. "Detective Valente interviewed Higgins' wife and discovered a link to the Church of a Sabbath Day's Journey. Since I was in the neighborhood, I decided to check it out. I believe both our missing persons could be here."

"Have you seen them?" Morrell asked cautiously.

"No, sir. The church won't allow us inside."

"And that's why the F.B.I is calling the Mayor?"

"Must be, sir. I tried to be polite in asking to make sure that

Peter and his daughter were okay, but the church won't release that information. I'm sure the mayor will understand that we want to make sure they're not in any danger or being held against their will."

"And the missing woman from the mortuary. Is she there, too?" asked the lieutenant, showing that his bullshit detector did actually work.

"I believe she is."

"But you haven't seen her either?"

"No, sir. The church is not being cooperative."

Lieutenant Morrell sighed heavily into the phone. "If I was to read between the lines, detective, would I be right in assuming that you're following the assumption that Peter Higgins is not only involved in the murder of his parents, but in an effort to elude justice he has kidnapped a possible eye witness and transported her to a remote church in North Dakota?"

"Something like that," Jersey said grudgingly

"But you have no solid evidence of either the murders or the kidnapping?"

"Apart from two dead bodies, a missing woman, and a suspect on the run, no."

Lieutenant Morrell sighed again. "You're out of your jurisdiction, detective, and there's nothing I can do from here to help. I'll pass the information on to the F.B.I. If you're right, the kidnapper has crossed several state lines, which automatically makes this a federal case. You will have to stand aside on this one."

Jersey gritted his teeth, and lobbed one last grenade. "Don't you think the mayor would be disappointed to find that not only did his interference help a multiple murderer escape arrest, but after tracking the suspect down, his only officer on the scene wasn't allowed to bring him into custody?"

There was a long pause before Morrell said, "You don't know that Peter Higgins murdered his parents or kidnapped your witness. You also don't know that he's where you say he is. Unless you find proof, I would say you're hanging from the end of a very thin rope. And just so we're clear, Detective Castle, I'm holding the fucking scissors."

AFTER MORRELL HUNG up, the phone automatically switched back to the first caller.

"You answered the damn phone, didn't you?" said Amarela.

Jersey laughed, releasing a gust of frustration. "Yeah, I answered the damn phone."

"I don't know why I try to help, you never listen. What did the lieutenant say?"

Jersey told her, and when he was finished, Amarela said, "The only help you're going to get is with cleaning out your desk. The boss is in full-blown, cover-his-own-ass mode."

"That's probably just as well," said Jersey. "I operate better when I've got nothing left to lose."

"ONE PIECE OF information," said Amarela. "I don't know if it helps."

"Go on."

"The Higgins family changed their name—twice."

"That's unusual," said Jersey. "What was it before?"

"Before Higgins, they went by Green. Peter was born under that name, but before Green, the late Mr. Higgins was Mr. Black. Mean anything?"

"The minister who runs the church is Father Black," mused Jersey. "Could be a relative. Brother, maybe?"

"So Peter's gone home."

"Yeah," Jersey sighed, "but why?"

80

Sally stood in front of the bathroom mirror and wiped tears from her eyes.

"You have your father's mouth and chin," said Helen from the doorway.

Sally turned. "And my mother's eyes."

"Yes," said Helen grimly, "unfortunately so."

Sally was led downstairs to the kitchen. Thick curtains had been drawn across the shutters to further block the windows and the room was dim. Behind her, curtains in the living room were also drawn.

Father Black took her arm and four large men took up position around them. Two in front, the second pair in the rear. If Sally had any thoughts of running, they were immediately dismissed.

Father Black led her out the back door and down a short flight of steps to a gravel path that curved around a perfectly mowed lawn. As they walked, Sally heard the heavy scrape of metal on wood. She turned to see the giant front gates being secured with a metal crossbar.

No one was getting in, she thought, and no one was getting out.

Father Black squeezed her arm and led her to the church.

81

Jersey watched the gates slam shut and felt a deep hollow open in his chest.

Beside him, Kameelah yanked the phone from her ear and cursed. "I've been ordered back to Seattle. The fucking F.B.I. called my lieutenant."

"What's the murder of a nun compared to the public relations nightmare of entering a church without an invite?" Jersey asked dryly.

"Man, if this was Stalinist Russia or Nazi Germany, we could just kick the fucking door down."

"Price we pay for freedom, I guess," said Jersey.

"So what's our plan?"

Jersey turned to Kameelah, his face devoid of humor. "We kick the fucking door down."

BEFORE EITHER OF them could make a move, the sound of thunder rolled in from the west, the rumble growing in intensity until seven gleaming Harley Davidson Fat Boys turned the corner and roared into the meadow.

The seven bikes formed a loose semi-circle in front of the detectives before the riders shut off their engines. Each mechanical beast was kitted out western style with dusty leather saddlebags, circular two-quart water canteens and, within easy reach, the stiff coils of a calf-roping lariat.

If the rodeo-grade lasso wasn't puzzling enough, strapped across each gas tank was a fringed leather scabbard that appeared to carry in the case of two of the riders, a Winchester rifle, and in the other five, a long-barreled Remington shotgun.

Jersey's hand moved away from his gun and his mouth twitched in relief when the leader of the leather-clad pack pulled a dusty bandanna from around her mouth and slipped off her helmet.

The woman's hair was the stark color of a canary.

82

Sally was led down concrete steps to the cellar beneath the church. Once she was inside, the four guards left to join their families in the sanctuary above.

Father Black checked the iron chain that bound Sally's ankle to the podium.

"It won't always be like this." His hand skimmed her bare ankle. "Once you accept your rightful place in our family, you'll see just how wonderful life here can be." His fingers ran up her calf and stroked the toned muscle. "The Seer is our link to God. You're the deliverer of His message. You are vital to our Journey."

"But I don't want to be a Seer," said Sally, her voice soft, non-combative. "I just want to go home."

"But you are home, dear." Father Black released her leg and stood tall. He stared deep into her eyes. "I know you were unprepared last time, that, in my excitement, I rushed you. I shoulder the blame for that decision. Twenty-five years without hearing the message made me impatient. But this time you must concentrate. You must bring us back the holy message."

"I would, if only I knew—"

Father Black snapped up his hand as if to strike, but he held it fast, the muscles in his arm quivering. His voice deepened into a growl. "You will know the message when you hear it. All you need do is listen."

Father Black reached out to place his hands on either side of Sally's face. He moved in quickly, his lips locking onto hers in a fierce kiss. Her eyes widened in shock as he sucked her lips between his own with an intense, bruising passion. When he released her, he spun away and moved quickly to his own podium.

Sally looked over at Helen in disbelief, but the woman's returning stare was so intense, Sally quickly turned away again.

83

Sister Mary Theresa slid off her bike and stretched her back. Her leathers creaked with every controlled movement and puffs of dust billowed around her like smoke. At the same time, her distractingly bright yellow hair reflected the sunlight like a ship's beacon.

The other sisters removed their helmets, too. Each one had dyed her hair a vibrant shade: purple, blue, green, red, orange, and pink. The hair was distracting, drawing you away from their faces.

Jersey looked past the hair, but didn't recognize any of the other six. They were all relatively young and looked in good physical shape—especially wrapped in leather.

"Sister Gillian couldn't make it?" Jersey asked while he tried to absorb and make sense of the unexpected scene.

Sister Mary Theresa smiled. "Sister Gillian takes care of the mission. She finds the longer road trips a touch tiring now."

Jersey raised an eyebrow, unable to picture the older nun on a bike. "But she rides, too?"

Sister Mary Theresa smiled wider. "Absolutely. She's one of our most devoted angels."

"Angels?"

Sister Mary Theresa spread her arms to encompass her pack. "What else would you call us?"

Jersey was at a loss for words, so Kameelah stepped in. "What brings you here?"

"Sister Fleur regained consciousness," said the nun. "She told us more about the Church of a Sabbath Day's Journey than what appeared in her notes. She also revealed more about Salvation, the woman you know as Sally."

"We found a few disturbing facts ourselves," said Kameelah.

"You know of Sally's gift?"

Kameelah nodded.

"And the blood sacrifice?" Sister Mary Theresa asked.

"We found a young girl's blog on the 'Net," said Jersey. "It was overly dramatic, but she was under the impression the church kills people in order to spark a vision."

Sister Mary Theresa steepled her fingers and leaned one hip against her bike. "That's what Sister Fleur was trying to stop when she took Salvation away from this place. She believed that without a Seer, the church would have no reason for being. It appears she was wrong and the sacrifices continued." She turned her head to look at the sealed gates. "This is an evil place."

"Created in the name of God," said Jersey.

Sister Mary Theresa faced front again. "Created by man for his own ego, detective. God has nothing to do with this."

Kameelah spoke up. "Do you believe Sally has this gift? Is it even possible?"

Sister Mary Theresa shrugged. "The Lord moves in mysterious ways, and if He gave her this gift it should be celebrated, not exploited for evil."

"So, as Kameelah already asked," said Jersey, "what brings you here?"

Sister Mary Theresa fixed her gaze on Jersey. "Do you have permission to enter?"

"No, we've been called off."

"But you believe Salvation is inside?"

"Yes."

"Are you planning to leave?"

Jersey glanced at Kameelah. "No."

Sister Mary Theresa smiled. "Then we're here to help."

Jersey turned to Kameelah again. "You should head back to Seattle. Staying here could mean your badge."

"You should come with me," she said.

Jersey shook his head. "That option ran out the instant Sally asked for my help."

Kameelah looked at the ground, her eyes hardening as she came to a decision. "I can't join you."

"I know," said Jersey. "Seattle needs all the good cops it can get."

Jersey turned to the nuns. "We know that Sally will be inside the church after the children are sent outside. At that time, the adult congregation will be preparing for their blood ceremony, and we need to be ready to move." He turned to face the gate. "The first order of business is getting those doors open so we can get inside."

Sister Mary Theresa turned to her pack of nuns and quickly gave instructions. Instantly, two nuns broke right and two went left. Each pair glided their bikes silently away from the gate until they reached the far side of the two homes. Hidden from view of anyone looking out, the nuns propped their sturdy machines against the eight-foot stone wall.

As Jersey watched, the ninja-black nuns hopped onto their saddles, stood up tall, and scrambled over the wall. One half of each pair carried a lariat, the other, a shotgun. The maneuver was so perfectly executed, Jersey wondered if the Mission of the Immaculate Heart had been recruiting women from the Navy Seals.

84

Sally could hear Father Black preaching to the crowd above. He was on fire, impassioned, telling them of his mistake in rushing the Seer to her task, begging their forgiveness, promising them glory and the rebirth of the church in God's everlasting light.

The crowd ate it up.

"He's a wonderful man." Helen moved in close to Sally until her lips were mere inches from her ear. "But he's consumed by the church and the legacy of his father. He doesn't realize that God already made His judgment. Your mother tricked him, and he's so blind he still doesn't see it, even after all these years."

"What do you mean?" Sally asked.

Helen moved behind Sally, her breath warm and moist on the young woman's neck. Her voice crackled with hatred. "Your mother was a liar, a witch, and a whore who wanted every man to lust over her."

Sally stayed mute. How could she honestly defend a woman she barely remembered?

Helen continued, "She twisted every message brought back from the Journey to suit her own needs. She told Father what he wanted to hear until he became putty in her hands and then her true colors shone. She molded him and slipped ideas into his mind. She was responsible for the death of the Whites. They were the bravest and the strongest of us, until your mother turned Father against them."

Helen continued to move in a circle until she was facing Sally. She licked her lips, but her tongue failed to provide moisture. "That was God's judgment. The death of the Whites was the death of our church. Your father knew that." Helen paused, then opened her lips to expose a jagged row of uneven teeth. "Why do you think he killed your mother? He was the kind one, the only one…" Her hand drifted to absently caress her crimson cheek, then she angrily snapped, "He knew exactly what an evil bitch she was."

Sally didn't rise to the taunt and Helen appeared disappointed. She cocked her head to one side, puzzled. "Did you know that, too?"

A roar erupted from above their heads as the audience cheered Father Black's announcement of the reopening of the Houses of Blue and Green. The cellar door opened amidst the noise and Aedan entered. He was dressed in his flowing black robes with the silk hangman's hood clutched in his hand.

He practically ran to Sally's side, his eagerness forcing his mother to one side.

"Are you ready?" Aedan asked. His frantic eyes bore into her, the white orbs a roadmap of red veins and his dark-matter pupils so large they practically swallowed the stormy brown of each iris.

Sally shook her head. "I'll never be ready."

He grabbed her right arm and squeezed the muscle, his sharp thumbnail cutting into flesh. "I can break this one, too."

Sally winced and groaned. "Okay, okay."

He let go and stood back. "Do you know what Father wants to hear?"

Sally shrugged and Aedan jerked forward so quickly, she feared he was going to snap her neck. Instead, he pushed his forehead against hers and locked his stare.

"I don't know what happens on the Journey," he said, his voice barely above a whisper yet sparking with malice. "I was too young to witness your mother's travels and hear the messages she delivered, but I know my father. He needs you to tell the congregation that their loved ones have traveled to the Promised Land where they are safe and happy and bathing in the glory of His light. You may receive messages for individuals from those who have crossed over, but the most important message is the one for Father. You need to tell him of the church's future, of its rebirth and renewed strength. If you remember nothing else, remember that or the pain you have experienced so far will be nothing to what is to come. Do you understand?"

Sally wanted to avert her gaze but there was no escaping Aedan's piercing coal-black eyes.

Aedan pressed his forehead harder against Sally's until her skull was about to crack.

"Yes," she blurted. "Yes, I understand."

Aedan released her. "I'll be watching."

He retreated to the cellar door just as Sally's podium shuddered in preparation to ascend.

85

Jersey gazed across the meadow parking lot to watch Kameelah climb into her Jaguar. Her body was stiff with reluctance, and her face dark with regret. Jersey offered up an encouraging smile as she waved goodbye before he swung the gates closed and crept onto church grounds.

It had only taken the four agile nuns a few short minutes to tie up the guards and unlock the gates, gaining him entry.

With the seven leather-clad angels on foot around him, Jersey quickly moved toward the front door of the central church building. Secure in the impregnability of their massive front gates, the church hadn't posted any other guards aside from the two, now unconscious, gatekeepers.

Once the pack reached the walls of the church, the angels spread out to peer through wooden slats and see inside.

From over the shoulders and heads of a packed audience, Jersey watched a massive wood-burning fire pit, contained inside a circular metal pan, rise to the ceiling on coiled strands of tensile steel.

Behind the fire, Father Black's face glowed with anticipation as he raised his hands to the ceiling in perfect pace with the fire. And then, filling the void where the hearth had been, a small woman in a flowing white dress, her left arm cradled in a matching white sling, ascended from a hole in the floor.

She had shock white hair and glistening green eyes: *Sally*.

When her podium locked into place, everyone inside the church jumped to their feet and applauded.

Jersey used the distraction to move to the side of Sister Mary Theresa.

"Sally's inside," he said.

"When do we move?"

Jersey mulled it over. "The children are a problem. Once they're outside and the real ceremony begins, we should be able to rush in, grab Sally and get the hell out before they have time to rally against us. I don't see any weapons, so if we can do it without violence, so much the better."

Sister Mary Theresa nodded. "We'll be ready."

Jersey moved back to his position and waited.

Once the crowd had settled down, Father Black indicated it was time for the children to leave.

Jersey and the nuns moved quickly out of sight as the front doors opened and at least forty pairs of tiny feet rushed down the steps and vanished in a thunderblust of excited noise into the maze of gardens.

86

After the children exited, Sally looked out upon the excited congregation and wondered what she was going to do.

The doors at the front of the church clanged shut and Father Black clapped his hands together. "Bring forward the Travelers."

From the last row, a young man stood and moved behind an elderly woman in a wheelchair. The woman wore an ill-fitting dress in a distressing shade of crimson that made her bloodless skin even whiter. Her head lolled onto her shoulder as though her neck muscles couldn't hold the weight, and her eyelids flickered, the tiny muscles stuck somewhere between asleep and awake. Her wrinkled face was obscured by a clear plastic oxygen mask, the life-giving tank affixed to the wheelchair.

The man nibbled his lower lip as he slowly pushed the wheelchair down the aisle to the stone altar. The congregation offered him words of encouragement and support as he passed each row.

Once they reached the altar, the man lifted the woman's limp arms onto the stone basin and removed her mask. The woman didn't fight him, her slack expression unchanged. The young man barely glanced at Sally as he placed the mask on top of the oxygen tank and twisted its valve closed.

He turned to the congregation and cleared his throat. "My

mama suffered a stroke while the surgeons operated on a tumor that hid undiscovered behind her liver until it was the size of my fist." He held up his fist to demonstrate, and his eyes fought back tears. "Cancer, the Devil's last laugh. Before the stroke, the doctors gave her six months to live. Since then, they say they don't know how she's still alive." The man wiped at his eyes and stood up tall, proud. "But I know. She didn't want to go on the Journey alone."

The crowd cheered and a chorus of Hallelujahs rang out.

The man glanced over his shoulder at Sally before continuing. "She wanted the Seer to guide her, to make sure she reached the other side without the Devil's tricks and lures making her take a wrong turn."

Amens erupted.

"My papa is waiting for her, and she's ready to go."

The crowd of onlookers stomped their feet and clapped their hands as the man walked back to his seat through a sea of reaching hands and smiling faces.

When the congregation had calmed down, a slim man in his mid-thirties stood up. He was dressed in an unusually fashionable monotone suit and his dark beard was perfectly sculpted to show off his cheekbones and hide a weak chin.

Standing next to him, dressed in a candied apple red gown, was April.

Sally shook her head and felt her whole body tremble as the man took April by the hand and led her down the aisle to the stone altar.

"No," Sally said weakly, "no, you can't do this."

Helen rushed to Sally's side.

"Hush, girl," she hissed. "This can be made painful for her if you wish it."

As father and daughter reached the altar, April looked up at Sally and beamed. "You're all clean and… and pretty. Do… do you like my dress?"

Sally swallowed a cry. "It's very pretty," she said.

April's father bent down and spoke in her ear, telling her to place her arms in the stone basin and to stay by the altar no matter what happened.

As he returned to his seat, he didn't say a word to support his decision to offer up his daughter, as if the obvious fact she had Down Syndrome was enough. Sally scanned the audience, desperate to find someone else who found this obscene. But everyone she saw was smiling.

Father Black clapped his hands together again. "Bring out the Deliverer."

A door opened at the rear of the hall, and Sally craned her neck to watch Aedan enter. His dark eyes burned behind slits in the hangman's hood.

The audience began to chant in prayer as Aedan moved closer to the altar.

Sally swung around to face Father Black, her back to the audience. "You can't do this," she said. "I won't let you."

Helen jumped onto Sally's podium and grabbed her forcibly by the shoulders. "We'll make the girl suffer if you cause us any trouble. Is that what you want?"

Sally didn't know how to answer, so in response, she did the only thing her terrified mind would let her: she opened her mouth and screamed.

87

Jersey was rushing the front doors when he heard Sally's scream. A further jolt of adrenaline instantly flooded his bloodstream, and he hit the doors with a full-fledged NFL-style shoulder tackle.

The tremendous blow made the doors shudder in their frames, but neither one flew open.

They were bolted solid from the inside.

SALLY STOPPED SCREAMING when, along with the rest of the congregation, she heard the heavy thud against the front door. But before she could process what it meant, her focus was diverted by Aedan's knife at her throat.

"No more fucking games," Aedan hissed. The thin silk hood was sucked so deep into his mouth it formed a bottomless well ringed with sharp black teeth. It could have been the gateway to Hell itself.

Sally screamed again as Aedan leapt from her podium with incredible energy and, with one powerful swing, slashed his long knife across the throat of the wheelchair-bound woman at the altar.

The cut was so deep, he almost decapitated her.

Blood sprayed from the woman's neck with such volcanic force, it was like a tsunami. Aedan, standing directly in its path, became drenched in it.

As the horrified congregation looked on, Aedan ripped off his blood-soaked hood. His eyes were wide, bulging, crazed, his mouth open wide in a silent, primal scream.

Then he rushed at April.

JERSEY SPUN TO Sister Mary Theresa, his shoulder rubbery and his eyes wide with panic.

"Get the bikes!" he yelled. "Break this fucking door down."

Jersey took off at a run, desperate to find another entrance to the church sanctuary.

SALLY YELLED, "STOP! Aedan please, I'll tell you everything if you spare her."

Aedan's knife hovered at the girl's throat, her hair bunched tightly in his other hand. The terrified girl was crying, begging, snot running from her nose to mix with the blood that was dripping off her executioner's arm.

Aedan glanced over his shoulder, his lips curled in a sneer.

Sally pleaded, "Please. I'll go on the Journey. I'll bring back the message, but you have to spare her." Her eyes turned hard and her voice grew cold. "If you harm her, I'll tell you nothing. Her death seals my silence forever."

"Listen to her, son," said Father Black. "We need her to cooperate. To be part of us."

"You'll stay?" Aedan asked. His eyes shifted as though suddenly regaining focus. "If I spare this girl, you'll join our family and become part of our church?"

"Yes," Sally said with desperate enthusiasm. "Yes, but no harm can come to April. She must be allowed to go home to her mother."

"What is this trickery?" yelled a voice from the congregation. It was April's father. "This is not our way. The Devil cursed the

House of Green with this mockery of a child. Her death lifts the curse and restores the House of Green to its rightful place."

"Silence!" boomed Father Black. "If the Seer portends a future for this child, we must respect her vision. *That* is our way."

Aedan shoved April away, sending her stumbling into Mother's arms. Returning to Sally's side, he slipped his gold-hilted knife back into its leather sheaf and grabbed her by the wrists.

"Time to travel," he hissed and plunged her face first into the stone altar that was already overflowing with the wheelchair woman's blood.

88

Near the rear of the church, Jersey found a door leading to the cellar. He darted down the stairs and yanked on the handle. Unlocked.

With a sigh of gratitude, he opened the door, but before he could dart inside a heavy hand locked onto his collar and yanked him back up the stairs.

Choking on his tightening collar, Jersey looked up to see a large man in a dark suit with a pointed, Egyptian-style beard. The man opened his mouth to offer a threat, but Jersey had already crossed the line of following any rules. Despite the awkward position, Jersey drove his elbow into the soft pillow of the man's throat and followed it with a bruising left elbow to the kidney.

The man released Jersey's collar to clutch at his own throat, his face turning purple. Back on proper footing, Jersey wasn't in the mood to fight clean. Instead, he brought his forehead smashing down onto the bridge of the man's nose. Blood gushed to either side as the nose snapped and the man's eyes rolled in his head.

Jersey took out his legs with a single sweep and shoved the guard away. The man tumbled silently into the garden as Jersey returned to the cellar.

Inside the cellar, Jersey quickly studied the layout, comparing it to what he had seen of the sanctuary above. The room was mostly empty space except for two steel pistons that connected with two circles on the ceiling.

Jersey studied the pistons and noticed two buttons, one green, one red, on the back wall near the smaller circle. He hit the red button and the piston began to sink into the ground with a hiss of escaping air. As it lowered, it brought with it a circular platform.

FATHER BLACK DIDN'T notice his podium sinking into the floor. He was too focused on Sally, having walked forward across the stage to be near her, to be the first to hear the holy message delivered from her lips.

She looked so much like her mother, especially now with her once-white hair turned crimson from the blood.

When she was first plunged into the stone basin, Sally had struggled for breath before her body shuddered and went limp.

Aedan gripped her under the arms, holding her slack body upright, as the Seer departed on the Journey.

JERSEY STEPPED ONTO the platform and hit the green button. The steel piston hissed again and began to rise.

When his head crested the surface, he saw the backs of three people, two men and a woman, huddled around a large stone altar. In front of them, the congregation was silent and open-mouthed as they stared at whatever was happening at the altar.

As soon as his shoulders cleared the hole, Jersey pulled out his Glock and fired into the ceiling.

The noise of the gunshot startled everyone, but the reaction of the priest was the last thing Jersey expected.

While the majority of the congregation jumped to their feet

and rushed for the exit in panic, Father Black spun on his heel and, with a mighty roar, charged directly at Jersey.

He screamed "How dare you!" as he bore down, his face a mask of unbridled fury.

Out of position, still rising through the hole in the stage, Jersey rushed to bring his gun to bear, but he wasn't quick enough.

The priest lashed out with his foot and kicked him in the jaw.

Jersey was knocked backwards and scrambled to grab the side of the circular opening before he lost his footing and went tumbling back into the cellar or was crushed by the rising podium.

Before he could regain his balance, the priest hit him again, the toe of his shoe connecting with Jersey's right wrist and sending the Glock flying from his grasp.

Jersey yelped in pain and rolled to one side as he scrambled out of the hole. In that same instant, the front doors of the church burst open and three angels astride Harley Fat Boys roared down the aisle.

SALLY OPENED HER eyes to chaos. She was clutched in Aedan's arms, her own arms dripping blood from the altar, and the church was in an uproar.

She swiveled her head groggily from side to side, desperate to refocus from her vision, and saw Jersey scrambling across the floor as Father Black lashed out with a sharp foot and sunk it deep into the detective's ribs. Jersey groaned as his body lifted from the impact and he was sent rolling into the rear wall.

Sally was about to call to him when Aedan gripped her tighter and said, "Hold on, this could be rough."

Sally screamed as Aedan buried his knife into an electronic panel and the podium they were standing on dropped like a stone.

•

JERSEY SPOTTED SALLY in the brief instant before her platform dropped out of sight and the giant fireplace plummeted from the ceiling.

The iron hearth hit the stage with an ear-splitting clang that contained all the force of a small bomb to spew massive burning logs and fiery coals in every direction. One of the larger logs hit Father Black square in the back, its velocity so great that Jersey swore he heard the man's spine snap.

The priest was thrown off the stage like dry kindling, any last words lost in a whoosh of flames as the backdrop of curtains ignited.

Alone on the burning stage, Jersey scrambled to his feet.

The church was quickly filling with smoke as the red-hot logs caught everything on fire: walls, floor, curtains, clothing. People screamed and rushed for the only exit, scrambling over and around the three Harleys to escape the building inferno.

Jersey caught Sister Mary Theresa's eye and mouthed, "Get out," before he slammed his hand against a red button and jumped back onto Father Black's podium.

The podium shuddered and dropped.

89

After the podium had descended about three feet, Jersey slid off and dropped the rest of the way to the floor. He landed on his feet and scanned the area just as the door leading outside slammed shut.

Jersey ran for the door and burst into the gardens. He turned to his right and saw dozens of panicked people running around in an attempt to gather up their children and flee the burning church. That way meant chaos. He went left instead.

When he cleared the church building, Jersey spotted movement on a gravel path leading to an eight-foot-tall dead end at the rear of the gardens. With a grateful smile, he yanked his backup Baby Glock from its ankle holster and gave chase.

SALLY TRIED TO fight her way out of Aedan's grasp, but his grip was too strong. He dragged her away from the church toward the stone wall that surrounded the grounds.

"You can't get away," she yelled. "The police will have this place surrounded."

"That's not the police," Aedan spat back. "It's one cop who doesn't know when he's outmatched and outplayed."

Sally wondered if that was true: Was Jersey on his own? Had she brought him here to face all these monsters without backup?

"What about your father?" she gasped as she bounced painfully on Aedan's shoulder. "He could be trapped inside the church. You can't just—"

Sally froze in mid-sentence when she spotted Jersey arriving on the path just a short distance behind them. Her heart soared. He was disheveled and beaten, tired and out of breath, but he also had an aura around him that said he was definitely not defeated.

"Jersey!" she gasped.

JERSEY LOOKED UP at the sound of his name and quickened his pace. He had the son-of-a-bitch cornered now, and there was no way he was letting him get away.

Hold on, Sally, he thought. I'm coming.

AEDAN TURNED LEFT at the end of the pathway and pulled Sally toward a steel door set into the stone wall. When they reached the door, Aedan activated a hidden panel and punched in a four-number code.

A lock clicked somewhere deep inside and the door swung open.

Sally tried to resist as Aedan pushed her through, but he was just too powerful.

JERSEY SPOTTED THE steel door and cursed. He bore down, putting every reserve of strength he had into his legs. His lungs were burning, his mind screaming: he was a fat fuck, and he was never going to make it.

The door slammed back into place just as he reached out to stop its swing, and he crashed into it, gasping, groaning, spitting obscenities in a machine-gun staccato.

He heard Sally call out his name from the other side of the door. Her tone was desperate, pleading. She was depending on him. Trusting him to save her.

Fuuuuuck!

Jersey, his face lashed with sweat, kicked the steel door in frustration and stepped back. The wall was at least eight-feet tall. How was he going to scale that?

A thunderous roar made him turn as two leather-clad angels rode up on their bikes.

Jersey pointed at the wall and wheezed, "I need to get over."

90

Mother held April tightly around the back of the neck, a small paring knife pressed against the girl's flesh. The knife had drawn a thin sliver of blood and it ran around the girl's throat like a scarlet necklace.

Five wild-haired women on motorbikes surrounded them in a loose circle—all but two twirled a lasso over their heads.

Sister Mary Theresa climbed off her bike, her Remington shotgun snug against her shoulder, its large barrel pointed threateningly at the snarling woman's head.

Mother kept trying to make herself smaller, to hide behind her terrified captive, but the nun's aim never wavered.

"Let the girl go, Helen," said Sister Mary Theresa. "It's over."

"How do you know my name?" Mother asked.

"Sister Fleur told me all about you. She said you're the true head of the church, the poison behind the throne."

Mother spat on the ground. "Fleur White was a whore."

"You murdered her husband… her children," said Sister Mary Theresa. "She told me you're the one who used to interpret the Seer's messages."

Mother cackled. "That is my gift. How could we trust anything those witches say? Most of it's nonsense anyway. I gave Father the messages that he needed to make the church strong, but he began to distrust me. He had to hear it directly from the source, so the source had to go. I would've got rid of Salvation, too, if she hadn't run away. I've been searching for years, but it was my own damn son who found her first."

"You killed those young women," said Sister Mary Theresa with a shake of her head. "Sister Fleur told me that when she read about their missing eyes, she suspected it was your hand behind it."

"They weren't Salvation," said Mother sadly, "but I couldn't take the chance that I might have missed something, that they might have possessed the gift. The Seer was our destruction, don't you see? She always had been."

"You cut out their eyes..." Sister Mary Theresa couldn't finish the sentence.

Mother shrugged dismissively. "I had to be sure."

"You're insane."

"And you're not?" Mother laughed again. "Look at you. What kind of nuns dress like this?"

Mother flicked her knife arm in a grand gesture to encompass all the nuns, but as soon as it was away from the girl's throat, a lariat snapped onto her wrist and was instantly pulled tight.

"What the hell?" Mother shook her wrist, but the snare held firm.

"Hey!" Mother yelled as a second lariat fell over her head and encircled her neck.

The second roper started to back up, forcing Mother to stagger backwards to stop from being strangled by the slick rope. Frightened, Mother suddenly moved her free hand to encircle April's throat and her strong fingers tightened like a vice on the girl's larynx.

April's face turned purple and her eyes bulged in panic.

"I'll break her neck," Mother yelled. "I've been strangling chickens all my life, one more don't mean a damned thing to me."

April's strangled whimper was drowned out by the *snap click* lever-action of a Winchester rifle.

Mother spun her head to see one of the bikers aiming the powerful rifle at her head. Beside her, a fourth biker continued to whirl a lariat above her head.

"I'm not kiddin' around," Mother seethed. "I'll break her—"

With a nod from Sister Mary Theresa, the rifle fired, spinning Mother 180-degrees as the large shell tore a chunk out of her shoulder, breaking bone, numbing muscle, and sending a spray of blood high into the air.

Mother screamed in frustration and pain as the third lariat encircled her dangling wrist and was pulled taut.

The three angels quickly backed up their bikes until Mother stood on the tips of her toes with her arms stretched out in right angles to her body as though being sacrificed on the cross.

Released from Mother's grip in the instant the bullet shattered her captor's arm, April stood frozen in shock.

Sister Mary Theresa slid her shotgun back into its scabbard and knelt down. She held out her arms to the scared girl and placed a peaceful, trusting smile on her lips.

After a moment of hesitation, April ran into the nun's arms, buried her face in the woman's shoulder and began to bawl.

Sister Mary Theresa lifted the girl onto her bike and then looked over at her angels, meeting each one's eye in turn. In a low, steady voice, she said, "You've all heard the evidence and her freely-given confession. What's it to be?"

Mother stared at the head nun in horror. "What do you mean? I'm injured, I need medical help, I—"

"Silence!" Sister Mary Theresa hissed. She snatched a palm-sized digital camcorder off the front of her bike and held it up until Mother recognized what it was. "This should give the authorities enough to convict, but will it appease God?"

Mother tried to spit out a retort, but the rope around her neck was suddenly too tight.

Sister Mary Theresa punched the ignition on her bike, its loud rumble drowning out the woman's gurgles of protest.

With the girl clutched tight to her chest, Sister Mary Theresa wheeled her bike around and said over her shoulder, "I'll leave it up to you."

As the nun departed, Mother's bowels loosened.

91

With two nuns standing on the seats of their Harleys and shoving his legs and buttocks into the air, Jersey scrambled on top of the stone wall. Once his belly was balanced, Jersey swung his legs around and let himself drop to the other side.

He landed with his knees bent and instantly went into a parachute roll. When he came out of the roll, he had his Baby Glock back in his hand.

The woods were thick, but a clear path of beaten grass and snapped branches showed the most likely way Sally and her captor had gone.

Jersey followed the path at a dangerous pace, knowing full well he was exposing himself as an easy target if the man who snatched Sally had a weapon of any kind. But he also didn't see that he had any other choice.

When the path broke into a clearing that contained a small A-frame cabin, Jersey slowed his pace and strained to listen. There were lights inside the cabin, but he couldn't see any movement.

He moved forward cautiously, alert, the sound of his own heartbeat loud in his ears.

A mechanical cough sputtered from his right. Silence. It sputtered again.

He hurried around the cabin and followed a secondary path that led off to the right.

SALLY GNASHED OUT with her teeth, trying to bite any inch of flesh that came near her mouth, as Aedan held her face-down across his lap on the plastic seat of a small four-wheeled off-road vehicle. He was having difficulty getting it started, and the more Sally fought, the more frustrating it became for him.

"Quit moving," he seethed as he twisted the throttle and turned the engine over. The engine coughed, sputtered, and died.

He tried again. Same result.

"We might need to walk," he cursed. He opened and closed the choke, settled at the half-open position, and tried again. This time the engine came to life with an unsettling bang and vomited a huge cloud of blue smoke out of the tailpipe.

Aedan allowed a wide grin to split his face. Nothing could stop him now.

JERSEY BURST INTO the clearing just as the Quad roared to life. He didn't yell a warning or even break stride, he simply sprinted forward and launched himself as though playing Australian Rules Football and the driver's head was the ball.

AEDAN TWISTED THE throttle and felt the vehicle's knobby tires start to spin when a punishing weight landed on his back and sent him crashing face-first into the tiny, useless plastic windshield.

When he bounced back, his nose was broken and his face was covered in blood. With a roar, he slammed his right elbow back and felt it connect with something meaty and soft. He reached for the throttle again, but a punch to the side of his face sent him sprawling one way while Sally tumbled the other.

Aedan recovered quickly, but not enough to avoid a brutal left hook and a swooping right overhand that knocked him into the dirt. He tried to scramble away, crab style, when Jersey stomped on his thigh, deadening his leg and making the muscle spasm.

He spat out a curse, but it lodged sideways in his throat when a thick leather heel landed on his testicles. When the heel twisted, sharp and brutal, he screamed once and passed out.

JERSEY TURNED HIS back on the unconscious man and rushed to the other side of the Quad where Sally lay sprawled in the dirt.

When Jersey touched her shoulder, Sally spun wildly, a large pointed rock clutched in her hand.

"Sally!" he yelled, jumping back, his hands rising to defend himself.

Sally recognized him and instantly broke down. She threw the rock away and clutched at him, her hands tearing at his shirt to pull him closer, to merge with him. She was crying so hard, Jersey didn't hear the faltering footfalls of the man coming up from behind until it was too late.

Aedan snapped up the sharp rock Sally had tossed aside and with both hands smashed it down hard on top of the detective's skull.

The sickening crunch was unmistakable.

Jersey's knees buckled, his eyes rolled into the back of his head, and he toppled backwards like a fallen tree as blood spewed from his broken head.

SALLY GASPED AS Jersey crumpled to the ground, the sudden deadweight pulling her down on top of him. In panic, she clutched at his throat, but felt no pulse. She dropped her head to his chest, but heard no heartbeat.

"No!" she screamed, her eyes practically bleeding with rage.

Ignoring the threat of Aedan looming above, Sally slammed

her hands on Jersey's chest and began CPR. She cursed the church for everything it had destroyed until her hands slipped and landed in the pool of warm blood widening around Jersey's head. The contact made her entire body shudder, and her eyes rolled in her head as she collapsed.

92

Everything was hazy as Jersey found himself in a long corridor lined with a hundred doors. The entire hallway was bathed in an omniscient white light that seemed to emanate from everywhere and everything simultaneously.

Without direction or source, the light cast no shadow.

He couldn't quite remember how he got here, the memory like an annoying fly buzzing just out of reach, but something was pulling at him from two directions. The stronger force was leading him down the corridor where doors opened as he approached. He glanced into rooms that contained strange objects and images, evocating clear memories of lives never lived, paths never taken. Some of the images were frightening, others sad or mundane, but some were glorious, filling him with yearning for what might have been if only...

Jersey forced himself to look away from the rooms and focus on the far end of the hallway where the light seemed, if possible, even brighter. A small cluster of vaguely familiar people was waiting in that light, but he couldn't make out their faces.

His pace quickened as he ignored the doors that swung open around him. He didn't want to look; didn't want to mourn for a life never lived. He strode on, his footfalls making no sound, an odd discrepancy only noticed when he heard his name being called from behind.

Reluctantly, Jersey stopped and turned to see Sally running after him. She glowed brighter than anything else around him and her aura was blue.

When she was close enough, Sally reached out her hand and Jersey grasped it, pulling her to him like a warm wave and kissing her with such passion he wanted the moment to last forever. This was a kiss you could place behind a million doors and he would walk the halls for eternity just to relive it.

"We have to go back," Sally said when they finally broke apart. "You still have a life to live."

Jersey glanced over his shoulder at the group of people waiting for him. They seemed familiar, and yet...

Sally tugged on his hand, leading him away, but just before he took another step, a violent scream shook the hallway and a cold hand suddenly materialized behind him to grab his shoulder.

Jersey was spun to meet the face of a woman with fiery red hair and electric emerald eyes. She looked like Sally but without the warmth... the woman latched onto him, fingers digging into his shoulder as her feet were lifted from the ground by some powerful force that wanted to drag her back.

"Let him go," Sally yelled, as she tugged Jersey the other way. "It's not his time."

With one last burst of strength, the red-haired woman drew herself close to Jersey's ear and whispered four short words. Then, she let go and vanished into the light.

93

When Jersey snapped open his eyes from the nightmare, he was lying on the ground, his head bleeding profusely, and with Sally laying deadweight and unconscious across his chest. The disfigured man who had snatched Sally was lifting a large rock over his head with the full intent of smashing it down again on Jersey's weakened skull.

Jersey didn't hesitate. He raised his Baby Glock and pointed it at the man's chest. Despite all he had been through, his hand was rock steady.

The man froze, stunned to see Jersey awake.

"They're waiting for you," said Jersey. "And they're fucking pissed."

He squeezed the trigger five times.

94

Sally had memorized Aedan's door code, and when she and Jersey re-entered the gardens, they found the church fully engulfed in flames. The heat emanating from the giant pyre kept them to the outskirts as they made their way at a slow pace to the open front gates.

Jersey's head throbbed, and he leaned on Sally in the pretense of keeping his balance, but mostly it was for the feel of her next to him, like a missing limb reattached.

As soon as they exited the gates, a young girl's squeal made them turn just in time to see April breaking the land-speed record to rush into Sally's arms.

Jersey reluctantly left Sally's side as the girl struggled to get all of her ordeal out in one jumbled breath. Jersey pushed through the crowd, searching for the nuns, when he spotted Kameelah leaning against her Jag. She had a handcuffed man lying face down at her feet.

When Jersey reached her, he recognized her captive as Peter Higgins, April's father and the prime suspect in setting his parents up for murder.

"Jerk tried to steal my car," said Kameelah.

"I thought you were heading home," said Jersey.

Kameelah shrugged. "Saw the smoke and figured I should turn back."

From the ground, Peter looked up at Jersey and groaned, "You."

"Should have shot him," Jersey said to Kameelah. "Amarela already threatened to do it once."

"Your partner's a clever girl," said Kameelah.

"I never settle for less."

Kameelah smiled, accepting the compliment. She indicated the blood congealing on his scalp and covering half his face. "That's a nasty wound, you okay?"

"I'm a drummer," said Jersey lightly, not wanting to contemplate how close he had actually come to losing it all. "Nothing in there to damage."

"HAVE YOU SEEN the nuns?" Jersey asked.

"They left in a hurry. Didn't want to get caught up in the local law." Kameelah held out a digital camcorder. "I was told to hand this over to the authorities when they get here."

"What is it?"

"Black's wife confessing to the murder and mutilation of several young women. The reporter was right, they were connected."

"Huh, I would have put money on it being the scumbag who kidnapped Sally."

"He's deeply involved, too, but never underestimate a woman's scorn. It seems she was trying to make sure the Seer *didn't* return."

"While her husband wanted the opposite," said Jersey with a shake of his head.

"Marriage," said Kameelah. "Who'd have it?"

Jersey looked over his shoulder at where Sally was hugging April, both their faces alight with happiness and joy.

"I don't know," he said. "It can't be all bad, can it?"

EPILOGUE

Sister Fleur opened her eyes to a miraculous sight—*Sally*.

The young woman clutched at the nun's hand. Sally's cheeks were red from wiping away tears, but her sparkling green eyes were alive with happiness.

"Thank God you're alright," said Sister Fleur in a hoarse voice. "I feared the worst."

Sally's voice broke with emotion, "I never knew what you sacrificed… to save me."

"How could I explain?" asked Sister Fleur. "It became so twisted and, for a time, I was a part of it."

"But you escaped," said Sally.

"No," said Sister Fleur quietly. "Like you, my family was murdered and I ran, but I never truly escaped."

Sally wiped at her eyes. "You returned for me," she said. "And all I ever gave you was grief."

The nun chuckled softly. "The truth wouldn't have changed that. I was over-protective and you were rebellious. And from what I understand that is the height of normalcy for mothers and daughters these days. And for a time that's what we were, what we had to be."

Fresh tears sprang to Sally's eyes. "I wish I had been a better daughter."

"And I, a better mother."

Sally launched herself across the bed, hugging the woman tight, sobs wracking her chest.

LATER, SALLY TOLD her that Mother Black, a bullet wound in her shoulder patched with field dressing, had been found trussed-up like a Thanksgiving turkey in the gardens.

She had confessed to the murder and mutilation of five women. Jersey had arranged for a young reporter out of Idaho to gain access for an exclusive interview that was picked up by every wire service in the country. The reporter was using the exposure to head for San Francisco where he heard a weekly news magazine was hiring.

Father Black's body was never found, but after the fire at the church had burned its course and the firefighters were able to drench the ashes, the skeletal remains of an unidentified male was recovered. The victim's back was broken, and although it was the right height and approximate right age, a dental comparison proved inconclusive.

The End

or is it?

ACKNOWLEDGEMENTS

THE JOURNEY OF any story is akin to the barrel escape scene in the second Hobbit movie: it starts with what seems to be a good idea, then becomes perilous as the raging current sweeps you from side to side until you feel sick with doubt. And that's before the jagged rocks and armed Orcs try to block your way on the long, turbulent journey to publication.

If you're lucky, however, you get a few people on your side who believe, not only in the writing, but also in the writer. I have been fortunate to be blessed with such friends. In the days when it's just me and the blank page, my family, who don't always understand this mad obsession, are my biggest support. My wife and daughter bring me cups of tea and the gift of time, my parents call with words of encouragement, and my pals pull me out of my creative fog for a night or two.

But when the story is told and I nervously await the verdict, it's my editor, Jason Pinter, and my agent, Amy Moore-Benson, who come to the forefront. The book you are holding in your hands is down to the belief and support of each and every one of these wonderful folk.

I want to thank the entire editorial and sales teams at Polis

Books for believing in my wee nail-biters—so much so that Polis is releasing many of my books in print for the very first time.

Most of all, I want to thank you, the reader, for taking a chance on a writer you may never have heard of before. I hope you've enjoyed *Speak The Dead* and will be rushing out to buy more of my stories for yourself, your family and friends, and even complete strangers: the mailman loves thrillers, I hear ;)

Without your support, these stories would only exist in my head—and it's already pretty crowded in there.

From the very bottom of my heart,

Thank you,

ABOUT THE AUTHOR

GRANT McKENZIE is the author of four edge-of-your-seat thrillers, plus an ongoing mystery series set in San Francisco. His riveting thrillers *The Fear in Her Eyes, Switch,* and *K.A.R.M.A.* are also available from Polis Books. Under the pen name M. C. Grant he writes the Dixie Flynn series that began with *Angel With a Bullet* and continued with *Devil With a Gun* and *Baby With a Bomb.* His short story "Underbelly" appeared in the *First Thrills* anthology edited by Lee Child from Tor/Forge. As a journalist, Grant has worked in virtually every area of the newspaper business, from the late-night "Dead Body Beat" at a feisty daily tabloid to senior copy/design editor at two of Canada's largest broadsheets and editor in chief of *Monday* magazine. He lives in Victoria, British Columbia. Follow him on Twitter at @AuthorGMcKenzie.